SCENES FROM
LATER LIFE

Works by the same author

SCENES FROM LATER LIFE

A Novel by

WILLIAM COOPER

MACMILLAN LONDON

ISBN 0 333 34204 6

First published 1983 by
Macmillan London Limited
London and Basingstoke

Associated companies in Auckland, Dallas,
Delhi, Dublin, Hong Kong, Johannesburg,
Lagos, Manzini, Melbourne, Nairobi,
New York, Singapore, Tokyo, Washington
and Zaria

Phototypeset in Great Britain by
WYVERN TYPESETTING LIMITED
Bristol

Printed in Hong Kong

This Book
is Dedicated to
Jonathan

CONTENTS

PART I

PART II

PART III

PART IV

PART V

PART I

CHAPTER I

NOT TEMPERING THE WIND

My mother said: 'Tell me how old I am!'
I said: 'I'll tell you how old you are if you want me to.
But you do know how old you are. And you know you know. In
fact ten minutes ago *you* told *me*.'

'Did I?'

'Yes, you did.'

'Well, you tell me now.'

'You're ninety-one. And when September comes you'll be
ninety-two.'

'*Ridiculous!*' She spoke in a loud firm voice. Surprisingly loud
and firm. I have to say that it always had been so. And the
comment '*Ridiculous!*' was not out of character, either; in fact it
was very much in character. I could never be sure that she was
not going to apply it to me.

'Ridiculous,' she repeated.

I said quietly, 'That's for you to say.' I could tell she didn't
hear me.

'I ought to have died ten years ago.'

What could I say to that, even quietly?

I was looking down at her, where she lay awkwardly in bed,
half-propped up on a pillow and leaning to one side. If I asked
the nurse to come and sit her more comfortably, she'd only slip
back. On the other hand she was being kept warm, though there
was a biting February wind outside.

She looked very old, very small, hollow-cheeked and frail. Her
hair, scraped back from her forehead into a little knot, was very
thin, yet it still gave signs, I don't quite know how, of having
once been reddish brown – carroty, she saw fit to call it, herself.

She couldn't see me.

3

'It's no fun, being old,' she said. 'You ought to die when you're young and happy.'

I could see the point of her remark, yet I didn't feel it would persuade many people to act on it.

'Not,' she went on, 'when you're old and miserable, and lonely.'

And lonely. Nowadays I came down to the convalescent home to see her every fortnight. Once it had been every week. It was the Matron, who, taking me for a grand *affairé* Civil Servant, was concerned by my having to leave my office early in the afternoon to come down to the South Coast. Once upon a time it actually had been a bit tiresome to get away; but it happened now that my present job, this my last and final job as a quasi-Civil Servant, could scarcely be more gentlemanly. My fellow Board Members sympathised with my absenting myself, while our Chairman, if he was not using his official car at the time, would instruct his driver to take me to Victoria.

The Matron suggested the change. 'Your mother won't know the difference, Mr Lunn.' She was a youngish woman, rather coarse-fibred but very sensible. What she said was true.

My mother often said she couldn't tell one day from another. In fact she couldn't tell one year from another – she often seemed to think she'd only been in the convalescent home for a few months, sometimes even a few weeks; when it was getting on for eight years.

I looked round the room. It was always newly swept and dusted – there was no reason why it shouldn't be, as I always gave a few hours' warning of my visit. The wallpaper, patterned with sage green stripes, was fresh and unspotted; the curtains, patterned with a crisscross of pink and yellow, were clean; the blue of the frill round the edge of the bedcover was dazzlingly royal; and the carpet, patterned with huge fawn roses on a glowing turquoise background, looked – unfortunately – brand-new. My mother couldn't see the room. A room to be lonely in.

In former days my mother had tried living with my sister in America. That didn't do. Then she had come back and lived near to us. That didn't do. Then she lived *with* us, which manifestly was not doing; till, coming into her room time after

4

time to find her fallen semiconscious on the floor, we'd had to give up.

Should we have given up? I wondered. (What we didn't know, what in the course of time the convalescent home discovered, was that a remarkable improvement was made by stopping her from being given a large gin-and-tonic before her evening meal and a couple of Tuinals at bedtime.) But living with us was *not* doing. Her effect on Elspeth, who had to be with her all the time, was alarming. It reached the pitch where I saw that I had to choose between my mother and my wife. There is only one choice a man can make.

When I explained it to Robert, that it was not doing, he said, with his usual insistence on comparative thought, 'What *would* do?' He knew my mother pretty well.

'There you have me,' I replied.

Yet now my mother was in this room, all day, every day. Old and miserable, and lonely.

'I only wish,' she said, 'I had a room of my own.'

'But you have a room of your own. There's another bed in this room, but it's unoccupied.' Over the years the Matron had alternated between trying her with company and without.

'Last night there were fifteen people in this room. You'd wonder how they could all get in. There were two men sat on this bed. Big, fat men, with beer bellies.' She paused. 'I don't know what you think, but I think beer-bellies are positively disgusting.'

Though I hadn't got a beer-belly myself, I didn't want to be unfair to men who had. I merely said:

'I think you must have been dreaming it.'

'Dreaming it? I saw them with my own eyes. There were fifteen of them. If you had been here, you'd have seen them, yourself. There's none so blind as those who won't see.'

As I'd been brought up on this sort of adage, I was at something of a loss.

There was another pause, during which she was thoughtful. Then she said fair-mindedly:

'I suppose old people do dream sometimes.'

I thought it wisest now not to agree, least of all to agree with enthusiasm. She went back to what she'd been thinking before.

5

'The trouble is,' she went on, 'that you can't die when you want to. You have to wait till you're called.'

I remembered the Matron's warning: 'She might go at any moment, Mr Lunn.' She'd been saying 'At any moment' for the last three years.

I said quietly, 'Perhaps it's as well.'

This time my mother heard perfectly. 'Well or ill, it makes no odds. You've got no option.'

'No.'

I found that I didn't care for her saying You all the time, rather than I or One. I thought she might at least have said One – though knowing my mother I suppose I knew she definitely might not. It was not that she had no capacity for tempering the wind to the shorn lamb: she didn't seem to recognise that lambs existed in the shorn state.

'But I suppose if people had the option,' she went on, 'they'd not use it sensibly.' She paused. 'I used to wonder why they'd never make it legal for you to finish yourself off, when it got too much of a burden. Just take a dose one night and not wake up in the morning . . . But I suppose people would have done it for silly reasons. Taking the easy way out, for any little thing.'

I was silent.

'You don't say anything,' she said.

I was thinking, There speak generations of Wesleyan Methodism. I agreed with her. Of course I agreed – I was only one generation of Wesleyan Methodism later. What a thing to be faced with at one's mother's bedside!

'I agree,' I said.

'I thought you would.'

Suddenly something in *The History of Mr Polly* went through my mind – I'd just been re-reading it in the train. I loved it, enshrining Wells's message of optimism – 'If the world does not please you, you can change it.' I loved the book, yes; but I could never really stomach Mr Polly's solution to his troubles – *running away*. Oh dear! Generations of Methodism.

Trapped by my upbringing, that's what I was. Trying to escape from this thought, I glanced at my watch. Then I glanced round the room. As usual I noticed on the dressing-table, a cheap little wooden dressing-table, the small statue of an elephant, mysteriously made of what appeared to be white soap. I didn't know whose it was. There was another bed in the corner of the room, but there was nobody in it. Whose elephant? And why an elephant?

'You've got to wait till you're called,' my mother said again.

I thought about it again. It implied the existence of a Maker, to call one. I, myself, didn't believe there was such a thing as a Maker. My mother did at least appear to believe in one after a somewhat distant fashion; yet I was quite sure that awe for Him didn't overwhelm her, even though it was not going to be long before she was summoned by His call.

'How old are *you* now?' she said next.

'I'm sixty-seven.'

'Good Heavens!' She weighed it. 'You're not a chicken any more.'

I didn't say anything to that. Suddenly she said:

'Do you *mind*?'

'Mind what?'

'Not being young any more.'

'It's not much use minding, is it?'

'I thought you might.'

'Of course I mind slowly losing my powers, who wouldn't?'

'I mind not being able to see. If only I could read!'

'I know, I know,' I murmured. She had cataracts in both eyes, one of long standing, the other of recent development.

'The doctor says I'm too old for them to do anything about it.' She'd said this often enough before.

'That's true,' I said inaudibly.

'What about *your* cataract?'

'They'll perhaps be able to do something about that, fortunately.' I felt curiously ashamed of myself because I was hedging. It was now definite that some time during the next few months I was going into hospital to have mine operated on.

Trapped by my upbringing. And trapped by my genes. From my childhood I could remember two maternal great-grandparents in their nineties (my mother's family lived to great ages), both more or less blind; simple country people outside the reach of up-to-date doctoring for cataracts, let alone free doctoring. They crept round their little house, feeling their

7

way by catching hold of familiar objects. I had a sudden vision of the great-grandmother, tiny, hollow-cheeked, frail, with her hair scraped back into a little knot . . . She was bent into a half-stooping posture by arthritis. My mother had arthritis in her hands, her knees, her feet. Arthritis had made its appearance in my left hip-joint. My mother had suffered with arthritis throughout the whole of her life; I not until the last couple of years. So I was one up on the genes! *Sod* the genes!

Did I mind?

It would have been nice not to be forced by my mother at this moment to think about such things. It would have been nice throughout the whole of my life for the wind to have been tempered just a little. Of course I minded. It was a bore not to be able to see out of my right eye – I could just about tell, with that eye, whether it was night or day. But I realised that there was more to it, in this case, than that. I minded the pupil of my right eye having turned milky in appearance – everyone could see it. The fact of the matter is that I was vain. I didn't want people to see that I was getting old.

Yet if vanity came to my aid in fighting off the sodding genes, what was wrong with that?

'How's Robert?' said my mother.

When I first arrived she always asked, 'How's the family?' When we were getting towards the end of my visit, when she seemed to have a grasp at least of an hour's passing, to the uncanny extent of guessing when I started to look at my watch, she asked after Robert.

'He's all right. I saw him a week ago and we're going to have a drink next Tuesday. He's very busy.'

'How's he getting on?'

'Well. Very well.'

'And how's Annette?'

'About the same.'

'Is she in or out? I can never remember which it is.'

'I think you'd be safest,' I said gently, 'to assume she's in.'

'I can remember, she first went in long before I ever came here.'

'That's true.' Long before . . .

'Poor girl. I'm sorry for her.'

I thought I was sorry for Robert, too. What a marriage! . .
'Tell me what they say's the matter with her!'
'A sort of schizophrenia.'
She didn't hear.
I bent down and said loudly, 'Schizophrenia.' It sounded
terrible, exaggeratedly so through being shouted. Too technical
and too meaningless to be launched on my poor old mother's
ears, and too technical and too meaningless for describing
Annette's agonising inability to cope with existence.
'I've heard you tell me that before, but I'm not much wiser.'
'I doubt if anybody is.'
She shook her head very slightly against her pillow. It was too
late in the day, both actually and metaphorically, for explana-
tions in psychiatry.
'I hope there'll be an improvement,' she said.
I said nothing, because it seemed to me that there couldn't be.
'Life's a funny thing. Nobody gets everything they want. Folk
who don't know about *her* must think Robert's got everything.'
'I don't know about that.' I changed my mind. 'Yes, I suppose
they must.'
'He's got money.'
'Yes, he's made a lot of that.'
Plainly thinking I'd made none, she said: 'I wish I'd more to
leave you when I go.'
'Oh, don't worry about that! I'll get by, somehow.' What she
had to leave was to be shared equally with my sister, anyway.
'I wish you'd got a pension coming.'
Now why had she to remind me of that? I said: 'Not half as
much as I do.'
'Elspeth works.'
'Yes.'
She was silent for a little while. She was getting tired.
'I know I ought to know,' she said. 'How much younger is she
than you?'
'Fifteen years.'
Silence again. I looked at my watch. In a few minutes a taxi
was due to come and take me to the railway station.
'How's Robert's lumbago?'
'It comes and goes.'

'He's lucky not to have it all the time, like me.'

I thought perhaps he had got it all the time. My mother was stoical but her stoicism was noisy. Robert's stoicism was silent, very silent – in my opinion too damned silent, since he expected me to be equally silent about my arthritis.

I stood up and she heard me. 'It's time for you to go.'

'Yes, I'm afraid it is.'

'You mustn't miss your train.'

'No . . .'

'And the Matron will be waiting to see you.' She always told me Matron was waiting to see me.

With liberation in sight I felt I ought to be staying another hour.

She said:

'You're very good, to come.'

I muttered, 'I want to come. I like to come.' I thought, I have to come.

'It's what keeps me going. I think if it weren't for you coming, I should die.'

This, after telling me she ought to have died ten years ago!

I bent down and kissed her forehead – the complexion looked transparent. 'Oh, come on! . .'

She didn't repeat it. Perhaps, after all that talk about having to wait till she was called by a presumed Maker, it was as well. Though I didn't believe in Him, I didn't like to think I was holding Him up in the pursuit of His proper avocations. You have to be fair to everybody.

I said: 'I'll come again.'

Did she ask me *when* I'd come again, how *soon*? Or make *any* demand upon me? Out of the question. Pride and diffidence had ruled her life.

I collected my coat and my shoulder-bag from a nearby chair (naturally it was a commode.) Then I went back to the bed. The front-door bell rang downstairs. My taxi. I kissed her again –

'I'll be back soon.'

'You mustn't miss that train.'

'I said I'd be back soon.'

'Good.'

I touched her forehead. 'Goodbye, my dear.'

'Goodbye.'

A minute later I was sitting in a taxi, on my way to the station, on my way back to London, home, Elspeth – to the two latter after I'd restored myself with a pint of beer at Victoria.

CHAPTER II
OUR HOUSE

Elspeth and I were sitting indoors on either side of the french windows, having turned our chairs so that we could look out over the garden. It was early evening during a warm spell in April. The sun was shining on to the lawn and through the trees, and we'd opened the windows a little, letting in the busy noise of bird-song – sparrows, wood-pigeons, a blackbird – and the rattle now and then of an Underground train passing along the top of the embankment. Elspeth was reading a novel. I was supposedly thinking.

Everybody who came to see us said, What a beautiful garden you've got!

I didn't deny it. When we bought the house, nineteen years ago, we'd decided, unlike our neighbours, to keep the trees, trees growing there since the house was built a hundred years earlier – sycamores, holm oaks and hollies, trees deciduous and ever-green, one or the other shedding leaves gracefully on to the lawn all the year round. And we'd made a lawn, irregular in shape, surrounded by flowering plants and bushes. A natural look was what we said we aimed at, though whether Nature ever generated such a thing as a lawn seemed to me open to question. It was beautiful, anyway.

Elspeth was reading and I was supposed to be thinking. What I was doing was letting my glance wander round the little crowds of daffodils and narcissi beside the grass, with a break for a patch of deep blue where the grape hyacinths were; then over the yellow sprays of forsythia and up the poplar-like cherry, which was beginning to show pink and white clusters along its stem; and so into the trees and the sky . . .

'My darling.' Elspeth had noticed what I was doing. She

stretched out her hand towards me. I stretched out my hand towards her. They were a foot and a half away from touching.

'I'm hanged if I'll put up with that,' I said, and rolled my chair on its castors so that I could catch hold of her fingers.

She laughed. Her mouth went up at the corners in a way that had entranced me for more than twenty-five years. The little brackets, the lines enclosing it, had deepened. Who cares? I had not got any better looking, either.

'What are you looking at?' she asked.

'You.' I looked at her. 'I'm in favour of this short hair-cut. It suits you.'

'You should have seen the number of grey hairs when Corinne cut it.' Elspeth's hair was fair, her eyes grey.

'It's when I see Jane sweep mine off the floor,' I said. Jane might tell me it was silver – to me it looked white as Santa Claus's. By God's Providence I hadn't gone bald.

Elspeth shook my fingers. 'We can't go on doing this.'

'Why not? I like it.'

'You'll get cramp.'

I let go. We resumed our previous occupations. I noticed that from time to time she was glancing at me, but nothing was said. I was now thinking about the sort of things I was supposed to be thinking about, the sort of things I'd been avoiding – not that I hadn't been thinking about them off and on for several years. The compulsory end of my working-days in the official world. Retirement, as it was called. Money, the sudden absence of it. And I found it, always had found it, difficult to think about money, even when there was the prospect of its being alarmingly absent. There was something wrong with me. I mean, there were many things wrong with me, but this was, very possibly, the most serious one. Why, when I was supposed to think about money, did a curious sort of languor steal into my thoughts?

The sun was shining, the shadow of the trees coming up the lawn imperceptibly like the tide on a shore. What a pretty sight! We went in for small daffodils, with pale-coloured petals. I noticed the camellias, and the blackbird fluting its evening song.

There was a sound in the room behind us – Viola, the elder of our daughters, just come home from work. (She was twenty-four; her sister Virginia, twenty-two.) Looking lively and pretty in a black velvet blazer, she came and kissed us both. 'All right?' she enquired. And went out again.

The room was quiet, warm and nice-smelling.

When people came to see us they said, What a beautiful house you've got!

I won't embark on a description of the house, but I have to mention it. It wasn't merely that we had far too many rooms in it for three people – only Viola lived at home. It was that we were not going to have enough money, not nearly enough money after I stopped working in the official world, to heat them, light them, paint them, pay the mortgage on them, the rates on them and all the rest of it.

I'll put it bluntly – the beautiful house and the beautiful garden had got to be *sold*.

For the present we were all right, of course. I was earning about four-fifths of an Under Secretary's salary – I worked about four-fifths time. It came to some £12,000 a year altogether, the year being 1977. But when my present working-days came to an end, I was going to get £0 a year. I was not eligible for a Government Service pension.

Any of our friends who heard about my plight thought it was terrible, incredible after my lifetime since the War in Government Service. I myself thought it was terrible, but I knew it was definitely not incredible. Several Chief Establishment Officers, those men of utmost knowledge and goodwill, had exercised their knowledge and goodwill on my behalf. But who could know better than I exactly how far knowledge and goodwill can take you in the face of Regulations, in the face of the Law? To a blank wall in my case.

Like most of the disasters that befall one in this world, my plight seemed to me to spring from choices I'd made myself, choices grounded no doubt in my own eternal nature. And yet, again like many disasters, there was an extraordinary element of chance in it. I had chosen first to be a 'temporary' in the Government Service, and then a 'part-timer', because my eternal nature was fixed on being a novelist – dammit, I *was* a novelist! If only it had been fixed on Regulations! Acting for the Government Service as an employer, I'd come across all too many men whose first impulse, when we were offering them a good full-time job for life, was to start haggling over the pension. In men I didn't know I'd found it very unappealing; in men I did know, somewhat embarrassing. Unappealing or embarrassing – how I wished now that I'd been one of them!

But that isn't telling all. The Regulations about 'temporaries' and 'part-timers', which made the blank wall in my case, had since my time been dropped. I felt I was not short of material about which to reflect on Choice and Chance in this world.

I had not been *without* luck. The official world, though I had a deplorable knack of saying sharp, bright things that disqualified me permanently from being one of its favourite sons, had found me a number of miscellaneous jobs that had kept me going beyond sixty, then beyond sixty-five, the last two years' jobs being particularly fascinating. At sixty-seven, and now only just about to be brought to a full-stop, I had to admit that I had not done so badly – perhaps in view of my disqualifications, pretty well. Even now I had two jobs, one as Board Member of a quasi-Governmental organisation, the other as consultant to a company the organisation owned.

I'd done pretty well to keep going till I was in my sixty-eighth year. But what about the years to come? That's what I wanted to know. There might be rather a lot of them. I thought of my mother's ninety one.

'Don't *worry*! . .' Elspeth must have glanced at me again. She spoke gently.

If you were me, you'd worry all right, I thought of saying; and realised that I couldn't. We'd been married so long that in a way we *were* each other. In this, anyway, she knew perfectly well what it was like to be me.

'You're worrying again about how we're going to live,' she said. She stretched out her arm and I took hold of her fingers again.

I nodded my head glumly, ashamedly.

'You mustn't. It's going to be all right. We shall manage somehow. You know that.'

I had some cause to nod my head ashamedly because she had gone out to work herself. She had taken a job that was bringing in about £3,000. And Viola, working too, paid us rent and keep.

'It isn't as if you won't have anything to do,' Elspeth said.

'Oh no! One can go on writing for ever – even if it doesn't bring in any money.'

'You're being unfair to yourself, my darling.'

I shrugged my shoulders, I'm sorry to say.

'And,' she said diffidently, 'unfair to me.'

That brought me down – or up, depending on which way you look at it. I crossed behind her chair and put my arms round her neck. The novel slipped off her lap onto the floor.

'Leave it!' I said, but she was already freeing herself to pick it up.

We stayed for a few moments.

'It does look pretty,' she said, meaning the garden.

'Yes.' This was one of the prettiest times of year.

'I do hope you're not going to go out and work in it again tomorrow.'

I laughed. 'What a woman!' I kissed the side of her cheek and went and sat down in my chair again.

The door behind us opened. 'Anything you'd like? A drink?' Brightly, Viola.

Elspeth shook her head.

I said, 'Not for the moment, thank you.'

The door shut again.

An Underground train passed along the embankment. Afterwards I said:

'The Blackwells' children are very quiet nowadays.'

The Blackwells lived in the house next door. Their children were extremely noisy, but not half as noisy as their mother and father, who respectively screamed and bellowed at them all the time.

Formerly we'd not seen very much of the Blackwells, nowadays even less; which was curious because we were united in a common purpose. The local Borough Council had put a Compulsory Purchase Order on our house and four others; we were united in a residents' organisation to contest the Order. The Council was controlled by the Labour Party, and all the residents, barring Elspeth and me, were True-Blue Conservatives.

Elspeth and I didn't think there was anything to be said for the Compulsory Purchase Order: the Council had a mania for buying up large houses in accordance with housing plans which they hadn't the money to carry out. The Borough was dotted with their purchases, most of them used for a while as temporary staging-posts for council tenants, and then boarded up indefinitely, inhabited by nobody and falling to pieces.

It was thought that the Council would give a lot of money to get the first of our houses, to break the tenants' front. But Elspeth and I had taken it as a matter of course that we should unite with our neighbours in their Appeal against the Order, even though we wanted to, we had to, put our own house on the market as soon as might be.

We duly joined the residents' organisation and contributed £150 to the Appeal Fund – to discover that our True-Blue neighbours had taken it as a matter of course that Elspeth and I, the local Reds, would sell out to the Labour Council. That was astonishing enough. What astonished us still more was that the general atmosphere we felt around us was what we might have expected if we actually had sold out to the Council.

The result of the Appeal was due in a month or so. I thought that we should lose it, Elspeth that perhaps we might not. If we lost we should have to take the 'fair' price laid down for the Council to offer in such circumstances: if we won we should get what we could on the open market. Before this hiatus an agent had told us he'd get us £60,000 for it – which I interpreted as meaning about £50,000. With that money we intended to buy a flat for some £20,000, spending, say, £5,000 on doing it up; leaving us with £25,000 with which to pay off our remaining £5,000 mortgage and then invest the remaining capital for income. An income for life.

Heigh ho, the way we live now!

Elspeth had taken on the detailed planning and estimating of our future finances. Washed to and fro by alternating anxiety and depression, I was not so lost to reason as to miss her skill and sense. She had run the house marvellously. She now made me understand the over-riding importance of Outgoings. ('Outgoings, the very word', I seemed to recall somebody saying, 'is like a knell.') Elspeth, although she must be washed to and fro by her own anxiety and depression, as well as by mine, demonstrated that our outgoings in a small, well-chosen flat could be halved.

17

Halved! I know it doesn't read like poetry, but it sounded like it to me.

I wondered how many other men in their sixties were listening to this sort of calculation. As the percentage of the aged in the population was going up, more and more of them, poor old sods.

'So you see,' said Elspeth.

'I do see.'

Actually if things went as we calculated, I was not in the least averse to the move. If only we had the money to buy a flat, the money to make it look pretty, and then the money to live in it! . . I could write novels in it, make love to Elspeth in it, and perhaps afford to have friends to supper with us in it.

'You won't have to do all the running up and down stairs,' Elspeth said.

'And *no gardening!*' said I. 'It kills my hip and my back and my knees.'

'Do try and take a rest from it this weekend, darling!'

'If we move into a flat I shall have a rest from it for ever.'

There was a slight pause. 'Perhaps,' said Elspeth, 'I can have some window-boxes.'

We both looked through the windows. The shadow of the trees had come further up the lawn, though the grass that was sunlit looked as brilliant as ever. Somehow there was a feeling of change in the air, exciting change. A strange antithesis to anxiety and depression.

Elspeth said: 'Let's go out in the garden before it begins to get cold!'

She held my elbow protectively while we went down the stone steps – being able to see with only one eye made it difficult for me to judge such distances. Then we walked down towards what the girls called The Dell. The buds on the silver birch we'd planted by the Blackwells' fence looked like spray. Beyond it, among the dark glossy leaves of a rhododendron, there were lots of flowers-to-be. Then, looking further into the depths, I spotted some fritillaries just coming into bloom. I left Elspeth and went to examine them – green hanging bells, some of them sinisterly checkerboarded. Snake's head lilies. Snakes in the grass . . .

'Joe!' Elspeth called me lightly.

I saw that she was looking over the fence. I thought she was looking at the Blackwells' garden, which they'd been neglecting of late.

'It looks to me,' she said, 'as if the Blackwells' house is empty.'

'It can't be.'

'I think it is.'

There was a moment of suspension. 'I'm going to see,' she said.

I said, 'You can't.'

She said, 'Yes, I can.' There was a gap in the fence up on the embankment. Swiftly Elspeth went up to it, through it, into the Blackwells' garden, and up to their house.

'It *is*!' I heard her with stupefaction. I went to the gap as she returned. We looked at each other.

'It's empty,' she said. 'They've gone.'

I still felt stupefaction. We knew nothing about it. We'd heard not a sound, seen nothing.

'It's incredible.'

'They must have sold out,' Elspeth said.

To the Council. To the Council secretly. For an inflated price. And then done a moonlight flit.

And then, then, the truth of our own situation hit us.

If we'd lost the Appeal, it wouldn't make any difference to what we were prepared for. The Blackwells would have got a jackpot, but we should still get our so-called 'fair price'.

But if we'd won the Appeal? If we'd won the Appeal the Council would pack that house with their tenants – and that would knock a good £5,000 off what we might have got for our house on the open market.

We went indoors.

A month after that we heard the result of the Appeal. Elspeth was right. We *had* won.

CHAPTER III

'IT'S THE BEST CLUB IN LONDON'

Robert was always very tactful about it. 'I know that *you* think we can't get any private conversation there,' he would begin, in the slightly hollow, emollient tone he had for such occasions – incidentally putting me on the wrong foot with the emphasised *you*. 'But it's the only time I can manage next week.' Truthfulness compelled him to add, 'With any sort of convenience.'

'Don't worry at all!' I'd reply with the magnanimity to be expected in a friendship of forty – no, well over forty – years' standing. (Yes, I really mean to be expected. Friendship doesn't stand for well over forty years without a show of magnanimity, at least sometimes, on both sides.)

Anyway, on this particular occasion I'd have met him for a drink in a public lavatory or a crematorium – assuming they sold drinks in those institutions. By the next week in question he'd have read the typescript of my latest novel. Is it to be wondered that I'd have met him for a drink in a public lavatory or a crematorium? After the moment when I finally and triumphantly got the book off my chest, it was the next peak in my literary year.

As I approached the neo-Gothic porch I made eye-contact with the policeman on duty outside. (Eye-contact – what an awful expression! It contrives to sound at once inhuman and indecent – perhaps that's why it has come into fashion.) Then I went into the large entrance-hall cum cloakroom, where I set down my shoulder-bag on the table in front of a majordomo with military ribbons across his chest.

I unzipped the bag. 'Do you want to inspect my bomb?'

'That's all right, sir,' he said, smiling with the bogus

sycophancy of his profession.

The bag contained my morning's copy of *The Times*, a couple of books I'd just got out of the London Library, and my swimming-kit. Judging by the way the bag was eyed by policemen and cloakroom attendants, I could only presume it must be one of the standard IRA bomb-sizes. (A very large bomb.)

At that moment I was aware of someone else's having come up to the table. It was a woman.

'Why, Veronica! Fancy seeing you here!'

I kissed her warmly on the cheek. She was a small woman, active and pretty, a Civil Servant of some distinction. It was she who for the last twelve months had been transforming Robert's desolate life. For that alone I'd have kissed her warmly. And her being active and pretty could only add to my warmth. She was what my mother would have called wiry, that is to say physically stronger than she looked. I'd never enquired her age, but I suspected that she must be a bit older than she seemed. She was thin-faced with a rather high forehead, sparkling eyes and a permanent bloomy colour in her cheeks. And she had a loud, firm voice.

She was just leaving.

'The Old Boy's up there, waiting for you,' she said. 'I've just been taking some manuscripts up to him.'

She had picked up my lifelong habit of referring to Robert, who in my eyes right from the time we first met was a Great Man, as the Old Boy.

At that moment someone else came up, also leaving. It was George Bantock. We saluted each other brightly and noisily.

'Joe!' he cried. 'How nice to see you, dear boy.'

I introduced him and Veronica to each other. She held out her hand and the bloomy colour in her cheeks deepened.

George asked me what I was doing here and I said I'd come to have a drink with Robert.

'I'll take you up to him, dear boy.'

His dear boy or not, I was about twenty years older than George. He was about the same size as me and he always reminded me of a lively small animal – he always seemed to be pointing his nose up a little in the air.

'There's no need, George. I know the way.'

'Oh, but I must.'

'George, you were obviously leaving. I know the way. One goes up that staircase, and then along a corridor that's too narrow and too lofty' – I was teasing him – 'with a crimson carpet down the middle of it, and grille-fronted bookshelves on either side made of rich, dark oak – exactly the colour my father used to stain the floorboards in our house when I was a boy.'

He burst into good-natured laughter.

I glanced round and realised that Veronica had gone. She was active and pretty, strong-willed, determined: I had forgotten that on some occasions she was shy.

George had capitulated. 'Give my love to Elspeth!'

'And mine to Liz!'

I made my way to the staircase and suddenly knew that I'd dropped my first brick of the evening. I was fond of George: he was lively, clever and fun. I hadn't the slightest desire to cause him chagrin. The place always struck me as astonishingly ugly, but that was my personal taste as an outsider: all the insiders I'd ever known simply loved it. George had recently been elevated to membership, so of course he wanted to show me, merely a visitor, the way. Oh dear!

Why did I have to try and be funny? It's never a good idea to tease anybody. And so on.

When I came to the institution's Piccadilly Circus or *Rundpunkt* or whatever they called it, I declared my intentions to one of a number of busy policemen and was duly appointed an escort to the visitors' bar, where Robert was sitting on the far side, waiting for me. It was at the beginning of the evening, so there were few people there – good!

I threaded my way between the tables. It was a large plain rectangular room, the floor-space crammed with square tables, each with four chairs to it – ineffably reminding me of a caff.

Robert was sitting in the corner of a high-backed, leather-upholstered bench, which occupied the space between two rows of neo-Gothic windows overlooking the river. I thought we got a little more privacy – what a thought! – by sitting side by side on this bench. Also I argued that the high-backed seat was better for his lumbagic back and my arthritic hip, though I never rehearsed the argument aloud to him as it would have offended against *his* stoicism and have called attention to *my* egocentricity.

We greeted each other. 'What would you like to drink?'

I heard the first call of the evening upon my magnanimity. We were looking across the room to where, between two doors at either end of the wall, was the bar – a sort of narrow cupboard behind which stood an elderly, nice-natured waitress ready to serve drinks.

The bar couldn't provide draught beer, only bottles of fizzy stuff. If I was willing to wait until six-thirty, or some such time, the waitress was willing to go across to another place and procure me a pint of draught beer. But I had to admit to myself, Robert's stoicism apart, that that was making too much of it. His own drink being whisky, Robert naturally thought I was being fussy.

I said graciously, 'I think I should like some whisky, please.'

Personally, I thought five-thirty was a bit early to start on the Scotch: but *autre locales, autre moeurs* . . . I watched him pottering across to the bar to order it.

In the high old days of 1945 it had struck me that Robert bore a physical resemblance to Franklyn D. Roosevelt. He was a big man, with the same sort of capacious cranium, the same sort of jaw that was not quite as heavy-boned as it looked, large bright grey eyes, a wide mouth with a gift from the genes that I didn't then appreciate – smallish gap-teeth. (However odd gap-teeth may look when you're young, you're not half so likely to lose them when you're old.)

As F.D.R. had never reached the age of seventy-two, I couldn't have a recollection of his appearance at that age with which to compare Robert's appearance now. Robert looked years older now, yet I didn't find it easy to say exactly why, being foxed by his having always looked older than he was. He had always looked older: I had always looked younger. Naturally taking 'the passive attitude to reality', as he called it, he'd never made any bones about how old he looked. I, in my imperfect way, had spent my time up to forty trying to look older, in order to qualify for better jobs; and after that trying to look younger, for reasons we won't go into. (At forty I had married.)

I watched him come back from the bar. He sat down beside

me. I looked at him. In the air echoed my unspoken $64,000 question of the moment – What do you think of it?

'I've read your book,' he said. His voice had its slightly hollow, slightly lofty tone. 'I think it's one of your best. One of your very best.'

Slightly hollow, slightly lofty; very thoughtful, characteristically judgmatic, overwhelmingly convincing.

I didn't speak – I couldn't. I just breathed.

Given time I might have said, I think so, too.

'It's very, very good,' he said.

If there's an opposite to piling Pelion on Ossa – piling Ossa on Pelion? – that's what it was in my case. I thought, he must be right.

The elderly, nice-natured waitress brought our whisky. We lifted our glasses and drank. I said:

'Here's to the silly-billies seeing it!'

The generic term for literary reviewers was not my own. It was the invention of one of our friends, a young writer who'd artlessly spent time living among down-and-outs in order to get it right in the novel he was writing. He did get it right – when you read the book you could see so with half an eye – and was promptly taken to task by literary reviewers for 'political tub-thumping'.

'They'll see it,' said Robert. Slightly hollow and lofty, and entirely confident.

That's what you want from a friend, I thought – in like circumstances I'd do the same by him. And it wasn't a matter of our buttering each other up about our novels: we saw in each other's books things we most enjoyed, most valued – we saw the *best* in each other's books. And what's better than that?

'David was unlucky,' Robert said. 'In your case they'll see it.'

That's what I wanted, and naturally I wanted more of the same. Having got appreciation in principle, I was ready to move on to appreciation in detail.

I picked up my glass. 'Now I know your general verdict, there are lots of things I want to ask you.' I drank some whisky. Lots of things were crowding into my mind.

Robert drank some of his whisky. In the pause a very tall, thin man, whom I'd half-noticed crossing the room, arrived at our table.

'R-r-robert,' he began. 'I do hope you won't mind my interrupting your p-p-private conversation for a moment.' His delivery was a shade drawly and stylised – presumably to minimise his stammer. 'I m-m-merely wanted to ask you, Are you going to be here during the next hour or so?' He glanced up at the Visual Display Unit whose screen announced in flickering green letters the name of the person who was speaking at present.

Robert looked at me. 'Yes.' Then he glanced at the screen.

Our newcomer, intruder, smiled amusedly. 'He's emptied the place, don't you know. No surprise there, no surprise at all.'

Robert smiled. The newcomer, stooping stiffly in a way more elderly than he actually was, stood holding his glass. Robert introduced us. Mr Lunn: Lord Faux. Robert obviously had no choice but to ask him to join us.

'I never congratulated you, Robert, on that intervention of yours. Very p-p-pertinent.' He smiled at me as if I knew what the debate was – something about education, I thought. 'We've got to make the highest p-p-provision for the *ablest*. M-m-most important.'

My magnanimity was being called upon for the second time. And if my past experience of the place was anything to go by, the second time was probably not the last, either. I wanted to talk about my novel, just that and nothing else in the world. Lord Faux sat down in the chair beside Robert and addressed himself to me.

'I'm positively delighted by this. Your books have given me p-p-pleasure, Mr Lunn, a *deal* of pleasure.' He glanced at Robert, to make sure that Robert was not letting his attention wander. And then he went on, to me. 'I hope you don't object to p-p-praise?'

I muttered the inane sort of thing one does mutter in such circumstances. I think I said, 'It's music.'

'Very r-r-real praise. I was once in publishing, so' – he paused, mocking himself – 'I know what I l-l-like.' He gave me a very engaging smile. 'I'd been farming for twenty years and I thought I needed a change. Now or never. I went into p-p-publishing.'

Comment seemed otiose. Actually his firm of publishers was quite good.

'In a way it was a r-r-real blow when I was called back to farming.'

I thought that must have been when he inherited.

Robert said to him, 'Joe has just finished another novel.' In a super-weighty tone of voice, 'It's very good.'

Could I reasonably have said, What did you think of the opening scene? and Don't you think I hit it off perfectly?

I could *not* reasonably have said that.

Lord F said to me: 'I'm not surprised. Please let me get you another drink. What is it, whisky?'

Third call on my magnanimity. 'Thank you, yes.'

He tried to beckon the waitress, with no success; so he went away to the bar. I looked at Robert and began to speak. A miniature gale blew up beside us –

'I must come over and say Hello to you, Robert. I'm just out of hospital.'

A hefty, athletic-looking man was standing there. He went on. 'I read your intervention in Hansard – you really got him on the hop! If you do something special for music and dancing, why not for mathematics? I *like* that.'

Robert laughed as he stood up to shake hands with him. 'Nice to see you back, Tony.'

'It's splendid! I see you're having a party with Tolly. May I join you?'

'Of course.' Robert introduced us. Mr Lunn: Lord Balderstoke.

Lord B sat down on the chair beside me with a powerful crash. 'Sorry!' he said. 'I'm now missing a cartilage – but they tell me it's going to be all right. If it isn't, I shall soon be missing a coccyx.' He looked expectantly at me. Goodness knows what he was expecting – I'd got all my cartilages, and my coccyx, too.

Robert intervened. 'Joe is a novelist.'

'*That's* where I've heard your name!' Lord B said triumphantly. 'My wife reads novels.'

'He's just finished a new novel.' Slightly hollow, etc. 'It's very good.' That, I thought, is what you want a friend to be – persistent, pertinacious, persevering. (The only other word that came to mind on the spur of the moment was persiflageous, but that wouldn't do.)

Lord Faux was back in his place.

'Hello, Tolly!' Lord Balderstoke addressed all of us. 'We're talking about novels. While I was lying on my back, reading my way through *The Pallisers* – '

'They're very good,' said Robert, gravely, to no avail.

' – I realised that what I was missing, you won't believe it, was Order Papers.'

'I prefer *The P-p-pallisers*,' Lord F said across the table to me.

Lord Faux's round of drinks arrived, fresh whisky for Robert and me and himself; and a bit of argy-bargy ensued over a drink for Lord B, who, to tide him over, instantly and with enthusiasm accepted the gift of Lord Faux's whisky.

Lord Balderstoke looked directly at me as he raised his glass. 'Will you celebrate with me?' It wasn't a simple question at all. There was a sudden shrewd look in his eye – I was being scrutinised.

'Love to,' I said. It may have been the fourth call. I had no idea if I'd answered satisfactorily.

Surely this must be the end, I thought.

Lord Balderstoke turned away from us all. 'There's Bert!' he said. He beckoned. 'Bert, come and join us!'

He was beckoning to none other than Bert Smith, former boss of the — — Union. The times one had seen photographs of him going into No 10, coming out of No 10, haranguing the masses in Trafalgar Square, marching with them down Park Lane! For fifteen years he'd been the Marxist menace, bogy of the Tories – if he'd come on the scene nowadays, he'd indubitably be called Red Bert. (Present-day Trade Unionists appeared to have strictly two modes of appellation for their heroes, either Red or Big.)

Bert, small and sturdy, was walking towards us with an old man's short steps. His face was beaming. It struck me as an internal beaming, as if it were directed inwardly. Perhaps he was beaming at himself being a Lord.

Lord Faux stood up to his tall, stooping height to call the waitress. 'A drink, my dear B-b-bert?'

'Thank you. I'll take a bottle of Watney's, if she's got one.' Lord Albert-Smith pulled up another chair, to sit between me and Lord Balderstoke – appropriately beside me, I thought; two men of the people together. He spoke rather slowly, as if it were cautiously, in the Redcar accent which through time and television had become mythological.

Lord F said: '*I* think Bert is looking rather pleased about something, don't you know.'

Lord Albert-Smith said: 'If you think I'm pleased about something, you know more about me than *I* know.'

Lord B said: 'Come on, Bert, there *is* something. Don't hold out on us!'

Robert had an amused, watchful expression.

'Well, if I've got to tell you, just among friends,' said Lord A-S, 'it's Lord Grimley as has asked me to go on his subcommittee.'

Lord Faux lifted his hands in playful horror. 'My dear Bert!'

'What did you say, Bert?' said Lord Balderstoke.

'I told him,' said Lord Albert-Smith, 'No Way.' He paused, savouring the literary flavour of his speech. 'No Way.'

'Good for you!' said Lord Faux. He looked up at the VDU, locally known as the Enunciator. We all looked up at the Enunciator.

'Aye,' said Lord A-S. 'I reckon it's 'im as has emptied the Chamber for this last twenty minutes.'

Everyone laughed. Lord A-S beamed some more. The waitress had brought his bottle of Watney's and she poured half of it into his glass.

How much longer would this sort of conversation go on? Indefinitely. The newspapers at the moment were full of high political argument about a 'Lib-Lab Pact' for the purpose of shoring up Mr Callaghan's Government. So much for the newspapers!

'At the present moment in time,' Lord A-S was telling us, 'I was fortunate enough to have a positive reason for telling him No Way.' He drank some of his Watney's. 'As you all know, I have an ongoing situation in another area.'

The times I'd seen him look straight into the television cameras and utter without a tremor these phrases. His political power had deserted him now, poor old chap, but not his egregious literary expression – that went marching on. All the same I had to give him credit for being a literary innovator of the highest order, once upon a time. It was Bert who had first launched that now immortal sentence – most perfect blend of Corn and Cant! – on the ending of a strike in which his Union, after the fashion for most Unions in recent years, had got more or less what it was striking for –

It isn't a victory for either side: it's a victory for commonsense

Nor, for that matter, had a guileful capacity for self-preservation deserted him. I couldn't help feeling drawn to him, though I wished him and the rest of them in Timbuctoo at the moment.

Lord Balderstoke said: 'You were right, Bert. Damn' right.'

Lord Albert-Smith said: 'I should like to have your view, Robert. You're keeping very quiet. Are you observing us all for your next book?'

I thought Robert was most likely being quiet because he was in pain.

Robert said: 'I suspect Grimley's is one of those committees that will never come to any conclusions; and if it did they would never be implemented.'

I was surprised by his acerbity. He usually kept a very firm check on his tongue in public. He must be in pain.

'There you are, Bert,' said Lord Balderstoke. 'Shows you know the ropes here, what?'

Lord Albert-Smith's rubicund face directed its inward beam upon me, the stranger present. 'The ropes are all the same, everywhere,' he told me.

I nodded my head in agreement. 'But this is a special place, all the same?'

I don't know what prompted me to say it. I couldn't have known it was going to provoke something which always caused me a particular happiness – the privilege of hearing somebody utter a judgement as if it were his very own, that one had been hearing from other lips as if it were *their* very own, time and again for thirty years.

'That's right,' he said. He turned his head slightly away, while still beaming. 'You know, this is the best club in London.'

Freshly-minted!

I didn't look at Robert. It was usual for him to enquire afterwards, in the cause of bringing comparative thought to bear, What other clubs would you say he's comparing it with? Pratts? Or Boodles? Or perhaps the RAC?

The others went on talking and I was beginning to feel desperate. I looked round the room, not that that was much consolation. We were sitting with our backs to the neo-Gothic windows: in front of the opposite wall was the drinks' cupboard with the nice, elderly waitress: and on each of the side-walls was a huge tapestry.

Suddenly, loudly, a bell rang. Division!

Everybody stood up, preparatory to moving off. 'We shan't be long!' As if that were good news to me!

I saw that Robert was hanging back, and then he returned.

'Aren't you going to vote?' I said.

'Yes, but I'll come straight out and meet you in the corridor, and we'll go to Vincent Square.' Vincent Square was where he lived.

CHAPTER IV

A HOUSE IN VINCENT SQUARE

'I'm sorry about that,' Robert said as he joined me again. 'I know you wanted to talk about your book.'

'I wanted to hear you talk about it.'

We made our way out of the building as fast as we could, and caught a taxi. The result was that in a surprisingly short time we were installed in Robert's sitting-room, in peace and quiet, with no likelihood of further calls upon my magnanimity. He handed me my typescript and went away to get water for our whiskies.

I made myself comfortable on a sofa, thinking At last! It was what could have been a comfortable room in a pleasant house. Yet it always struck me with sadness because Robert lived there alone and gave no thought whatsoever to keeping it comfortable and pleasant – such as by giving it a lick of fresh paint for a start.

I hadn't the nerve to tell my mother how many years Annette had been away, because they were so many; or how agonising it had been for Robert, too, while she was still here. He'd loved her deeply. That was readily understandable: she was intelligent and beautiful, with, in the early days, an appealing quaintness of 'living in a world of her own'. They married about six months before I married Elspeth – Elspeth had been very taken with her, Elspeth then being twenty-five and Annette twenty-nine. I realised at the time that Robert was allured by what I thought of as her quaintness, by the promise – dangerous – of a strange internal world to explore. I didn't realise that when her retirement into that world began to close in, he would be joined in a heart-rending struggle to draw her out of it. A fatal, useless struggle

There was no question of divorce. Privately he seemed to have settled down to a sort of Thackeray-like existence – apart from

Thackeray's having had two daughters while Robert and Annette had two sons. (The sons had long since flown the nest: Arthur, the elder, was a surgeon in Toronto; while Harry, the younger, was in banking in New York.) Robert had a house-keeper, a Spanish woman who ran the house. And that appeared to be that.

Unlike Thackeray, though, Robert had not been without a string of young women who were prepared to console him – their offers were readily accepted. Veronica was the most recent of them. And although the earlier ones had come and gone, none of them had gone entirely. Although the present incumbent was usually unaware of it, Robert never lost touch with any of her predecessors. Open and friendly by nature, he was all the same a peculiarly secretive man.

'Here you are. Sorry I was so long.' My reverie was broken. I shifted my typescript in my lap. He sat down on the sofa facing the one I was sitting on.

So began the most delightful of literary interchanges, in which one gives the other person the opening to say what he thinks about one's work, and then says oneself why it is so good. There was a beautiful absence of let or hindrance to this interchange because, although he didn't necessarily think everything was so amazingly good as I thought it, he nevertheless thought it was pretty good. Is it to be wondered at, that before long I was getting well above myself? Oh Art, Art, what heights of vanity do we rise to in thy name! (Also what abysses of disaster do other people push us into later!)

We got over the opening scenes of the book, the introduction of the main characters, the beauties of this and that, the profundities of the other. I made notes in the margin of any improvements he suggested. Till we came to what I most of all wanted to know.

'What about the love-affair of the doctor and the girl?'

The doctor, the narrator and chief character, was a widower aged sixty-two; the girl, the youngest daughter of one of his friends, was twenty-two. It really was a love-affair, as much of a love-affair as any I'd ever known anything about, on both sides – if anything, she led him on more than he her. And the love-affair was the core of the novel.

'I thought it was very good,' he said.

'Did you believe it?'

For me that was the most important question of all. About this novel or about any other, it was, Do I believe it? If I didn't believe it, I really felt at the bottom of my heart that everything else about it, the author's intention, the author's language, the author's art, had been wasted.

'Yes.' Robert grinned wryly – 'I believed it all right.'

I was satisfied. In the burst of relief I embarked on fulsome talking.

'I had no idea, when I began the book, that it was going to take over the way it did. And then I didn't even know if I could do it, without its having actually happened to me now . . . I decided to work on the principle that what it's like to fall in love is the same at any age. What it's like to *make* love doesn't lose its edge.' (A private spark came and went in Robert's eye.) 'Therefore what it's like to *fall* in love doesn't.'

I secretly thought I'd made a discovery. As I couldn't announce it in the novel I wanted to boast about it to Robert.

'What it's like to fall in love at sixty-two,' I said, not worrying about re-iteration, intent on establishing my claim to the discovery and its proof by demonstration in my book, 'is really no different from what it's like to fall in love at twenty-two.'

Robert thought about it. We both drank some whisky, to encourage thought. It always seemed to me that Robert's capacious cranium was ideally designed for thought on the grandest scale. He gravely nodded his head.

Inflated beyond measure I suddenly saw my discovery taking its place alongside, say, Dostoievski's discovery of the double motive. What it's like is no different at twenty-two, forty-two, sixty-two, eighty-two. (Little did I know what Mr Auberon Waugh, the reviewer, was going to write!)

'Once I'd got over that,' I said, 'I enjoyed writing it. I had a marvellous time.'

'Yes,' said Robert. 'I think that shines through.'

Wanting to continue with How I did it, I was just about to embark on another confidence. While writing the love-scenes I'd resorted to artificial stimulants in the form of incessant playing on the gramophone of Rachmaninov symphonies. Yearning music, lush, romantic, twisting one's very soul between its fingers, I thought – just like being in love . . . I thought perhaps I'd better not tell Robert that. For one thing he was more or less tone-deaf. For another I was sure he would think it showed my typical incapacity for sustaining a serious attitude. And most risky of all – when he knew how I did it he might think less of what I'd done than he thought of it before.

'There is just one thing,' he said. 'I don't think it's a very good title.'

I'd called the book *Happier Days*. I didn't think it was a good title, myself, but I couldn't think of a better one. I tried to justify this one to myself by saying that the happier days were what the elderly doctor miraculously came to find ahead of him. Oh, happier days!

'Anyway, I suppose your publisher can change it,' Robert said. His American publisher had changed the title of his last novel from a title that we were agreed was not especially good to one that was both meaningless and excruciatingly flat.

'Sarcastic, aren't you?'

Robert did not reply.

We sat in silence for a little while, quietly finishing our whiskies. Robert was thinking about something. It suddenly crossed my mind – was he, by any chance, thinking about the next Division bell?

He said: 'The book itself, though, is quite certainly as good as anything you've ever written.'

'Or ever shall write?'

I think he took my question for a statement.

I put my typescript into its envelope. I said: 'As she thought you wouldn't be in, Dolores won't have put anything out for you to eat?'

He shook his head. Alas, he was incapable of boiling himself an egg. I thought Great Men were incapable of boiling themselves eggs – which was one of the reasons why I could only feel less than a Great Man, myself. *I* could boil an egg with anybody.

'Then you'd better go back,' I said. 'We'll get a taxi in the Square.'

He stood up. 'Yes, I think I'll do that.'

34

CHAPTER V

MENTION OF A LIFELINE

Although I saw Steve irregularly, I don't suppose a few months went by without my running into him. I knew the pub in Old Compton Street that he frequented; and sometimes, when I was 'taking an extended lunch-hour' from my office in order to go swimming at Marshall Street Public Baths, I dropped in at the pub after my exercise. I was a great believer in doing myself good, but determined not to let it get me down. The good of a half-mile swim could be mitigated by a drink afterwards, especially by a drink with Steve.

Steve's profession was that of stage-director. After the War he'd gone to a drama school and trained as an actor. To tell the truth, Steve was not a very good actor, but in fairness it has to be said that Steve didn't seem to mind telling the truth himself, not that particular truth, anyway.

In some plays he'd given a tolerable, perhaps a more than tolerable performance. In other plays – well, it was a different matter. When Elspeth and I went round to see him afterwards, sitting at his dressing-table with a half-finished bottle of Guinness beside him, he'd say, with a characteristic engagingly rueful smile, 'I'm afraid, Elspeth, I was' – spacing the words out – 'not . . . very . . . good.' What could one say to that?

Gradually Steve's career as an actor had petered out. However Steve was nothing if not an engaging cove. His rueful smile had a touch of pathos, it had many touches of intelligence and fun. He was an attractive man to have around, whether in the theatre or anywhere else. As his career in acting petered out, a career in directing petered in. To Elspeth and me he was wont to paraphrase George Bernard Shaw – If you can't act a play, direct it! (We doubted if he was wont to say it in the theatre.)

35

Steve's career as a director had petered in, but it still maintained a permanent petering quality. He seemed to spend a lot of time resting. And when he was working it was in 'fringe' theatre, very fringey theatre, very odd plays. The last production of his that Elspeth and I had been to see was performed in an upstairs room at a public-house in N11 of all places.

That performance had been devoted to improvisation. The actors were improvising as they went along – which was very apparent. Equally apparent was their enjoyment of their activities. They were getting a magnificent exercise in thespian art. Unfortunately we, the audience, couldn't help noticing that we weren't getting a play.

Steve was standing in the corner of the room, his chin resting on his fist while he listened intently. We were not surprised by his listening intently, since much of what was being said he couldn't have heard before. The evening set me meditating on how ineradicable is the conditioning of one's youthful days. Nothing now, I realised, could eradicate my expectation, when I came into a theatre, of seeing a play, of seeing some human beings conflicting with one another in a drama shaped and heightened by Art. I could readily see that in terms of current popular cant about *élitism* it was democratic to remove shaping and heightening by Art – artists are by definition an *élite*. But then I found that I didn't care for the performance in the same way, that is to say at all.

I dropped into the Old Compton Street pub one day, wondering if Steve would be there. The room had been decorated all round the ceiling with red, white and blue bunting for Jubilee Year. I saw that Steve actually was there. He was leaning against the bar, which had been permitted by some quirk in modernising brewery management to retain its Victorian row of swivelling little windows round the counters. He saw me.

'Joe!'

Obviously recalling the last performance, he went through a sort of shrinking gesture. It was a gesture he'd gone through ever since I first remembered him, when he was a youth of seventeen. The shrinking had not been due to any physical weakness – anyone could see that he was normally healthy and well set-up –

36

but had indicated his sensitive artistic nature and his consequent need to be taken care of. Such a need at that time had been met, shall we say (not taking too high a moral line) to the full, by an ebullient accountant ten years older than himself, patron and boss rolled into one, a friend of mine called Tom. All that happened in 1939.

Steve, still occasionally shrinking ruefully, must be in his mid-fifties now; and although not fat, he was at least a couple of stones heavier. He was tall and fair-haired and presentable. His fine-textured complexion had not stood up well over the years to alcohol; it looked pinker and shinier: and his nose, always inclined to be a bit shapeless, looked more shapeless – but persons under twenty-five ought not to take a high line about that: an ugly fate overtakes most of us. And in fact Steve, though obviously looking older with the years, surprisingly showed none of the more desperate signs of ageing, so I thought.

'Wasn't that play awful?' He was getting it over at the beginning.

I laughed and said nothing. Theatre people always delighted me with their capacity for finding the show in which they were currently performing Marvellous, Amazing, Fantastic! . . But of the previous show they now had no qualms whatsoever in coming out with the reasonable opinion that it was Awful.

'Let me buy you a drink,' he said, grinning. 'I think I ought to.'

He ordered a drink for me and I let him buy it, though my earnings, not yet reduced to £o per annum, were, if I was right in thinking Steve's earnings actually were £o per annum, an infinite number of times greater than his. (For the moment I had forgotten what he'd told me a year or so previously, that he'd inherited a little money – more than he expected – from his father.)

He handed me the drink, saying, 'You're looking terribly fit.'

'I've just been swimming.'

'You always look terribly fit.'

'Constant vigilance, my dear Steve.'

'How do you manage to go on looking so young?'

Not a question I could answer.

He looked at me speculatively. 'You dress young.'

'Nonsense.' I was at that moment wearing my suit for Board meetings, expensive black material with a chaste – yet interesting – fine stripe. 'This is what I call my banker's suit.'

'But you're not always wearing that suit, Joe.' He was dressed in ancient blue denim.

'That's true.' I thought about it.

I said: 'I can't resist telling you an incident that happened last Saturday afternoon. One of our Canadian friends brought his daughter to meet us. Afternoon tea on the terrace, and all that. I was wearing some whitish Levis I bought in San Francisco more than ten years ago. What do you think she said to her father when they got away? She said, "He wears trousers too tight for his age." '

Steve burst into laughter.

'For my age!' I repeated.

'Are they too tight?'

'No tighter than they were when I bought them. Close-fitting, perhaps. No different from what everybody else was wearing.'

Steve went on laughing.

'Censorious girl,' I muttered. Then I realised I was dangerously near to standing on my dignity. (When I was young I once wrote a poem that began, *Don't stand on your dignity / Till it's flat!*)

Steve said, 'I think she must have been attracted by you.'

'She was not.' I slammed my glass on the counter. 'Look, I was going to offer you another drink.'

'Was she attractive?' His eyes were brighter.

'I'm not prepared to tell you. Will you have the same again?'

He nodded his head, the brightness lingering reminiscently. Presumably he was thinking about some fresh girl he'd got his eye on.

Since his liberation, first by the War from the passionate attentions of Tom, and then by his initiation after the War in the *moeurs* of drama school, Steve had never ceased to have his eye on a fresh girl. After the drama school he married a girl who'd been there at the same time as himself, and they'd had two children. She'd become a very good actress. And she, it seemed, had never ceased to want Steve. I've already said that he was an attractive man. I don't know what his sexual powers were like, but they must have been satisfactory: I do know what his company was like – it was typically engaging, fluid, relaxing.

A little while after their second child was born his wife had become a Roman Catholic.

To Robert I observed, 'I should have thought for a girl who's married to Steve, becoming a Roman Catholic is the reverse of appropriate.'

Robert said immediately, 'It means he'll never be able to get away from her by divorce.'

(You see why I venerated Robert's capacity for perceiving the heart of the matter?)

Steve had never been divorced, but it was many years since he'd lived with his wife and family. He had lived with a succession of other ladies.

I have remarked that from his youth, Steve's manner, even when he was absorbed in entertaining, had continued to preserve something which indicated his sensitive artistic nature and his consequent need to be taken care of. In the psychological sense his need to be taken care of may have been illusory if not frankly bogus: in the financial sense, while his career in the theatre stayed permanently at the petering level, it was hard fact.

Such was Steve's charm that each of the ladies in succession appeared to have been happy to oblige in taking care of him. For a time. It was for that reason that I tended not to encourage his having his eye on a fresh girl. To put it crudely, I thought he ought to watch his step. (On the other hand, people who do watch their step all the time rarely endear themselves, alas! to other people.)

Refusing to indulge him by discussing that censorious girl, I handed his glass to him and said, 'Do you mind if we sit down?'

The outer walls of the room were pleasantly divided into compartments which offered a little privacy. Turning, we were confronted with a huge coloured photograph, on the wall above the compartments, of Her Majesty; under it, the legend in huge letters –

LIZ RULES OK?

Steve carried his glass across. 'I noticed you limping as you came in.'

'This bloody arthritic hip.'

'Can't anything be done for it?'

'It *is* being done. I'm going to the Westminster Hospital for physiotherapy twice a week.'

'And is it making it better?'

'If anything, worse.'

'Doctors!' (His elder son had become a doctor. A pleasing turn of fate, I thought it – conventional as any other doctor, the young man disapproved of his father.)

We sat down facing each other. He was looking at me directly.

'Joe, your eye!' His face, pinker and shinier than it used to be, was changed, almost distorted, by its look of youthful sympathy. 'The pupil's much whiter than it was last time I saw it.'

In the ordinary way I tried to pretend to myself that people didn't notice it. It was showing. Oh dear! I said:

'You don't have to worry about that so much. Last time I saw him, the eye-surgeon said it's ripe.'

'Ripe – how terrifying! What does it mean?'

'Ripe for excision.'

'I'm a terrible coward, Joe. What do they do?'

'They excise the eye-lens, which has gone opaque. And as you don't have that inside your eye afterwards, to focus with, you wear a contact lens on the outside.' Something, I don't know what, made me hear the tone of voice of my mother.

Steve looked puzzled by the science of it.

I said I was going into hospital sometime in August. Steve asked me if I was having it done privately.

I explained that I'd had a stroke of luck. For some years I'd gone to the surgeon as one of his private patients – he was one of the most distinguished in London – while the cataract 'ripened'. When the time for action had come we'd discussed how much it was going to cost, and he suddenly offered to do it on the NHS.

'He must be a nice man.'

'He's an excellent man. I think he's wonderful. And I'm sure *he* thinks he's wonderful. And he thinks *I'm* a bit out of the ordinary – being terrified neither by the operation nor by him.' I smiled at the thought of him. 'He's large and handsome, very efficient and very impressive. Getting on for sixty. Always wears a rose in his lapel. Very grand. He looks as if he used to play rugby football – he did.'

'How do you know?'

'I asked him, one day. There was a silver-framed photograph of two healthy-looking young men on the table beside where you sit. I guessed they were his sons, guessed they were rugby football-players, and asked him. One thing led to another, in a hearty sort of badinage. He doesn't play rugby football any more.' I couldn't resist adding, 'On the other hand he still leads a vigorous married life.'

'Joe, how on earth did you find out that?'

'I didn't find it out, it just sort of fell out. Let me see . . . I suppose it must have been when he was finding out how physically fit I am, my regular swimming and all that. I suppose there must have been a bit of fun in the air. After all, when you get down to bodily functions and think of their enjoyability, what else? I favoured him with my advice for the ageing – *The essential thing to do is to keep on doing what you've been doing*. He laughed at that, and gave me a look. Message exchanged – to the satisfaction and pleasure of both parties! He's a fine man. He's known to Elspeth and me as His Majesty.'

Steve was amused. 'So he's going to do you free of charge.'

'He probably feels it's taking the mickey out of the NHS at the same time.'

We sat for a moment, reflecting. The pub was not especially crowded or noisy. It was a fine day outside and the doors were wedged open. I glanced at my watch.

Steve looked at my glass.

I didn't think I had time for another. My personal assistant had his instructions, how to deal with importunate telephoners, but I thought I'd better give him a break.

Steve seemed to have changed in mood. I said:

'We've talked all the time about my affairs. How are things with you?'

He lifted his shoulders, another gesture I'd seen in the past. As if his shoulders were weighed down.

'What's the matter?'

'It's Marìa.'

'What's the matter?' Marìa was the latest lady in the succession, an Argentinian lady living in London. She'd been contributing to the fulfilment of Steve's need for some two years. He was installed in her flat in Regent's Park. I gathered that she was rich and interested in the theatre – the happiest of combinations for Steve. On the few occasions when Elspeth and I had met her we'd thought she was perhaps a shade predatory, but not unamiable. But how could Steve hope to be taken care of by someone who was not a shade predatory?

'I'm afraid that she's not as free as she used to be.'

'Free?' I said. 'What do you mean by free?'

Steve didn't reply, as if I'd merely been asking the question to tease.

Free?

'We've started to have quarrels,' he said. 'I mean serious quarrels. I mean not just love quarrels, where all you have to do is to get into bed.'

'I'm sorry.'

'She's started to find terrible fault with me, Joe.'

'Oh dear.'

'She says I'm lacking in seriousness.'

'Steve!'

'I mean seriousness as far as she's concerned.' A tone almost of anguish came into his voice. 'I *am* serious.' He looked at me with extraordinary sincerity. 'She's my *lifeline*, Joe.'

I could think of nothing to say.

At last Steve thought of something to say. He said:

'Do you think I shall find another?'

'I'm sure you will, Steve.'

Another lifeline.

After a pause he stood up and I did the same. It was time to part. He stayed beside me on the pavement while I waited for a taxi.

'By the way,' he said suddenly. 'Do you know Tom's coming to London?'

I looked at him, so surprised that I let a taxi pass.

'When?'

'Some time later in the year.'

'It must be the first time for ten years.'

'I know. Shall you see him?'

'I shall make no moves to do so.'

42

Passers-by were buffeting us. Steve said:

'He can't still be a menace to you, Joe.'

'I don't suppose he is, but why give him the chance?'

'You're much more strong-minded than me.'

Another taxi came up. 'We'll see,' I said. I got into the taxi and it drove off.

In Shaftesbury Avenue the taxi was held up by traffic and I was given time for thought.

So Tom was going to re-appear. Actually I didn't feel menaced, but I meant to keep him at a distance. In the past I'd been amused by his bounding, bombinating activity. No, that wasn't fair – there was a good deal more to it than that. There had been friendship between us. He'd always been ready with an unusual fund of human sympathy and, it seemed to me then, an unusual fund of human wisdom. Not that he was modest about possessing those unusual funds, especially the latter. 'I understand you better than you understand yourself,' was his line, even though he was a year younger than me. In those days I was shy of thinking I understood myself. His line was menacing yet it was comforting. Now I hope this hasn't made him sound pompous and over-bearing: he actually was pompous and over-bearing, yet he was also funny and frequently comical. He was a bit of a clown.

He was coming to England. If he'd been here during the last ten years I hadn't heard of it. And when I'd been in New York I'd made no effort to get in touch with him.

I had decided the most sensible thing I could do was let our friendship lapse. In this case distance had lent disenchantment. Thinking over the goings-on during the years of our close friendship, it seemed to me that in spite of his sympathy and his wisdom, in spite of his empathy, he was a destructive person. Only too often his clowning made trouble, did harm. On one occasion, when I really was in trouble already, it had made matters more troubling, more painful for me – and also for the young woman with whom I was having a love-affair that was coming to an end.

It was coming to an end because *she* wanted us to marry and *I* didn't. Tom, in the midst of pursuing Steve from pillar to post, conceived, in empathy for her, the idea of marrying her himself.

After the War he had resolved to make his future in the USA. In addition to bounding energy he had a great deal of ability, a great deal of shrewdness. He'd gone through the hoops of qualifying as an American accountant with distinguished success. After a few hard years, which he was helped through by marrying a rich American girl, his career had taken wing. He now lived in New York and was rich himself. His marriage had ended in divorce and he had not married again. When he travelled abroad nowadays it was invariably with an entourage of young men – some of them with wives – who were junior partners, personal assistants and so on, one of them clearly occupying a chosen rôle.

When Tom was young I'd made fun of his seeing himself as a great understander of human nature, a great writer – he wrote a couple of novels – a great connoisseur of the good things in life, and a great lover. He did not see himself as a great chartered accountant. Well, Destiny had lain in wait for him. It was a great chartered accountant that he'd become – a high bigwig in Boyce Peterhouse New York!

It had been part of Tom's tactics in America deliberately to loosen his ties with his native country. He must have been in the USA for five years before he came back to England, and he merely returned then to attend Robert's wedding to Annette.

It went without saying that Annette roused his empathy irresistibly.

'I've know Robert all his life, my dear. I'm sure you'll be very happy with him.' He smiled at her, his pop-eyes shining through his spectacles with understanding and wisdom, his arm warmly enclosing her waist. 'You'll have to be prepared for a string of petty infidelities, but I *know*, my dear, you'll be able to tide them over.'

I resolved to keep him out of Elspeth's way.

CHAPTER VI

GOODBYE TO A CATARACT

His Majesty had a ward of his own, His Kingdom, on the first floor of the hospital. It was a large handsome room with about seven beds ranged round three of its walls, the fourth being taken up by wide bay windows giving a splendid view of suburban countryside – a low valley, gleaming down below with half-hidden roof-tops and rising to a skyline of distant trees.

All but two of the beds were occupied when I arrived, occupied mostly but not entirely by men who were elderly, some of them with dressings fastened over an eye, others without. One of the two empty beds was mine: in the next was a tall Sikh, complete with beard and turban as well as a patch over the eye.

I was taken into a private office, Elspeth with me, and inducted with great tact into the whole plan of procedure – presumably on the principle that both of us would be less frightened if we knew exactly what was going to happen. At the same time it was clear that I had entered His Majesty's realm and was one of his subjects. Mr Harrison likes you to do this, and Mr Harrison will want you to do that. I didn't fancy the chances of anybody who didn't do them.

In due course Elspeth left and I enmeshed myself in the routine, a sequence of trips from one place to another for one test or another.

And then, 'Now, Mr Lunn, we shall want to cut off your eyelashes.'

'Oh!' I discovered I'd got a Samson complex.

The snipping felt very odd. I'd been used to imagining that I had long eyelashes. 'They'll grow again,' the nurse said. 'Yes, of course,' I replied, as if I believed her.

I was returned to the ward, where I observed the routine for those patients who had had the operation.

At lunchtime I had been given a decent meal. Now I was approached by a smiling, Chinesey little nurse with a basin and a spoon. 'I've come to feed you, Mr Runn. So you get used to it before the opelation.'

A delicious little creature with large, flat eyes and shining teeth. I prepared myself to be fed by her.

It was part of the procedure. After the operation you were placed in a sitting-up position, where you had to stay, sleeping in that position. Your head was not sandbagged down, but you had to keep it still. For a few days you had to be spoon-fed, and there was an absolute ban on brushing your teeth afterwards: if you had false teeth you were given the choice between not having them in at all for the four days, and having them in but on no account taking them out. Mr Harrison's orders.

I began to find spoon-feeding inordinately slow, and was suddenly visited, across twenty-odd years, by remorse – I'd done my younger daughter an injustice! When she was a baby, being spoon-fed, she'd given up eating after a while apparently out of boredom, and we'd been impatient with her. She was right. I'd been very unjust. Being spoon-fed really is boring and I felt inclined to give up. 'Some more, please, Mr Runn.'

Virginia hadn't had the encouragement I was getting. Slightly giggly and quite delicious. She told me she came from Malaysia, and her name was Marìa.

Marìa – I thought of Steve's lifeline! I'd had a drink with him before I came into hospital. He was not sanguine. Marìa's doubts about his seriousness had not diminished. I understood there had been no change in her being less 'free' than she used to be. If I hadn't been going into hospital he would have wanted me to see her, to help convince her of his seriousness. Poor old Steve, things were going to be serious for him if she wasn't convinced. So far he could still pay for his drinks. (In all the years I'd known him, throughout all his vicissitudes, he'd never proposed borrowing money from me and I'd never heard of his borrowing money from anyone else.)

Steve had no further news of Tom.

'Not much more now, Mr Runn.'

'A pity,' I said. 'I think you feed me very nicely, Marìa.'

46

Giggles and smiles. I wondered what it would be like to have a wife who was small and delicious and who came from Malaysia. Such wonderings were brought to an abrupt close. Maria – she must be a Roman Catholic! That wouldn't do for a Protestant atheist like me, Methodism coming with the genes. You can't giggle and smile away a great divide like that.

The meal ended, and in due course, rather early I must say, the day ended. With ablutions over, the ward composed itself for sleep. The Sikh in the next bed went to sleep – and began to snore like a steam locomotive. It was an incredible noise. Every so often one of the nurses would come and try to rouse him.

'Mr Singh, Mr Singh, stop *snoring!*'

It didn't have the slightest effect. Some of the other patients who were used to it managed to get off to sleep. Not I. In the early hours of the morning an Irish night nurse took pity on me. 'Will I be making you a nice cup of tea, Mr Lunn?' She brought it and chatted with me comfortably while I drank it. The Sikh, it transpired, had some kind of obstruction in his nose: there was no hope of a quiet night for the ward till he was discharged.

In the morning a visit from His Majesty, wearing a beautiful yellow rose: he was accompanied by the Sister.

'I expect you've met Sister Curtis,' he said.

I said Yes.

'Sister Curtis and I are old colleagues. She's been working with me for many years, more years than I'm going to tell you.'

I bowed politely. After all, I hadn't asked him.

'Sister Curtis knows as much about all this as I do. Probably more. Isn't that so, Sister?'

The Sister smiled – with a flick of her eyelids. 'Yes, Mr Harrison.'

His Majesty glanced at me. 'You see?' We laughed. The two of them looked briefly at my eye and then they swept on to the next bed. 'Good morning, Mr Singh.'

Poor Mr Singh, because of his nasal obstruction, had had to have his operation with a local, instead of a general, anaesthetic. He was somehow not made for hospital life – apart from his getting a good night's sleep. In bed he still wore the baggy trousers ordained by his religion: I saw them when he got out of bed to use his bottle. It was forbidden for him to get out of bed at present. Whether it was because of religious rules about cleanliness or because his baggy trousers made it impossible, he wouldn't use his bottle in bed. So he got out of bed – and immediately came up against his rules about exposing himself. Looking tall and proud he tried to use his bottle while hiding it behind the bed-curtains. Poor Mr Singh . . . How much better for everyone not to have *any* religion!

In the evening, though, Mr Singh had some compensations. He was visited by a wife and daughter, beautiful, dusky women dressed in beautiful, silk saris. Elspeth, sitting beside me, felt eclipsed. She concentrated on how far my own appearance fell short of what was desirable. This hinged on my pyjamas. After the War, when clothing required coupons, I'd ceased to wear pyjamas altogether. I absolutely refused to buy new ones now, solely to wear in hospital. Consequently I was dressed in a pair that had been hidden away in a drawer for thirty-five years.

'It's super silk,' I said to Elspeth, feeling my cuff. 'They' – I nodded towards the Sikh ladies – 'would agree.'

'They,' said Elspeth, 'can't see it's so thin that the jacket's already split down the back.'

'If they can't see, what does it matter?'

I took hold of her hand and squeezed it. One ought not to bicker with one's most loved person on the edge of general anaesthesia. You never know. I was to be operated on next morning.

His Majesty operated on me next morning and by the following evening I'd come out of the general anaesthesia and Elspeth was sitting beside me again. This time it was she who took hold of my hand. I was keeping still, pretty firmly held in position by the sheets. There was a dressing over my eye and I had no headache nor any pain at all. Now we had to wait and see – literally. Put your trust in His Majesty! The Sister came and chatted with us and reassured Elspeth. Four days to wait.

The four days passed, with spoon-feeding, drinking-cups, bottles and bedpans. I even began to sleep through Mr Singh's snoring. If I didn't sleep I had a job to get a cup of tea, as we now had an African night nurse who confounded the universally received idea that black people are indolent and ever ready to please. She was highly efficient and seemed intent, with success, on pleasing nobody. With Mr Singh her technique was to wake him up every hour. Poor Mr Singh, turbanned and bearded and handsome, proud and shy and not very sure of the language; I think she hated him. In my opinion he was lucky that she never saw his beautiful wife and beautiful daughter.

I began to get interested in the next lot of patients to come in. There were two old gentlemen put into adjoining beds, Mr Griffiths and Mr Davies. It was fortuitous not only that they were both Welsh but that they bore a physical resemblance to each other. They were small and wiry, wearing straggly little beards. In their brand-new Marks and Spencer's pyjamas they were constantly nipping in and out of bed, and they'd seen fit to bring in with them some bottles of Guinness which they surreptitiously stowed away in their lockers. Working on the inverse of another universally received idea, that to us pinko-greys all Orientals look alike, I thought our delicious little Malaysian nurses were going to have some difficulty in telling Mr Griffiths and Mr Davies from each other.

The previously empty bed, next to mine, was now occupied by a stocky fellow who looked about forty-five: he told me he was a Post Office engineer, name of Brian. He'd come in for the first of two cataract operations. I was astonished. Two cataracts by the age of forty-five. He explained that cataracts were common in his mother's family.

'The sodding genes!'

'That's right,' he said.

We were both taken aback by rapport.

I explained the concept of *Sod the genes!* I scarcely needed to. 'That's right,' he said as soon as I paused. 'That's how I feel.'

He stood beside my bed in a rather glorious dressing-gown – not M & S, possibly Austin Reed. 'Sod the genes!' he repeated. 'That's right.'

There was a pause.

'This man Harrison,' he said.

'What?'

'Is he OK?'

'Very.'

'S'what I thought.'

I felt I'd found a mate. I looked forward to the evening, to see what his wife looked like. Alas! I was to be disappointed. He was working temporarily at Dollis Hill: his wife and children were up on Tyneside. He told me about them. I told him about Elspeth and the girls. I also told him that time was when my Civil Service job had taken me on visits to Dollis Hill.

'Did it really?' he said with wonderment and delight. He too had found a mate! He sat on the edge of his bed and we talked about Dollis Hill.

Then there was another pause. He looked round the ward.

'You ever been in hospital before?'

'No.'

'Me neither.' He went on. 'What's it like?'

'I've survived so far. I've had the operation and I'm still in possession of my faculties.'

He gave me a quick look. Shrewd brown eyes and a blunt nose – who did he remind me of?

'Such faculties,' I said, 'as I've had the opportunity to exercise.'

He grinned at me. I knew who it was whom he reminded me of – none other than the Noble Lord Balderstoke. I thought of Robert, then of *Happier Days* . . .

I shifted under the sheets. 'If you'll excuse me,' I said, 'there's a faculty I'll have to exercise pretty soon.' I began to fumble for my bottle.

'Let me get it for you!'

'Thank you, I must do it for myself, though I still find it a bloody nuisance, trying to find it without leaning over to look for it.'

He said, 'I suppost it's something I'll have to learn to do.'

'It's either this or bust.'

He politely looked away. 'I suppose there's nothing to it.'

'Not if you've set your heart on it.'

We both laughed.

I thought of Mr Singh's difficulties and decided not to mention them.

Poor Mr Singh, there was no longer any objection to his getting out of bed, but that was no help to his modesty: he was still trying to hide behind the curtains. But then I thought of his dusky wife and daughter in their saris – not poor Mr Singh, lucky Mr Singh!

Mr Griffiths and Mr Davies returned from having their operations. Then Brian. One felt the sort of bond men are supposed to feel who have gone through the same initiation ceremony.

The wives of Mr Griffiths and Mr Davies continued to make regular appearances in the afternoon. They were short, bustling women with the sort of unquenchable cheeriness that reminded me of our office-cleaning ladies. They brought with them, as instructed by the hospital, clean sets of pyjamas: they also brought more bottles of Guinness. They were extremely adept at stowing the bottles away when there was no nurse in sight.

Elspeth saw what was going on. 'Are they *allowed* to bring in all those bottles of drink?'

'I don't know. I've never asked.'

'It looks as if they're *not*.'

'They give that impression,' I agreed, 'but it may not be so.' I embarked on high psychological speculation. 'Isn't it just their instinctive behaviour? Confronted with a system, they instinctively set about circumventing it. Whereas if they only learnt to play the system, they could get what they want without circumventing it.' I paused. 'How about that?'

I wondered what Brian, lying unvisited in the next bed, thought about it. I knew perfectly well that you weren't allowed to say such things in democratic society. Elspeth frowned and I wasn't surprised. She said:

'Anyway, what about *you*? And your pyjamas?'

'I've brought some. I'm not instinctively circumventing the system, not being able to comprehend it.'

'They're indecent.'

'Only from the back.' Now that I was returned from the brink, there was no harm in a bit of marital bickering. I heard a slight snigger from the next bed and realised that I'd got the Trades Union of Men going.

'What about when you get out of bed?'

'I shall put on my dressing-gown. And that'll be a pity – my pyjamas are super silk. You can't buy silk like that, nowadays.'

Elspeth began to laugh. 'You're getting above yourself.'

I stopped. Tomorrow morning I was due to have my bandages off. I felt frightened.

Elspeth squeezed my hand. 'It's all right,' she whispered.

That night there was a rumpus in the ward. The African night nurse had come on duty and was making her first round. I'd begun to think less ill of her, though all the other men hated her. Her cool *de-haut-en-bas* manner struck me as explicable – I'd have been prepared to bet she came from the Nigerian aristocracy. Furthermore she really did know her job.

She was at the other end of the ward.

'Good evening, Mr Griffiths. How are you feeling this evening?'

'Very well, thank you, Nurse.' Earlier on one of the ambulant patients had surreptitiously poured him a night-cap of Guinness.

The nurse went through her routine. 'There you are, Mr Griffiths. Good night.'

As she was moving away, he called after her, 'Nurse!'

She turned.

'Can you pass me that, please, Nurse?'

I have to say that Mr Griffiths and Mr Davies had brought in with them receptacles for their false teeth, receptacles that looked like plastic butter-dishes with lids. It was at one of them, on top of his locker, that Mr Griffiths was pointing.

'What do you want that for, Mr Griffiths?'

'To put my teeth in, like, for the night.'

'Mr Griffiths, you know that if you chose to keep your teeth *in* you're not allowed to take them *out*. Not until Sister gives you permission.'

'I didn't choose to keep them in, Nurse, no indeed. I always have them out, like, to sleep in . . . '

'Well, you've got them *in* now.' She suddenly stopped as the significance of what he'd said struck her. 'Mr Griffiths,' she said, 'I'm going to look up in the records where your teeth ought to be.'

She turned and walked out. Horrors! There was silence in the ward. I felt my diaphragm shaking with suppressed laughter.

She came back. 'Mr Griffiths, you did choose to keep your teeth out after the operation. In that case you should never have had them *in*.'

'No, Nurse.'

She looked at him. 'I suppose the best thing we can do with you now is take them out, and keep them out, until you're given permission to put them in. Do you understand, Mr Griffiths?'

'Yes, Nurse.'

She passed him the plastic butter-dish and there was a rattling sound.

'Thank you. Now good night, Mr Griffiths.'

She moved on to the next bed. She was a tall, good-looking girl. I thought she was perhaps a chieftain's daughter, doing hospital training in this country: she spoke English like someone who had been educated here.

'And now, Mr Davies.'

Mr Davies said nothing. His straggly little beard was outside the sheet: his unoccluded eye was wide open.

'According to our records, Mr Davies, your teeth should be *out*. Are they?'

Mr Davies screwed up his mouth tight. Everyone else in the ward, and the night nurse as well by now, guessed where Mr Davies's teeth were.

'As you don't reply, Mr Davies, we can soon find out.' With a simple gesture she lifted the lid of his plastic butter-dish.

'Mr Davies, I think your teeth are *in*.' It suddenly occurred to me that she, too, was having a job not to laugh.

Mr Davies nodded his head without speaking.

She held out the butter-dish in front of him. 'Mr Davies, please – *out*!'

Mr Davies made a movement, and there was a second rattling sound.

'Thank you, Mr Davies. You understand? You're not to put them in again until you have permission.'

Mr Davies's one eye remained wide open, very bright. I wouldn't have trusted him for an instant.

She went on her way. It was one of the duties of the night nurse to rub baby-powder on the bottoms, as a precaution against bed-sores, of everybody who had had their operations a few days earlier. At length I saw the curtains being whisked round Mr Singh's bed, and a *sotto voce* conversation ensued as it did every night. From it I could overhear as usual, 'All right, Mr Singh. If you'll promise to do it properly, I'll let you do it yourself.'

Poor Mr Singh, with those baggy pantaloons! How on earth could he do the job properly in those garments? As for allowing the nurse to see, let alone touch, his bottom! . . At length the curtains were whisked back and the night nurse finished her round without further trouble. Instead of going to her illuminated desk in the corner of the room, she went out.

Silence.

Then, 'Psst! . . Mr Thoroughgood! Psst! . .' It was Mr Davies, now capable of speech. Mr Thoroughgood was his next-door neighbour, an ambulant patient soon to be discharged.

'Yes,' Mr Thoroughgood answered.

'Mr Thoroughgood.' Mr Davies's voice was quavery. 'Mr Thoroughgood, I can't get to sleep. Can you pour me a little drop of my Guinness?'

There was the noise of Thoroughgood getting out of his bed and padding across to Mr Davies's locker. Clinking, a brief glug-glugging, and a pause.

'Mr Thoroughgood! . . ' It was Mr Griffiths now. 'Can you give *me* a drop of *mine*? Just to help me off, like. That's a friend.'

I heard Brian mutter from the next bed, 'They're like Tweedledum and Tweedledee.'

At last the diversions were over and everyone finally composed himself for sleep. The night nurse came back to her desk. Blessèd silence.

Then Mr Singh began to snore.

I shouldn't have got off to sleep so very quickly, myself, that night. I was wondering how things would turn out in the morning.

I must have slept, because the day had dawned when I was awakened by the start of the morning's routine. In the grey light, a cup of tea. A farewell to the night nurse and a welcome to the day shift. We had to go through washing and breakfasting before the time for the crucial test would come.

At last the time did come. The Staff Nurse appeared, accompanied by one of the older, non-giggly, non-Chinesey nurses. They drew my curtains and gathered round me. Sister Curtis appeared.

'Now, Mr Lunn,' said the Staff Nurse, 'just lie quietly!'

I did as I was told. I felt them undo the bandage, then unwind it, and then gently loosen the sticky plaster that held the dressing. And then, with a smooth skilful stroke they took the dressing away –

I could *see*!

Where I'd only just been able to tell if it were night or day, now I could see, softly blurred, the pink shape of the nurse's cheek, and her nose, and the dark bit where her eye was, the white rectangle of her cap.

'It's amazing! I can *see* . . . '

'Yes, Mr Lunn. That's how it should be. Don't get too excited!' Pause. 'Mr Harrison will be coming to see you later this morning.'

His Majesty – the greatest king I'd ever met. How soon could I let Elspeth know? I lay patiently, gradually recovering, while they took it in turns to look into my eye and then collogue over me.

When they'd gone away Brian congratulated me.

'In a couple of days it'll be your turn,' I said. 'You'll be all right.'

'I hope so.'

In due course there was a stir outside the door, as of heralds trumpeting soundlessly. His Majesty came in, accompanied by Sister Curtis.

He reached me. 'It's amazing,' I said.

'I'd like to have a look at it.'

He examined it, leaning over my bed from one side while the Sister leaned over from the other. He said to her:

'His iris peaked, as you'll have noted.'

'Yes, Mr Harrison.'

'A nuisance, but it couldn't be helped.' He addressed himself to me. 'It's nothing to worry about, Mr Lunn. It sometimes happens. Instead of your pupil being circular you'll notice that at one point there's a little dark peak from it into the iris. It's my fault . . . It won't affect your being able to see.'

I made some acquiescent sound or other. If His Majesty said so, it must be so.

He stood up. 'You'll be able to see just as well.' He gave me an amused glance. 'But you just won't be quite as beautiful as you were before.'

In the nick of time I suppressed a facetious rejoinder – he'd said seriously that it was his fault . . .

I said: 'I expect I'll manage, somehow.'

'I expect you will.' He laughed. 'Somehow.'

Then he went on his way.

The eye was covered up again and I had permission to get out of bed. When the state visit was over I made a circuit of the ward and then went over to the window to stare at the sunlit vista of roofs and treetops stretching downwards and then up again into the distance. Though I was occluded again, I knew I could see. I thought of my poor old mother, too old for her cataracts to be operated on. Sometimes she said, 'It's a sunny day, isn't it?' How she could tell, I didn't know.

I thought about the peaking of my iris and felt a momentary, after-the-event qualm. Things *could* go wrong . . . But they hadn't.

I joined the group of ambulant patients who found themselves something to do by giving the nurses a hand with passing round meals and cups of tea, and generally by doing minor services for patients still confined to their beds.

The latter services in my case included attending Mr Griffiths and Mr Davies. They were irredeemably naughty. I interfered with them and needless to say they got the better of me. They sustained themselves with frequent nips of Guinness. They had been told that they were to sit up in bed and on no account lean over sideways. One day I saw each of them leaning out of bed to pick up a bottle of Guinness from the lowest shelf of the locker.

'Mr Griffiths! Mr Davies!' I expostulated. 'You know you're not supposed to lean out of bed like that.'

They looked at me mutely with one bright eye apiece. They reminded me terribly of a little long-haired dachshund we'd bought for the girls: *his* way of exerting his individuality on a system he was in the grip of, i.e. us, was exactly by this mixture of wilfulness and cunning.

'If you'd only asked me,' I said, 'I would have got your bottles of Guinness for you.' I proceeded to get the bottles. In my expostulations for one thing, and in my psycho-sociological reflections for another, I'd entirely forgotten that I was not supposed to stoop down to the ground, myself.

But just as wilfulness and cunning didn't always avail Silky against us – inexorably we would put him out in the garden even though he was convincingly pretending that he didn't need to go – so it didn't avail Mr Griffiths and Mr Davies every time.

It was an occasion for blanket-baths. The nurses usually began a fresh round of them at the window-end of the room, where Mr Griffiths's and Mr Davies's beds were. The nurses were always hard-pressed with work and they were frequently interrupted for long periods to do other jobs. On this particular day the beginning of the round was entrusted to the two delicious little Malaysian girls. Everyone was envious when they saw somebody's bed-curtains being drawn – there was something to look forward to.

The daily life of the ward had been rolling on, and nobody was paying much attention, when unusual sounds began to come from behind the curtains round Mr Davies's bed.

'Mr Davies, where are your crean pyjamas?' It was Maria's voice. 'In your rocker?'

'I had them *on*, Nurse.'

'No. Your *crean* pyjamas, Mr Davies.'

'Yes indeed, Nurse. I had them on.'

'No. Those were your dirty pyjamas. We took them off. Now we put on your crean pyjamas. You have crean pyjamas? Where are they?'

The curtains opened at the corner near to Thoroughgood and the second little nurse threw out a pile of soiled sheets and a blue-striped pair of pyjamas. At the opposite corner, next to Mr Griffiths, there was already another pile, which had been lying there for some time, including an orange-striped pair of pyjamas.

'You've just taken them away, Nurse,' said Mr Davies.

'Mr Davies, you joking.' There were giggles.

'No indeed, I'm not.'

'Then where are your dirty pyjamas?'

'You took them away, the first time.'

'Mr Davies, you really joking.'

Silence from Mr Davies.

'What colour your crean pyjamas, Mr Davies?'
'Blue, Nurse.'
'What colour your dirty pyjamas?'
'Orange, Nurse.'

A delicious little Chinese head appeared out of either corner of the curtains. It was Marìa's head nearer to Mr Griffiths's bed. She picked up the orange-striped pyjamas. (The whole ward were now listening with riveted attention. The truth had dawned to delirious effect.)

Marìa picked up the orange-striped pyjamas. 'These Mr Gliffiths' pyjamas,' she said confidently.

Mr Griffiths joined in. 'No, Nurse. Those aren't *my* pyjamas. Mine are green, like. And purple.'

Marìa began to giggle. She took the orange-striped pyjamas inside. 'Yes, Nurse,' came Mr Davies's voice. 'Those are my dirty pyjamas.'

Chu-Yin took the blue-striped pyjamas inside. 'And those are my clean ones.'

Now there were gales of giggles. Through them we could hear Mr Davies say:

'You've given me *two* blanket-baths, Nurse.'

While outside, his curtains still not drawn, Mr Davies said in a quavery voice:

'And I haven't had *one*.'

The sound of general hilarity brought in the Staff Nurse – Brian was commenting 'Lucky Mr Davies!' Instantly everyone piped down. I was thinking, Crafty Mr Davies.

After that incident any patient felt at liberty to invite Marìa and Chu-Yin to give him a blanket-bath twice-over. Giggles and giggles.

The days rolled on further and discharge began to be a definite proposition, first for me and then for Brian. Mr Singh had already gone.

We heard His Majesty deliver a pre-discharge admonishment to Mr Singh –

'Remember, Mr Singh, *No violent exertion.*'

Brian and I had listened from our adjacent beds with great attention.

'Did you hear that?' Brian said to me afterwards.

'Of course I did.'

'Do you think he means? . .'

'I should think he does.'

A brief silence. 'That's a bugger, isn't it?'

'It is.'

'What are we going to do?'

I said brightly, to tease him: 'Do without.'

He groaned.

Smitten by pity, I said: 'It doesn't have to be violent, does it?'

'You mean if we go at it gently, it'll be all right?'

'More likely to be all right than if we go at it violently,' I said, thinking it was a good idea to inject a little comparative thought into the discussion.

He glanced at me with amusement. 'You're an educated chap, aren't you?'

'Up to a point.'

We both laughed. Then we lapsed into thought.

Two days later I had my penultimate inspection from His Majesty and Sister Curtis. He gave me his list of recommendations, instructions and injunctions.

'And remember, Mr Lunn, no violent exercise or exertion to begin with.'

I nodded my head. I have to admit I put one interpretation on the word 'exertion'.

After His Majesty had left the ward, Brian said:

'You got sentenced today. In a few days' time it will be my turn.'

'That seems very likely.'

He paused. 'We're in the shits, aren't we?'

'Well, remember, Brian, *we can see*.' I paused. 'Furthermore we've not got to go back to work for six weeks – that's nice.'

Brian grinned reluctantly. 'It'd be better if it weren't so vague. How long do you think we shall have to wait? Assuming, like you said, we go at it gently.'

'Like *I* said? It was your *immortal* phrase.'

'It's a reasonable phrase.'

'I thought it was an excellent phrase. An excellent idea.'

'Well, about how many nights would you think?'

'I haven't the faintest idea.'

Silence.

Suddenly I was inspired. 'I'll ask him!'

'You will?'

'Why not? I'm sure I can. He isn't God – he's only a man the same as us. He's human, he's fun . . .' I felt bold. Brian was impressed. I was impressed, myself.

So when the day came I was ready. I hadn't actually prepared my form of words. If one referred to it as 'intercourse' that removed from it any air of impropriety, but made it sound rather unlike what I was thinking of.

There was a good deal of scurrying round by the nurses that morning. They even took away dead flowers and put fresh water in the vases of the flowers that were still alive. Finally there was the stir as of a whole corps of heralds trumpeting soundlessly.

His Majesty swept in – at the head of a squadron of retinue, three baby doctors, the Sister, the Staff Nurse, three nurses including our African friend, and goodness knows who. He was wearing a glowing tangerine-coloured rose in his buttonhole and a glowing regal expression on his large handsome face.

I thought, *I shan't be able to do it.* In front of all those people. It was sheer ill luck.

His Majesty came and looked into my eye, talking to me in his usual un-stuffy way – I could have asked him easily had we been alone. Then he held forth to the audience. The baby doctors looked at my peak and learnt that it didn't affect my vision and so on. Finally when, this time from a distance, I received the well-known instructions and injunctions, I couldn't say a thing, other than Thank you, to him.

At last the grand visitation was over and the ward settled down to routine. I had to say something to Brian.

'I'm sorry, Brian. I let you down.'

'No problem, Joe.'

'I think my spirit was broken by sheer weight of numbers.'

'Mine would've been the same. That shower made it impossible.'

'So we're no forrarder, alas!'

There was a pause.

Brian said: 'We'll just have to play it by ear, Joe.'

I smiled at that. By *ear* . . . 'Don't we always?' I said to him.

Brian turned to look at me. 'Joe,' he said, 'I think you must be a good husband.'

'I don't know about that,' I said. 'I doubt it. What about you? I think you probably aren't so bad.'

'Maybe. Maybe not.'

The following day I was discharged. Kind friends came to take me back to London by car, so that I shouldn't be jolted by a train. Elspeth came with them, bringing presents for the nurses. Brian and I shook each other firmly by the hand. In a sudden outflow of emotion I kissed Sister Curtis on both cheeks. (Marìa and Chu-Yin were off-duty, unfortunately.)

So I came back again to our house and our garden – now up for sale. And to a special lunch that the girls had spent all morning preparing. It was like a celebration. The girls examined my peak and disagreed with His Majesty's opinion that I wasn't quite as beautiful as before – that's the sort of daughters to have!

After lunch Elspeth said: 'You'd better have a rest this afternoon. And go to bed early.'

'Go to bed early!' I cried enthusiastically.

'I've made up a bed for you in the other room.'

'I shan't have to go to it straight away?'

'You know what His Majesty said.'

'As if I could forget!'

'I'm not so sure of that . . .'

'Oh, all right.'

In the event I didn't go to it straight away, but we both behaved with utmost circumspection. Elspeth held my hands in a very firm grip. The minutes passed, bringing happiness. 'It's wonderful to be in bed again,' I said.

'Yes . . .'

A long pause.

'Wonderful.'

No reply. 'Isn't it?' I said.

'I think you'd better be going. I don't want you to. But you know . . .'

'Not so soon.'

'Darling, you must be sensible.'

61

A call to my better nature. I had to answer.

'All right.' I got up, and after a lingering exchange of lesser civilities went to the other room.

So far so good.

The following night we were naturally a bit more easy-going about it.

'Isn't it wonderful to be in bed?'

'Yes . . .'

The minutes passed. Elspeth was not holding my hands firmly. She wasn't holding them at all.

'Wonderful . . .'

I listened for her to say 'No.' She breathed, 'Yes . . .'

One thing began to lead to another. I said:

'This is more than flesh and blood can bear.'

I listened again for her to say No. I could have sworn I heard her breathe, 'Yes . . .'

I said: 'If we go at it gently, very gently, I'm sure it will be all right.'

'Are you really sure? My darling?'

I said: 'I'll tell you what. I'll stay absolutely still, and keep my eyes shut. Then I'm sure it will be all right.'

Looking back on it I can see that it was sensible to stay absolutely still, but I don't know what good I thought keeping my eyes shut was going to do me.

I rolled carefully on to my non-operated side, and shut my eyes. 'There! . . .'

It was bliss, bliss every moment up to and including the last, especially the last. It was incredible.

And then, then I opened my eyes. 'Darling, I can *still see*!'

PART II

PART II

CHAPTER I

ABOUT PROPERTY

O ur house was up for sale.

The Blackwells actually had sold out to the Council. Our joint agent's professional discretion – or slyness – which had prevented his telling us what they were up to, and how much they were likely to get thereby, didn't stop him letting us know now that they had got an inflated price. Meanwhile, having originally encouraged us with the proposition that he would get us £60,000 for our house, he suggested, now that he'd got to prove his proposition, that we should put it on the market for £50,000. House-prices were falling everywhere, he said.

We learnt to speak the language of house-selling. We learnt to speak of Asking Price, which was an entirely false price, being neither what we hoped we might get nor what we'd be willing to take. It was a price from which one Came Down to the price one was forced to sell for. I'd always told Elspeth I thought house-agents were crooks: it came to us now that in house-selling and house-buying, the behaviour of all parties concerned could scarcely be called straight. We had our first intimations of that Great Truth –

Buying And Selling Property Brings Out The Worst In Human Nature

Our tenants' organisation held a party to celebrate its victory over the Council, the Labour Council. The Blackwells, now living miles away, were nevertheless present, large as life and universally received as true as blue. Elspeth and I, likely to drop £5,000 or more as a result of their manoeuvre – which was known to everybody present – were received as ever like the cads of the party, the local Reds. Knowing the ways of the world, what else could we expect? We were wondering, as the organisation had been awarded costs, if we should ever get our £150 back – fools that we still were! It was a jolly party.

With six weeks' convalescent leave under His Majesty's orders, I was conveniently at home to show prospective purchasers round. I was astonished by how many prospective purchasers turned up. I was not allowed by His Majesty to do much reading, so I'd resolved to spend my time listening to some of all those gramophone records I'd bought, played a few times, and then filed away. I'd decided to work my way through all the Beethoven quartets, then all the Bartók quartets, the Schubert song-cycles – not to mention whole operas, for instance *The Ring*. Did they give me a chance to do it? Not likely.

I have called the people who interrupted me prospective purchasers. I was coming to realise more clearly than ever how innocent I was. More than half of the people I showed round hadn't the faintest intention of buying the house, of buying our house or any other. For some of them it was purely a sight-seeing tour – why not charge them an entrance-fee, I wanted to know, for visiting an Unstately Home? There was another lot, though, who sounded more serious. They held most encouraging conversations among themselves – 'We should have to have that wall down, shouldn't we, dear?' or 'We could just fit the cocktail-cabinet in there, don't you think?' or 'It's so *light*, darling, we could paint the walls *blue*!' It was all fantasy. I've no doubt some of them went home and spent happy weeks decorating and furnishing our house – in imagination.

Occasionally there were what appeared to be bona fide prospective purchasers. After the grand tour they sat down in the sitting-room to talk to me, and in due course they asked politely:

'And who are your neighbours?'

The Blackwells' house was in full swing as a staging-post for Council tenants on their way to more permanent homes – or further staging-posts. There were usually about three families in the house at once. In fact they were quieter than the Blackwells, for the most part leading much more vocally-restrained lives. (One night somebody woke us all up by crashing through one of the huge plate-glass sliding doors that gave on to the Blackwells' terrace, but that was exceptional. The glass was not replaced for a long time, and we wondered if the tenants were counting on being moved on to their next port of call before the Council found out.)

'And who are your neighbours?' It was a little embarrassing if the prospective purchasers, while inspecting the garden, looked through the Blackwells' wire fence and saw the family of little Ghanaians at play.

The Ghanaian children didn't make a great deal of noise, but they had a habit of tearing off any of our plants that grew through the fence or that they could grab from their side of it. They seemed to have a special taste for shredding.

'They are rather destructive,' I said to our younger daughter, Annie, one day when we saw a lot of shredded rose-petals on the ground. Our roses flowered all the year.

(You may have noticed some time ago I said she was called Virginia. She was. When we decided on names for our children we knew that a time would come when they would reproach us for our choice. So we told them that when they were old enough they could choose fresh names for themselves and we would abide by their choice. At the ages of ten and eight, respectively, they got together and came to us with the information that they *both* wanted to be called Anne. Such confusion arose that in the end they agreed to give up. Viola remained Viola. But when Virginia went to a School of Art she moved into up-to-date circles – there's nothing so up-to-date as a School of Art – from which she emerged as Annie.)

'You must admit it's destructive,' I persisted.

'It's the result of deprivation,' she said, because they were black.

'Deprivation?' I cried. 'Look at their toys!'

Their garden was littered with expensive toys – a red plastic tricycle, a yellow plastic dolls' pram, a red and yellow and blue plastic roundabout or something that looked like a roundabout, and God knows what else in the way of broken plastic bits and pieces.

'If it's the result of anything,' I said, 'it's the result of indulgence!'

She turned away. Her current principles forbade her admitting it, but I could tell from the curving of her cheek, where it showed beside her hair, that she was trying not to laugh. (She was a pretty girl, with long silky fair hair that swayed when she walked.) I thought it was sweet of her to give up the argument, but of course I didn't say anything.

However it was no laughing matter when prospective purchasers of the house wanted to know who the neighbours were. The most we could do was to assure them that, whoever the neighbours were, they would not be in residence for long.

So the weeks passed and we began to get offers. A new phrase in the language – Offering Price. I was going to say it was neither more nor less false than Asking Price. But it could be, in its way, more imaginative. We discovered there were *soi-disant* purchasers who made offers without for a moment meaning it. They bought houses, in contrast merely to decorating and furnishing them, in imagination. I should have liked to put up a notice on the front gate –

NO FANTASISTS ADMITTED

In due course there were Offering Prices convincing enough for us to consider them, only to learn that they were contingent upon the offerers selling an unsaleable property elsewhere or raising a colossal mortgage on negligible security.

The weeks changed into months. I was back again for my final term at the office, and we had got nowhere, apart from devoting our Saturdays and Sundays to behaving like attendants at Madame Tussaud's. Then winter came along and our stream of visitors diminished because it was cold – and that was worse still.

'Never mind!' wiseacres who had been through the mill consoled us. 'Some day someone will come along who'll fall in love with the house.'

Fall in love with the house? In a long life I'd seen love take so many forms, mostly bizarre, that I supposed I couldn't profess to being surprised by this one.

In the meantime I refused absolutely to countenance our buying a flat before we'd sold the house. Robert had once been the not-so-proud owner of two monumental properties for over a year.

Elspeth nevertheless went out looking at flats – on 'a recce', as Field Marshal Montgomery might have called it. There was a dismaying recce after she had read in *The Daily Telegraph* that lots of smart people were going to live in Parson's Green. 'Peregrine

Worsthorne's gone to live there!'

'I know,' I said. 'He got into the Underground there, the other morning, in his scarlet socks.'

One Saturday afternoon she took me to look at a house there that *we* could afford. Street upon street of little red-brick petty bourgeois houses with bay-windows –

'Do you realise,' I said, 'this is the sort of house I spent my childhood in? It'd be going back to square one.' I was stirred to eloquence. '*Say the struggle nought availeth,*' I cried, 'if I've got to end my days in Parson's Green!'

That was that.

I had offended Elspeth. On the way home she sat beside me in the Underground, silently looking straight through the window on the opposite side. My offence dawned on me: after she'd gone to all the trouble of finding the house, I'd thoughtlessly dismissed it out of hand.

I leaned sideways towards her. 'Let's have something nice for supper this evening. Let's go out, shall we?'

'Why did you say that?'

'To try and cheer you up.'

No response.

'I'm sorry,' I said, 'that I turned it down so hastily.'

'Oh, that's all right . . .'

It looked as if tears had come into her eyes.

She had to locate houses and flats, arrange to go round and see them – all after she'd done a full week's work. It's something that doesn't seem to get mentioned in novels, I thought, how exhausted we all get with doing things.

At home Viola was waiting for us.

'Those people, the Poults, who came to see the house last Sunday, telephoned. They said they're going to make an offer – '

'Did they say how much?' I interrupted.

'Thirty-eight.'

We simply can't accept that, I thought. We had put £40,000 as our very lowest – whatever that might mean. I could have asked, Do you think they've fallen in love with the house? but I hadn't the heart. I remembered the Poults, nice people, and I fancied they might mean it.

I didn't doubt that the agent would advise us to take £38,000.

Or £36,000. Or any other number of thousands that constituted an offer which was likely to be honoured. He just wanted to take his 2% commission and clear out. The difference between 2% of £38,000 and 2% of £36,000 was £40 – who'd do a stroke of work for that?

'Are you going to tell those other people, the Eulers?' Viola asked. 'They were very enthusiastic.'

'They may have been enthusiastic but they didn't make an offer.'

'They said they were going to come and see it again.'

That was true.

Could the Eulers have fallen in love with the house? They were nice people, as well.

'If you tell them we've got a definite offer of 38,' said our darling offspring, 'they may come up with 40 to get it.'

The deplorable voice of experience came from her having worked, in her very first job after secretarial college, for a firm of property tycoons in its heyday. (In the five years since then they had of course progressed from boom to bust.)

For a moment I wished the voice of experience would be quiet. Elspeth and I had subsided on to a sofa: we were worn and depressed.

'We'll see,' I said.

Pause.

Brightly – 'Can I get you anything? A drink?'

There's a pitch of being worn and depressed at which one even refuses a drink. Fortunately we hadn't reached it. We said we'd like gin-and-tonics.

The effect of the drinks was faintly reviving. I began to feel that possibly all was not lost. What's £2,000? I asked myself. The answer was £2,000, of course. But the worth of £2,000 seemed to vary according to how one looked at it. I wished the way I was looking at it were not so dark.

I finished my drink. 'I'll start getting the supper,' I said masochistically, the idea of going out having been abandoned.

'Oh Daddy, *I'll* do it!'

Elspeth said: 'I think perhaps we *should* telephone the Eulers.' She scanned my expression. 'All right. I'll do it.'

It was not long before she came back from the telephone.

'Keep your fingers crossed! The Eulers were definitely thrown by the news. They're upset because they can't come and see the house again tomorrow afternoon. They can't manage it till Sunday week.' She paused. 'Since they saw *this* house, they've sold *theirs*.'

'Oh,' I said, not permitting myself to go any further. We'd concluded that the Eulers could raise the money. They had told us about their jobs: they both worked, and they were having a mother-in-law to live with them – it sounded as if she had money.

How could one think of fellow human-beings in those terms? As names, to which were attached sums of money, money that one was hoping to get *off* them.

We held our breath for a week. Will the Eulers or won't they?

Sunday week came, and so did the Eulers.

'We *love* this house!' said Mrs Euler as they came down the hall.

They offered our ultimate in Asking Price, £40,000.

It seemed unbelievable. The house was sold. Or as good as. We got our breath back.

60, 50, 40 – it scarcely bore thinking of in cold blood. Best not to think of it!

And would those nice people, the Poults, feel we'd Gazumped them? As indeed we had. Best not to think of that, either.

The Eulers, having sold their own house, wanted to move into ours as soon as they could get a survey done and the contracts exchanged. Everyone knew that exchange of contracts took weeks, if not months, since it involved lawyers. All the same we began to hold our breath again – *we* now had to find somewhere to live. We thought of all the places Elspeth had explored – mostly no longer for sale, of course. But we knew where to look: I'd said I thought I could live there. Mansion flats on the Embankment by the bridge. When you came out of them you had only to cross the road to find yourself beside a lovely curving stretch of the river. On the near side was a row of boat-houses leading to a long rural towpath; on the far side a long river-wall overhung by the trees of a park: in the foreground was a jetty and then a line of little boats moored in mid-stream; and far away the gleaming turrets of Harrods' Depository, sometimes flying Union Jacks –

'It's pure Monet,' said someone we knew who lived there.

We telephoned the place. Extraordinary. There was a flat going of the size we wanted. We arranged to go and see it, holding our breath still harder.

We were shown into the sitting-room. A small, stuffy room with a gas-fire burning . . . My spirits sank beyond recall, while Elspeth and Viola toured the other rooms. My hip began to be nastily painful.

Afterwards, when we were outside, Elspeth said: 'Why did you give up? Did you think it wouldn't do? Viola and I thought it might.'

'Really?' That little room, that gas-fire . . .

'It's got the right number of rooms. They're a fair size and well-disposed. And they're bigger than they look.' Elspeth paused emphatically. 'We could do all sorts of things with it.' She paused again. 'And at £18,000 for a 78-year lease, it's a snip.' She paused for the third time. 'The poor dears have got to sell in a hurry.'

At that I began to think again. £18,000, instead of the £20,000 we'd allowed for in our calculations. Could one profit by the disadvantage of fellow human beings who'd got to get out in a hurry? What about *Buying And Selling Property*? We could.

'Of course if *you* don't like it, we'll have to look for somewhere else.'

We could do all sorts of things with it . . . I began to think about it. We had joined the happy band of fantasists.

The flat was on the top floor and there was a lift – no more running up and down stairs for me. And one thing I had noticed was that the windows gave a splendid view of the sky. (At the house we'd kept the trees, at the cost of never having an unimpeded view of the sky, even from the attics.)

'I'm prepared to look at it again.'

So we made another appointment.

'And this time, darling, look at all the rooms properly! They're *not* small. And *think* about what we could do with them!'

We went. I looked. I thought.

We went again.

We were going to buy it; we were going to buy it . . . We did.

CHAPTER II

MY MOTHER AGAIN

I was in two minds about telling my mother we had sold our house and bought a flat. I always felt short of news to give her, but this particular news could easily revive an old row. After she'd been in the convalescent home for nearly three years, expensively keeping on her own flat nearby and a woman to look after it, it was quite apparent that she would never be able to leave a place where there was somebody on call night and day. Constantly she talked of going back to her flat – she still did – but there had been a brief spell during which she came near enough to recognising the truth to agree with a case for selling it. With my power of attorney I promptly sold it. And then she reverted to her fantasy of going back to it.

One day she said something to which I could only fail to disclose what I'd done by lying grossly: I couldn't do it. Hence the row. 'You've got rid of my home!'

The row was apparently forgotten, but I felt wary all the same.

I was let in to the convalescent home by one of the part-time helpers. I enquired how my mother was.

'Not quite so well today, Mr Lunn.' From the way she looked at me I suspected I was in for a bad time.

I went up to my mother's room. The door was propped open and there was a smell of wee. My mother was lying askew, as usual. Her mouth was in motion as if she were chewing. I pulled up a chair close to the bed.

'I'm glad to see you,' she said. 'But you shouldn't keep on coming here like this. You'll tire yourself.'

I went into my usual explanation. 'It's perfectly easy for me to leave the office early, and there's often a car to take me to Victoria.'

'Well, that's good. But I don't want you to tire yourself.'

'No, I won't do that.'

There was a pause. She said: 'So you're still going to the office.'

'Yes. But not much longer, I'm afraid.'

'How much longer?'

'Till the end of the year. I had a two-year contract and that's when it ends.' My spirits sank as I said it. That, I thought, is when my capacity for earning a living ends.

'And then you'll be pensioned-off?'

'You can't say pensioned-off when I don't get a pension.'

'I know that. What do *you* say?'

'I suppose you'd say I'm retiring, or being retired.'

She thought for a moment –

'You won't *like* it.'

I tried to laugh. I failed.

'You'll miss having an office to go to. And a secretary. And people to take orders from you. *And* a car to take you to Victoria.'

I thought, Oh God! I said:

'Those won't be the only things I shall miss.'

'You'll miss the money.'

'Well, if you must put it like that, yes.'

I don't think she heard me.

She said: 'I wish I had more to leave you.'

'I don't think about that. *You* shouldn't think about it, either.'

We were interrupted by the girl who'd let me in, bringing me a tray with a small pot of tea and a little cake. She went round the other side of the bed. 'Now, Mrs Lunn, let me help you to sit up a bit while your son's here!' She began hoisting my mother up, plumping the pillows and straightening the sheets.

I poured some tea, and glanced round. The elephant apparently made of white soap still decorated the dressing-table. Why on earth of white soap? Why on earth an elephant?

My mother said: 'Who was that? The Matron?'

'No. One of the girls who helps here.'

'That's funny – she wants to see you.'

'Who wants to see me?'

'The Matron, of course.'

I'd heard this story before and found there was no substance

in it. It was my constant fear that the Matron really did want to
see me – to ask me to find a place for my mother elsewhere.
However I said:

'What for?'

'She's always wanting to see you. You can tell from the way
she looks at you, she thinks the light of the sun shines out of *your*
eyes.'

'Oh,' I said, rejecting the idea of asking how she could see the
Matron's facial expression.

There was a pause, and I began to drink my tea and eat my
cake.

'What did she bring you?'

I told her.

'I could do with a cup of tea, myself.'

'I expect you had your tea a little while before I came, and it
will soon be time for your supper.'

'I don't see what that's got to do with me thinking I could do
with a cup of tea now.'

'Well no,' I said patiently. Oh dear! This was a bad day.
Something told me she was further round the bend than usual.
Yet I was surprised by her energy, which seemed undiminished.
I said: 'I'll put some of my tea in your drinking-cup, if you like.'

'No. I don't want to rob you of *your* tea. You need it.'

Saying Oh God! under my breath again, I poured some tea
into her plastic cup with its serrated drinking-spout. I put it in
her hand, and helped her to bring it to her mouth.

'Here you are!'

'Thank you.' She drank. 'You'd make a good nurse.'

There was a longish pause. I listened to the fluctuating sound
of the traffic on the main road. There was somebody talking to a
deaf patient in the next room. The tea was good, anyway

'What were we talking about when the Matron came in?'

Taken by surprise I said like a fool: 'Money.'

'What I want to know is, How much longer am I going to be
able to afford to live here?'

This was a topic I'd met before, and had no desire to meet
again.

'Look here,' I said mildly, 'I've told you before not to worry
about that.' I put my hand on hers.

75

'But I do worry about it. I've got nothing else to do – just lying here, all day and all night.'

'Well, don't worry about how you're to go on living here! You're managing all right. I've explained it to you before.'

'I suppose you have, but I can't remember it.'

'I'll explain it to you. You get your Old Age Pension. You get a Blind Person's Allowance. You get an allowance for Night and Day Attendance. And you have the income from your investments. If you add all those together, it's enough to keep you here.'

The place was no great shakes, I thought, but she conceded that the food was good and the bed comfortable. It happened that there was even a little money left over after her bills had been settled, and we were paying it into her Building Society account.

Suddenly I thought of all the old people who couldn't add up enough to keep them somewhere. My mother's investments were small, inherited from an old childless aunt. How fortunate she was! How fortunate *we* were! (Actually we should all have been more fortunate if she'd let our stockbroker advise her, but she refused to hear of it.)

'Have I got any money in the bank?'

'Yes.'

'How much?'

'I don't know. I'll tell you when the next statement comes in.'

I had no intention of doing so. She was now completely out of touch with the current value of money, which was decreasing at the rate of about 15% every year, and she hadn't had to buy anything for herself for eight years. She was appalled by the increasing charges of the convalescent home, which were perfectly justifiable; and when I told her the magnitude of the sums of money she held, she was too incredulous to take it in.

I leaned closer to her. 'Listen, my dear . . . You just mustn't worry. You're all right. Do you understand that? You're all right.'

Suddenly I heard the echo of Elspeth's saying exactly the same thing to me, trying to make *me* believe that *we* were all right.

'I suppose *you*'re worried about money?'

'We shall be all right, too. You mustn't worry about us.'

'I can't help it.'

I was in no position to make any comment. To shift the line of conversation I decided to risk uttering the word 'flat'. I said:

'I've got some news for you this week. We've sold the house at last. And we've bought a flat.'

'A flat?'

I thought, Here it comes – You've got rid of my flat and now I haven't got a home. I merely said, 'Yes.'

My mother said:

'I suppose it's for you and the Matron to live in.'

'*What!*'

'What I want to know is, what Elspeth thinks about the divorce.'

'What divorce?'

'Yours and hers. You're not going to set up with the Matron without marrying her, are you?'

To laugh or to cry, to scream or to shut up? I took hold of myself. I said:

'I think you've got everything mixed up again.'

'Have I?'

'You have,' I said. 'Now listen to this! Stop thinking about the Matron – I don't know anything about her; I'm not interested in her; I don't even see her every time I come here. Provided she runs this place properly, that's all that concerns me about her. Have you understood that?'

Silence.

'As for the flat,' I went on, 'we've bought that so that we can cut down our living expenses. It's quite a nice flat – at least it will be when we've done it up. And the people who are going to live in it are Elspeth and me and Viola –

'What's become of Virginia, then?'

'Virginia doesn't live at home. She lives in a studio with some other artists.'

'Oh.'

'So the people who are going to live in the flat are Elspeth and me and Viola. Do you understand that? Elspeth and me. Elspeth and me . . . and we're very happy with each other.'

'I'm glad to hear it.'

'We're very happy.'

'I've always liked Elspeth.' My mother paused. 'Though when you married her I thought you were baby-snatching.'

'Baby-snatching? She was twenty-five!'

'Ar, but how old were *you*?'

Should I refuse to disclose my age at the time, or blushingly say Forty? While I was trying to make up my mind I realised that she wasn't waiting for an answer. She wasn't waiting for anything – apart from the one thing . . . You have to wait till you're called.

I looked down at her in pity. And the question hovered over my mind, the question I was always trying not to hear when I went to see her – *Is this what's going to happen to me?*

I looked at my watch. When was the doorbell going to ring, to release me? It was nearly time.

'You mustn't miss your train,' she said.

'That's all right.' I stood up and began to collect my impedimenta.

The doorbell rang. I didn't know if she heard it. I said, 'There's the taxi now.'

I paused, and then bent down and kissed her goodbye.

'Thank you for coming,' she said.

'I'll be here again soon. I'll come and see you again.'

'I know you will. You're very good to me.'

To avoid saying anything I kissed her forehead again and then left.

In the train I tried to read, and at Victoria I made straight for the nearest public-house.

By the time I'd put down a pint of beer, I was feeling slightly better. Going over it all again I began to see that the fugue over the Matron had a comic side. In fact it was funny. I thought it was so funny that I began to rehearse telling it to Elspeth.

When I got home I told it to Elspeth. By that time it seemed to me extremely funny. I have to admit it didn't seem so to Elspeth. It's true, what they say – women are strange creatures.

CHAPTER III

TWO CONVERSATIONS AND A LETTER

The arrangement was that I should pick up Robert at his house in Vincent Square and we should then stroll round the corner and have a drink at his local pub. The period was during the Christmas Recess. I arrived punctually at five-fifteen. It was a dark, blowy evening and rather mild. There were wet leaves on the pavement, even at this time of year. In the humid air the streetlamps seemed dim.

To my surprise the door was opened not by Robert – it was Dolores's evening off – but by Veronica.

'Come in!' I kissed her on the cheek. 'The Old Boy's just gone out to buy the evening papers. You know what he's like about newspapers.' She led the way to the staircase. 'I'm to entertain you to a drink while you're waiting. That's if you'd like a drink. I expect you would.' She gave her loud characteristic laugh, nervous yet attractive, somewhere between a hoot and a giggle.

'*I* should.'

We went upstairs to the sitting-room, and I sat down on a sofa while Veronica made two sizable whisky-and-sodas. I watched her. She had a remarkably trim, small figure – pretty legs, I thought. How *old* was she? Mid-forties? She was an Assistant Secretary in the Civil Service, wondering if she was going to make Under Secretary, so Robert told me. Her hair was dressed in a French pleat, with a few wisps allowed to stray over her ears. She turned and came to me. I stood up. Her narrow grey eyes were sparkling with amusement.

'I know *you* think that five-fifteen is too early for Scotch. The Old Boy told me.' She handed me my glass and I sat down. 'You needn't be alarmed. When he comes back he's going to take you out to the pub to drink some beer.' She looked at me a shade

79

wryly. 'So the two of you will have time together on your own.'

There was a pause. Over my glass I looked at her. Her cheeks were their usual bloomy pink, surprisingly unlined. Her tall forehead was rather pale. The pause felt odd to me. Suddenly she gave me a slightly nervous glance and said:

'Has he told you I'm now living here?' She gave her laugh again. 'Since yesterday.'

My face must have shown that I didn't know.

'He was going to tell you today.'

I grinned. 'He doesn't tell me everything.'

She was thoughtful. If I'd been given to thought-reading, I should have wondered if she was convincing herself that in future he *would* tell *her* everything. If so, then I thought she could be wrong.

I said in a friendly way, 'I'm very glad, anyway, that you've moved in.'

'He needs it.' Her glance moved round the room. 'Living here all these years on his own. It's not good for him.'

I said, 'No, it isn't,' thanking my lucky stars that she was not looking at me. The fact of the matter was that Robert had *not* been living here all these years on his own all the time. I had seen several women come, and go. Veronica appeared to be the strongest contender up to now for permanent residence, but she was far from being the first.

She drank some of her whisky-and-soda, and said:

'I'm glad I've got this chance to talk to you, Joe.'

I wondered what was coming now.

She said: 'I want to ask you something. Why does Robert carry this terrific burden of guilt about his marriage to Annette?'

I couldn't possibly have expected the question – nor have answered it. I said:

'I know what you're talking about, but I shouldn't put it to myself in quite that way.' Her phrase 'burden of guilt' was exactly the sort of phrase I could never have used, a phrase summing-up something that was to my mind un-summable. Though Veronica was not one of such people, the phrase satisfied those people who wanted, as Robert contemptuously put it, psychological explanations that could be expressed on the back of a postcard.

80

'What way would you put it in?' Her eyes were sharply bright. (I suddenly had intimations of why Robert thought she might make Under Secretary.) I said:

'I should like to think it over for a moment.'

'Come on, Joe! You'll be telling me next that you want to sleep on it.'

'No, no,' I said easily.

'Well, don't! Because the Old Boy will be back in a few minutes.' She looked at me. 'I do want to know. And I do think you know more about it than anyone else.'

I said: 'In the first place you have to accept the idea that I believe some people are more given by nature to guilt than others. The strength of your predisposition probably comes with your genes.'

'That's what you and Robert think about everything that matters.'

'That doesn't prove we're wrong.'

She said nothing for a moment. 'Then Robert's predisposition must be stronger than anyone else's I've ever known.' She gave me a shrewd, amused glance. 'Stronger than yours.'

'How clever of you!' I cried. 'Do you know that Anthony Burgess once criticised one of my novels on the grounds that I, the writer, suffered from *insufficient sexual guilt?*'

Veronica gave a hooting laugh. 'Did he really? Oh, how killing!'

I didn't think it was quite so funny – nor literary criticism, if it came to that. Nor did I think she was right about Robert, generally speaking. But I wasn't prepared to argue. I set the conversation back on the rails by saying:

'I suppose you might say Robert feels some kind of guilt, among other things, you know, over his marriage to Annette.'

'Was she beautiful? He says she was.'

'Yes.'

'Was it obvious she was schizoid? Did he know?' She corrected herself. 'Of course he must have known.'

'Yes, of course. In a way, that was one of the attractions, I'm sad to say. Her inner world was quaint and remote, and fragmented . . . Robert spent years exploring it – he got drawn in.'

'Poor devil!' She went on: 'Do you think he did understand her? I'm sure he must have.'

I thought, He fell deeply in love with her, which may be a different matter, almost always is. But I said, 'Yes.' I went on. 'He got a pretty clear idea of how severe the split was – between living in the world of her own and living in the world other people were living in.'

'Did he think it was dangerous for her to marry?'

Now we were getting towards the sort of ground it was more usual for me to tread. I knew how deeply and how long Robert had pondered the question. And how uselessly. 'He thought it might be. Or it might not.'

'But he went ahead.'

Robert was in love with Annette. I could only say to Veronica, 'Yes.' What neither Robert nor I nor anyone knew was what difference it would have made to Annette's fate if he had left her to herself. I had a terrible feeling that, after all the suffering – and all the joy, which was not to be overlooked – for both of them, it had ultimately made none.

Veronica went on incisively: 'How did she get on? I mean as a wife.'

'Pretty bizarrely, as you might expect. Her ideas about running the *menage* were idiosyncratic, to put it mildly. For a start she had moral objections to employing servants. Coupled with a negative talent for house-keeping. In a house like this.'

'I suppose Robert wanted her to entertain. That's what they must have bought this house for.' She thought about it for a moment. 'I suppose it *might* have helped her to come out of her shell?'

I said nothing. I was suddenly grasped by memories, memories of this room and strange parties – of Annette dressed brilliantly, behaving like a duchess; and of Annette not appearing for hours, then, dressed in scruffy old jeans, passing wraithlike through the room as if there were nobody else there. That was in the days before she had drinking-spells.

'Was it Robert who persuaded her to have children?'

I could see the case Veronica was building up. I said:

'You know, for the first years after the children were born she was distinctly better, more able to cope with life. Don't forget she was a highly intelligent woman.' I paused. 'But that spell was the last remission before the inner cold – '

'Clamped down.'

I couldn't bring myself to say anything.

There was a long pause. Our drinks stood beside us, for the time being untouched. Veronica said:

'I suppose she was treated for it?'

I said: 'You don't think Robert neglected anything, even if he didn't have any faith in it? Or still does neglect anything, for that matter? Psychiatry, chemotherapy, the lot . . . In the Home, where she now is, it still goes on, so far as I know. He never talks about it.'

There was another long pause. This time it was not Veronica who spoke first. I said:

'I can see where you think the burden comes in.' I had dropped the word 'guilt' – who was I to single it out from regret, remorse, responsibility, love? . .

'We've got to get him out of it!'

I picked up my drink again.

'It's not *good* for him, Joe, going on like this for years.'

I had a suspicion that I was being at least half-accused, as his closest friend, for letting it go on. As if *I* were able to influence Robert!

'You do see that, don't you, Joe?'

'I do.'

She picked up her glass again. 'It's this terrific burden of guilt,' she said with fresh energy, 'that prevents him getting divorced.'

Ah! I thought.

I behaved as if I didn't know I was required to comment. I was not sure what I wanted to say in any case. I liked Veronica; I thought she was a good woman; I could see that she was determined to make Robert happier – I was prepared to give her every credit for doing her best for him. But was *her* best *his* best? . . Of course I'd thought about these things. I'd seen Robert's feelings about his marriage to Annette as a cause for his not getting a divorce. When, a moment ago, I had listed to myself guilt, regret, remorse, responsibility, love, I had momentarily forgotten conscience. Conscience came into it strongly.

But I'd also seen – and this I couldn't say to Veronica now – that the unattached, quasi-unmarried state was not without its appeal to him. (After all, he hadn't married, in the first place, till he was forty-five.) Disloyal to him though it might seem for me to say so, I admitted to myself that 'not without its appeal' could well be the understatement of the evening.

Veronica was drinking the last of her whisky-and-soda. I wished Robert would come back. I thought he was taking an extraordinarily long time to buy a *Star* and a *Standard*. She said:

'We've got to try and get him out of it. For his own sake.'

I drank some of my whisky.

'You do agree, don't you?'

'Yes.'

'Joe, I want you to back me up.'

So we'd reached the aim of the conversation. I said, 'All right.' I raised my glass to her, silently signifying that I was willing to be her ally. (It really was a tremendous difference – for the better – that she had made to Robert's life during the last year.)

'Good!'

Actually, while this had been going on, it had dawned on me that I was the victim of a put-up job. Robert had been sent out so that she could have this conversation with me. Oh well! . .

Veronica stood up, holding her glass. 'I won't offer you another one as Robert will be here at any moment to take you out.' She was having another one, herself.

As she came back to me she was looking critically round the room.

'Tell me – has this place ever been re-decorated since *her* time?'

I felt it would be disloyal to Robert to say No, but disloyal to Universal Truth to say Yes. She went on.

'Have you noticed the colour of the paint?' She suddenly gave her laugh. 'It's filthy dirty!'

'Dolores looks after him quite well,' I said peaceably.

At that moment I was relieved to hear the sound of Robert coming upstairs. The conversation was at an end.

'Hello, love!' Robert put his arm round her waist and kissed her. 'Everything all right?' he asked her – I thought it was a bit cool of him.

'I was just telling Joe it's time you had this place re-decorated.'

Years ago I'd told him many a time that the place needed re-decoration, and he'd looked so pained that I gave up.

'Good!' He hugged her. I thought, You old humbug!

'We'll get it done without disturbing you. I've got just the little man to do it.'

I thought, in view of the size of the place and the state it was in, that it would take a 'little man' the best part of three years. Robert was looking down into her eyes adoringly.

'It won't cost you half', Veronica was saying, 'of what it would cost to have an expensive firm of decorators.' (And probably wouldn't be done half so well, I thought.)

Robert was nodding his head in agreement. He could easily have afforded the best firm of decorators in London. It crossed my mind that in Veronica's Civil Servant's efficiency there might be a touch of parsimony.

Veronica disengaged herself from him. 'It's time for you and Joe to go to the pub.' She smiled up at him. 'I shall just sit down and finish my drink, and then I'll start cooking something for supper.'

What a transformation for him! Someone to cook his supper on Dolores's night off. Someone to be in the house when he came home. I thought of Elspeth and me – years and years of comforting happiness. And that made me think of Jonathan, who seemed to feel that comforting marital happiness of that sort stifled the spark of Divine Discontent which generates Art. Perhaps he was right. And perhaps he wasn't. Dickens didn't know comforting marital happiness: George Eliot and Trollope did. (Yes, I know George Eliot never knew the actual marriage ceremony with George Henry Lewes.)

'Come on!' Robert crammed on a shapeless hat. And we set off to the pub. When we were outside the house he stood still on the pavement. 'The pub hasn't opened. I passed it.'

I cursed. It was one of the signs of the times: some local pubs seemed to open when they felt like it. The upshot was that two elderly men, one of them an elderly man of considerable distinction, might be seen trailing round at five-thirty from one public-house to another, or else standing disconsolately still in the doorway of one that wasn't going to open till six o'clock.

Actually on this occasion we were lucky with the second one we came to. It was neither small nor cosy nor free from juke-box music, but at this stage of the evening it was open; and the beer it served didn't offend what Robert regarded as my inexplicably pernickety taste for beer that was pumped by hand.

We settled down. First of all he asked, 'What about the house and the flat?' It was out of pure friendship: it was the sort of thing he had no interest in. I told him we'd triumphantly arranged to exchange contracts for sale of the house and purchase of the flat on the same day.

'We shall have to find somewhere temporary to live,' I said, 'for four or five weeks to begin with. While we have the flat done up – '

'What for?'

'You wouldn't understand.' I paused. 'But Veronica would.'

He grinned distantly in acknowledgement of my having made a minor score. We drank some of our beer.

'The flat's got to be re-wired for electricity; have central heating put in; have a fresh bathroom and cloakroom, and a fresh kitchen; and be re-decorated throughout.' I thought it served him right, to have to listen to all that.

He paused for a while, then said hollowly, 'Any news?'

I shook my head. 'I've now received my last monthly pay-cheque but one.'

He was silent, looking pained on my behalf.

I felt pained on my own behalf. Elspeth wanted me to ask our doctor for something to alleviate depression – retirement depression!

Robert said:

'Any news of *Happier Days*?'

I shook my head. Then I thought of something. 'Yes, there is.'

I asked if he remembered the American woman who'd published (with no success) my last novel but one – a very nice woman who liked my books and who understood what I thought of as my sort of novel. He did remember her. I said:

'Well, she read the typescript of *Happier Days* and wrote to my agent, saying she couldn't publish it – but "it's such an adorable book, do you think Joe would let me have a copy of it, when it comes out in England, to keep for myself?" Isn't that the best American publishing story you've ever heard?'

Robert smiled wintrily. 'It's explicable.'

'Entirely explicable.' I had a very fair idea of what I thought of as my sort of novel and what I thought of as the American sort of publishing industry – never the twain shall meet. I'd had a string of American publishers who'd tried me, not unlike many another English writer. Some of them had not *lost* money on me, but that was not the point of industry: profit was what was required – I could see that.

'I shall send her a copy,' I said. 'She's a good sort.' It wasn't her fault that large numbers of Americans didn't want to read my books. Come to that, were there large numbers of English who wanted to read them?

'It's a very good book,' Robert said. 'One of your very best.'

My spirits revived a little. Writers live for praise, I'm afraid. Afraid – fiddlesticks! It's perfectly natural and honourable.

I drank a fair amount of my beer – it was quite good. 'We'll see what happens in this country.'

'Have you thought what you're going to write next?'

'Give me a chance!' I then asked him a question I didn't usually ask him. 'Have *you* decided what *you*'re going to write next?'

As he'd got an American Book of the Month choice with his last book, he must have made a fair amount of money with it in the USA, but I wasn't by any means sure that it had done as well as he hoped in this country. Someone was being employed to turn some of his earlier novels into a television serial; but we'd had enough experience to know that you believed in a television serial when you actually saw it on the television screen, not before. (If you did see it on the television screen, though, that meant you stood to make a lot of money out of your novel as *The Book Of The TV Serial*.)

I said, 'What about another beer?'

'Yes . . . Will *you* get it?' He gave me a one pound note from his wallet. I thought his back must be painful.

I came back from the bar and put our two pints on the table, gave him his eighteen pence change, and noticed that he was looking unusually thoughtful.

'What are you thinking about now?'

'Books.'

'What, about books?'

He began his fresh beer.

'Oh, how publishing is changing. How books are changing. How people are changing.'

'How are people changing?'

'I was thinking about your books to begin with. One of the things you were original in, was not being especially prudish about sex.' He eyed me with an ironic look.

'That's as may be. I've been wildly overtaken since then.'

'Just so. Books, and people, have become steadily less prudish about sex.'

I interrupted. 'You'd sometimes think they were no longer prudish about sex at all.'

'Books and people,' he went on, 'have become less prudish about sex.' He paused. 'They've become *more* prudish about money. And *more* prudish about death.'

We thought about it.

'I'm taking as the standard for comparison,' he said, 'the degree to which people were prudish at the time of the classic Victorian novelists.'

True. The people around *us* were chary of talking about money in their private affairs, and of talking about death in their personal lives. It occurred to me that I didn't like the idea of making my will. And I thought of what happened if I asked people what their incomes were – the hunted look that came into their eyes!

As we drank our second pint – we never drank more than two – we talked on. Robert said:

'The Victorian novelists were much less prudish about money than we are. And much less prudish about death.'

'And somewhat more prudish about sex, you might say.'

'They wrote better books than we do.'

'Agreed.' What else could I say?

Towards the end of the conversation I said:

'This has given me an idea, for when I'm writing my next book.'

'What?'

'As I made a bit of headway in not being prudish about sex' – I paused – 'I might have a shot now at not being prudish about death and about money.'

Robert did not say anything. He never agreed over-hastily with my ideas.

I could see, myself, that there must be plenty of arguments against as well as for. One against money, that struck me there and then, sprang from my having just recently read in the *FT* or somewhere that 'with the annual rate of inflation running at 12%' the worth of money halved in six years. So £10,000 in a novel written this year would have to be equated, for worth, with £20,000 by a reader in 1984.

'Well,' I said, not letting Robert get away with silence, 'what do you think of that?'

He drank some of his beer. 'Your luck might hold,' he said distantly.

That set me thinking again. Perhaps I'd made a bit of headway over sex because I was swimming with a tide, even if I was unaware of it, or even if I was unconsciously helping to generate it. But – here was the worry! – might it be that that tide had set up, in the dialectical nature of things, counter-tides in people's attitudes to money and to death? (The question was simply asking for Freudians to give an answer, mechanical and jejune, no doubt.) If that were so, when I tried writing unprudishly about money and about death, I might find myself in trouble.

I realised that it was time for us to go. We drank up.

Robert seemed to be lingering. Suddenly he said:

'Look here, old boy – I want to talk to *you* about money.'

I couldn't think what was coming next. 'Yes?'

'I've just set up a Trust.' He looked away. 'And *you* are to be one of the beneficiaries.'

I tried breathlessly to intervene with Thank Yous, but he went on.

'It's a Discretionary Trust. The other beneficiaries are members of my family. Not Arthur and Harry, I've taken care of them already. But my brothers and sisters. Veronica, if her position doesn't change; and one or two other persons.'

I felt a fantastic mixture of happiness and embarrassment.

'It should relieve your anxieties and Elspeth's just a little.'

'It will. I couldn't be more grateful – it's wonderfully generous of you.' And so on!

I followed him out of the pub in a state of uplifted spirits. I left him to go to Vincent Square while I went towards the Underground. I walked along the dark windy streets, thinking, I shan't be entirely destitute in my old age – there'll be something to save me! The moon was up now, sailing through the clouds with its halo of rainbow colours.

When I let myself into our house, I found a letter lying on the hall-table. I picked it up. From George Bantock – on the front of the envelope it said *From The Vice-Chancellor*, and it had the crest on the back. I opened it.

> Dear Joe,
> For some years my Council and the Senate has been perturbed by the low level of literacy on the part of our students, predominantly scientists and engineers, as you know. We are taking steps to have them taught how to write their professional papers, but this does not affect their ignorance of literature. They are not lacking in intelligence or curiosity. Their need is for someone to make them read literature, and to talk to them about it as someone talks who knows how to write literature. I can think of no one better equipped to do this than you. Would you be interested? A single course per term, involving not more than 3 hours teaching per week, would not interfere seriously with your writing, would it? You could more or less please yourself in telling them what to read. I expect you would choose novels. Why not include one of your own?
> I am off to Islamabad immediately after Christmas, so it would be a blessing if you could telephone me during the next few days. If you are willing to do it, we could agree terms, an honorarium in the region of £2,000 a year perhaps. I could then get a formal letter of invitation out to you before I leave.
> I do hope you are willing.
> > Yours ever
> > George

By the time I got to the end of it I felt I was practically reeling with high spirits.

After the number of times I'd made fun of George Bantock for always being on the look-out for people to offer *him* jobs – that was why his nose pointed up in the air – he'd offered *me* one.

CHAPTER IV

GOODBYE TO A HOUSE

'We *must* start getting rid of things we don't want.'
'Yes, darling.'

I don't need to say which of us made which of those remarks. The exchange took place as soon as selling the house and buying the flat were settled. The house had been advertised as having 3 recep, 6/7 bdrm, 2 bthrm and so on: it was a 5-roomed flat we were moving into. (Why so many as five rooms? Because Annie, while saying she didn't mean to live with us again, insisted on there being a room for her to come home to. There's nothing one can do about one's children, especially when their behaviour is touching.) 10 into 5 won't go: we had an awful lot to get rid of.

'We can keep all the pictures,' I said helpfully. At that point I hadn't counted them – eighty odd, it turned out, two of them very large. 'And the big mirrors,' I went on. 'We shall need *them* to make the rooms in the flat look bigger.' I considered I was doing rather well. 'And the Eulers are buying all the curtains and carpets.'

'What,' said Elspeth, 'about all the furniture?'

'Can't everything we don't propose to keep go to auction? It's just the chance to get rid of that dining-table.' I'd never sat down at it without noticing it was really a reproduction. 'We'll use my Ma's old table in its place.' A plain eighteenth century breakfast-table my mother had thrown out because in her view it was rickety. I went on. 'And all those Victorian dining-chairs can go, in favour of the Regency ones.' I was becoming enthusiastic about getting rid of things.

'You,' said Elspeth, 'don't know the sort of things auction-rooms will take and won't take. They'll never take that bamboo bedroom furniture. And all those beds. Nobody wants second-hand beds.'

'Why not?'

'They'd rather buy new ones.'

I thought about it.

'And don't forget,' she went on more mildly, 'I want a decent new bed. You must have had that one for nearly thirty years.'

I thought of that bed over nearly thirty years . . . However I said:

'Won't that make one more to get rid of?'

Elspeth said: 'Sandra thinks she knows somebody who'll take it.' (Sandra came in to clean for us.)

'Then we'll have a new bed.' The present one must have cost about £50: the sort she had in mind, its present-day equivalent, would cost £200.

'I don't think you know how much *stuff* we've accumulated in this house.'

'Probably not.'

'And don't want to know.'

'What sensible man would?'

'Well, darling, you'll really have to. I can't do it all.'

'Of course I'll help.'

'Then I suggest you make a start by sorting out the stuff in the roof-space.'

The roof-space! It wasn't even mentioned in the house-agent's brochure. I wouldn't have mentioned it, either. It was crammed with an unspeakable amount of stuff. There were cases of wine in store; large parcels of remaindered copies of my novels (do you wonder I didn't want to go up there?); cabin trunks filled with blankets and sheets; boxes of plates and glasses we kept for parties; discarded pictures; toys the girls wouldn't part with, including a dolls' house; a camp-bed; and that was only the start of it.

Elspeth went on. 'And there's the garden furniture.'

'That's pretty,' I said defensively. It was painted white, of cast-iron designed on the lines of Chinese Chippendale.

'The only way I can see of getting rid of it is by advertising it.'

'Let's advertise it!'

'How about you putting an advertisement in the local paper?'

'Which local paper?'

'You know there's only one local paper.'

'I suppose I can do it by telephone. I'll draft an advertisement.'

Elspeth began to laugh. 'Do you have to have a draft?'

'Of course I do – how'm I to dictate something over the telephone if I haven't got anything to dictate it from?'

'What about from your head?'

We were both laughing. Elspeth said: 'We're wasting time, darling. You were going up to the roof-space.'

'All right. I'll need a notebook . . . . ' I looked round hopefully.

'That's a good idea,' she said and walked away.

So we embarked on getting rid of things we didn't want. A man came round from Phillips's and told us what they would deign to auction. One or two local junk-dealers came round and offered to take everything else away, for sums of money appropriate to the occasion of their doing us a favour. Our advertisements and Elspeth's personal negotiations provided an incessant stream of telephone-calls followed by an incessant stream of people to the house. We decided it was best not to regard the price they offered us for things as in any way related to their intrinsic value.

The weeks passed by. The amount of stuff was getting less, but not less enough. My retirement depression, although I had not yet retired, got worse, much worse when I contemplated all the stuff.

'Please God,' I cried, 'take away this property from me!'

And addressing Elspeth I cried: 'Now I understand why people renounce possessions and become tramps and hippies. What did Jesus of Nazareth say? Lay not up for yourselves treasures on earth? *I* say, Lay not up for yourselves rubbish on earth, either! In fact, Lay not up for yourselves!'

She took my hand. 'It's all right . . . We've got rid of a tremendous amount. We're really doing quite well. And when we get to the flat you'll be glad of the possessions we've kept. You really will.'

'Just a sleeping-bag under the stars,' I said. 'That's all *I* want.'

She looked upset.

'With just you and me in it,' I said.

That was better.

94

And of course that made me think of the sleeping-bag scene in *For Whom The Bell Tolls*. I reminded Elspeth. 'I always think that bit, "and the earth moved", was rather overdoing it, don't you?'

After a moment Elspeth said, 'Perhaps.'

And that made both of us laugh.

Elspeth extended her getting-rid scope. People came to the house from the Red Cross, the St John Ambulance, Oxfam, the Salvation Army – we were now giving things away. The final stage lay before us, when, to get people to take things away, *we* should be having to pay *them*. Oh, lay not up for yourselves!

The last day was notable for the triumph of logistic skill on the part of Elspeth and of slapdash behaviour on that of the removal men. They came half an hour late, having been drinking tea at a caff on the main road. They were in possession of a pantechnicon with scraps of old carpet lying on the floor and containing a huge number of tea-chests partially filled with crumpled newspaper. There were four men; one, older than the others and smelling rather more strongly, appeared to be the foreman. He assured us that although they were starting half an hour late they would finish early. Early, if you please! It was immediately obvious how they were going to achieve that desirable end, when the house resounded with the noise of our chosen pieces of furniture crashing against the bannisters and banging into door-posts on their high-speed way to the pantechnicon.

'Don't you wrap the pieces of furniture in old sacking or something?' I asked, as I observed the purpose for which the token scraps of carpet were used.

'They'll be all right when they get into store, sir. They'll be unpacked straight away.'

'What about now?'

'That's all right, sir.'

I said to Elspeth: 'Is this what other people have to put up with?'

'Of course it is. Everybody will tell you that moving house is traumatic.'

'Traumatic, indeed – it's obviously one of the deepest human experiences. Doubting the existence of God is obviously nothing compared with it!'

When the men came to the pictures an altercation took place.

I'd ascertained that by special arrangement they'd brought wooden containers for the two very big pictures. The rest of the pictures they took off the walls and dumped straight into the tea-chests.

'Aren't you going to wrap the pictures in newspaper?' I said.
'No, sir.'

'Then what's the newspaper for?' I pointed to the crumpled balls of it lying on the floor.

'That's for your china, sir.'

'But you'll ruin the picture-frames by doing this.'

'That's the way we do it, sir.'

'Then you'd better stop doing it.'

He shook his head – possibly to induce thought, I hoped. Not so. He said: 'You'd have to speak to the Area Manager about that, sir. I can't instruct my men to do it no other way.'

'Then I'll telephone the Area Manager.'

I hastened to the telephone – *he* went on as before. It was Saturday morning and the Area Manager was not in his office of course.

Elspeth thought I'd better go out.

'Yes, Daddy,' said Viola. '*You* go out!'

'I won't go without you two. And somebody's got to stay.'

Elspeth was listening to something else. 'I think that's Sandra's friends come to collect the bed.'

Viola said: 'Daddy, why don't *you* make the elevenses?'

So the trauma took its course. The men finished half an hour early – thanks to the vast amount of preliminary stacking and packing we'd done ourselves – and promptly hinted at the consequent appropriateness of an augmented tip.

Desperate, we gave them an augmented tip. Catching the wing of the pantechnicon on one of the gateposts, they drove away. It said on the back of the pantechnicon –

A HOUSEHOLD NAME IN FURNITURE REMOVAL

We were left alone. The house was empty – apart from a small stack of baggage we were taking to sustain us through the four or five weeks we were going to spend living hugger-mugger in a very expensive two-roomed flat, on which my office had a lien, in Westminster – we'd had no time to look for anywhere else.

'Do you want to have a last look round?' I said to Elspeth.

She shook her head – she couldn't bear it.

I looked at Viola. 'I've been,' she said.

So I set off on a last tour, making my way first of all to the roof-space, now empty – believe it or not! Then to the attic bedrooms, Virginia's with paintings on the back of her door – a talented girl. Then through the present guest-room where first of all the four of us had slept in mid-winter, nineteen years ago, without furniture or carpets or curtains. (You'll never get the workmen out until you move in, wiseacres had told us.) The girls were very small, then, and very sweet, tucked up together in a single bed. The past, the past! . .

Nobody who has seen *The Cherry Orchard* can forget when the characters make their last tour of the house they're leaving. 'Goodbye, old home!' I could almost hear a pre-echo of some future owners chopping down the sycamores, the holm oaks and the hollies.

I heard Elspeth's – 'The taxi's come!'

I skipped the other rooms.

CHAPTER V

THE LAST LUNCHEON

Henry was sitting in the centre of the picture, at the head of the table, our Chairman – tall and good-looking as well! On either wing, down the two long sides of the table, were sitting the rest of us, his Board Members and his Directors, and at the far end of the table, opposite to him and separated from him by a fair distance, the Chief Executive of the Company we owned. (Lightning, one knows from experience, can leap any distance.)

The Members of the Board were a collection mostly of retired people, appointed by the Minister. Part-timers we were, who met once a month but sometimes oftener, to do as Boards do, that is to say, listen to what the Chairman had in mind, discuss it, criticise it if we had the nerve, veto it if we wanted to be out on our necks – not that Henry, throughout whatever we were saying or doing, didn't behave with the utmost suavity.

The Directors of this, that and the other, were the bosses who under Henry ran the place: they worked full-time, of course. And the Chief Executive of the Company we owned? Sebastian, always known as Baz. Henry was *his* Chairman, too; and *he* worked passionately, dementedly . . . full-time and a half. In our quasi-governmental organisation, Henry had the status of Permanent Secretary, Baz of Deputy Secretary, the rest of us of Under Secretary.

Henry was aged about fifty, Baz a few years older: they had both worked previously in the private sector, as they called it; now they were in the public sector, and the question always floated in the air, Would they or wouldn't they go back to the private sector? My fellow Board Members came mainly from the private sector – I was the exception – as one would expect in a Board properly constituted according to the current rules to run an organisation in the public sector. One of them was an elderly retired banker, a friendly chap but a bit of a dodo: another was an able lawyer of about Henry's age, who sometimes deputised for him: not one of us thought the Minister had chosen badly. And Henry appeared inclined to agree with us –

'I should like to have kept the same team,' he said.

He said it again *à propos* of today's monthly Board luncheon, which was the last one at which I and Alice Hargreaves, another Board Member, were going to be present, because our two-year contracts had run out. I was sitting on Henry's left, Alice on his right.

'I thought we'd have something nice to eat today,' he said with a consoling smile at Alice and me.

The waitresses had just served us with plates of smoked salmon. Being quasi, we didn't have to employ the Civil Service's corps of caterers.

'Delicious, Henry,' said Alice. (She was Dame Alice.) 'Can we afford it?' She was teasing him.

'I was thinking,' Henry said, 'of proposing that we should all contribute.' He had a way of saying something slyly amusing as if he were serious about it. 'Have you some views, Alice?'

He knew she had views, must have views, since she always had views on every conceivable subject. Alice was one of the only two Members of the Board whom I'd seen ruffle Henry's suavity. (The other one was our Trade Unionist.)

Current fashion decreed that every Royal Commission, every Governmental Board, every quasi-Governmental Board, should include a woman and a Trade Unionist. (I always presumed it must have something to do with the democratic representation of ethnic minorities.) When Henry and I were alone he referred to Alice as our Statutory Woman. Jock Williamson, our retired Trade Unionist, was unvociferous with his views, and so escaped being called our Statutory Trade Unionist – he ruffled Henry's suavity by seeming disinclined to produce any views at all.

'I meant,' Henry continued with his line of thought about our making contributions to the cost of the meal, 'according to our means.'

Alice was an old Socialist. Henry never made clear what *he* was.

'Very good idea,' said Alice. 'Lend me a pound, will you, Henry?'

I could see there was no need for me to intervene on either side.

In the Board Members' room, Alice and I usually got on with each other pretty well as two old Socialists together – she was about my age. She was a long-standing bigwig in Family Planning among other things, and was currently engaged in a battle for the recognition of pre-menstrual tension. And she was a magistrate, of course.

Alice and I sometimes got some fun in the Board Members' room, I'm ashamed to say, out of teasing Jock. (We often met in the Board Members' room because Henry found us all useful and interesting tasks.)

'We want your advice, Jock,' she said to him. 'Joe and I think we need a union of our own, here. To fight for better pay and working-conditions.'

'Eh?' said Jock.

'We think our pay of £1,000 a year could be improved.' She used the Trade Union term 'improved' which means 'increased'.

'Aye?' said Jock.

I didn't know how she dared mention working-conditions, since our Board Members' room was as palatial as the Board room itself.

'So,' said Alice, 'what do you think of it? Would you consider organising a little union for us, and leading it?'

Jock gave her a shrewd look. Though he was never going to be Lord Jock-Williamson, he was by no means daft.

'You won't get anywhere, nowadays, unless you join the big battalions.'

As Jock had skilfully carried his original Union – the Dry Cleaners' and Pressers' I think it was – first into the bigger Union, then into one of the big battalions, without loss of office for himself, he knew what he was talking about.

'Sorry, Dame Alice. Y'see – that's my advice.' And there was a look on his face that could well have been read as saying, That's settled *her* hash!

Alice began to talk about something else.

While we were eating the smoked salmon at this, our last,

Board luncheon, I was recalling other conversations in the Board Members' room, when Alice and I hadn't concealed from each other that we wanted our contracts to be renewed for another two years.

'I hope you'll like the next course,' Henry was saying to us. 'I don't know how good their *chicken kiev* is. I hope it's all right.' He poured some more wine into Alice's glass and mine, some more Perrier water into his own. He caught my eye on the Perrier water: he glanced down to the opposite end of the table and said to me *sotto voce*: 'I've got a meeting immediately after with Baz.'

I laughed, ruefully on his behalf, more ruefully on my own. For the last two years my four-fifths time job had been as personnel consultant to Baz's company, which meant to Baz. Now it happened that Baz was one of those men, passionate, energetic, given to paranoia, who don't want to consult anybody about anything. Characteristically he'd made a brave and dashing Army officer during the War: he'd been decorated with a medal – also with a wound across the cheek which looked dramatically like a duelling-scar.

I glanced down to the other end of the table, to see Baz with one of his own directors on each side of him, eating his smoked salmon perfectly undementedly.

Henry said to me: 'I know it must be a consolation for *you* not to have any more of them.'

He was smiling at me in a friendly way. He knew that it was the opposite of a consolation to me – I wanted to go on working: I didn't want to be retired: I'd gladly have gone on having meetings with Baz every day of the week. (Actually one of my secondary difficulties had been to get hold of Baz for any sort of meeting at all.)

Henry knew it was the opposite of a consolation – but he couldn't resist saying it. I smiled back at him, said nothing. Recurrently I reflected on what a strange man he was. I was fascinated, as well as admiring. There were so many things in his nature which one might have thought couldn't exist together, but which in Henry did exist together. He was ruthless, restless, ambitious, and very able: everybody recognised those. But as friendship between us came into the atmosphere, I recognised the degree to which he was sensitive, thin-skinned, fastidious.

Henry's rôle in affairs was to be sent for to put things right, in one organisation after another, that other people had got into an impossible mess. What more appropriate for a man who was ruthless, restless, ambitious and very able? So far, so explicable. Yet he struck me as sensitive in the way an artist is sensitive. (His younger son, like our younger daughter, had become a painter, and it would not surprise me if Henry were going to take, one day, to some form of art.) He was, I was sure, inherently thin-skinned. He made me think of Ian's dictum that a life in the Civil Service teaches you to be resilient, if not thick-skinned: under that tuition Henry's skin had thickened enough for survival, and yet . . . it sometimes blushed. And his fastidiousness? We all noticed his *frisson* when Alice got on to her campaign of the moment.

But what exercised me most was that he displayed flashes of innocence. (Actually Robert, that other Great Man in my life, did the same; always to my astonishment, because I thought of myself in the world of affairs as the most innocent of men while all other men around me were the least.)

It could only have been in a flash of innocence that Henry had arranged for me to be Baz's personnel consultant. Certainly Baz's personnel was in such a state of chaos that it was nothing if not sensible for him to have somebody to come in and do something about it. And it was not unreasonable for Henry to hope I'd succeed. I liked Baz, admired him in a way, wanted to try and sort things out for him, even to protect him; and to begin with Baz at least didn't dislike me. Where Henry had been innocent was in not taking account of Baz's streak of paranoia. That was now proven only too conclusively. The present situation, after my two years, was that Baz believed I'd been planted in his Company to spy on him for Henry.

'You've been unlucky,' Baz's chief lieutenant on his Board had once said to me, 'caught in the crossfire between those two.'

Those two! Where it came to firing, I didn't doubt which of them carried the bigger guns. But that was no help to me with Baz. Now that I'd come to the end of my two years, Henry might have wished to keep the same team: Baz couldn't wait for me to go. Relief tinged with triumph. (Triumph – yes, Baz had his flashes of innocence, too!)

One of the troubles with paranoia isn't only that it doesn't make you happy, but that it won't let you alone. Poor old Baz found himself constantly impelled to write drafts of the terms of reference of his job – in order to demarcate where Henry mightn't interfere. (I'd never heard of his showing his drafts to Henry, but I might have been wrong.) It seemed to give him a greater certainty of his job being preserved from Henry's interference if he saw its terms of reference written down in black and white.

Henry had said: 'I know it must be a consolation to *you* not to have any more.' Meetings with Baz.

Friendship in the atmosphere didn't preclude the occasional tiny cut. What a complex man! I said nothing.

Henry said: 'Now we shall see what the *chicken kiev* is like.' He drank some of his Perrier water.

I drank some of my wine. He'd chosen a very pleasant wine for the occasion. Alice, on the other side of him, was drinking it at a fine pace.

While the waitresses were moving between us I looked round the room, the palatial Board room, for the last time . . . Parallel to the long table was a wall taken up by tall windows with a splendid view; opposite to it a beam across the ceiling, supported by handsome pillars, marked out a kind of alcove – this was where a table for today's drinks had been placed. All the paint was a pale creamy colour, and on the floor was a very worn but still beautiful persian carpet. And to complete the room, but perhaps not to complete a palace, there were on the wall facing us, where we sat at the top of the table, what looked like two large school honours-boards: they bore the names of past Board Members and the dates of their reigns.

Henry noticed me looking up at the honours-boards.

'Next week,' he said, 'they'll be entering up your name and Alice's' – he turned his sly smile from me to Alice – 'in gold.'

I said nothing again, smiling to myself. He really couldn't resist it! I didn't think any the less of him for it.

'I shall insist,' said Alice, 'on coming in to see it.'

'I hope you'll come in to see us often,' said Henry.

Our *chicken kiev* had been served and we fell to. It was good. The hubbub of the party was reduced by everybody's falling to.

The sun shone upon us all through the tall windows.

The last luncheon. More wine. A rather superior fruit salad. Coffee.

'I don't propose,' Henry said to me, 'to make a formal speech of farewell. I know it would embarrass you.'

'It would.' All things considered, as one might say, it certainly would.

'It wouldn't embarrass me,' said Alice.

The men near to us laughed.

The occasion had come to an end. There was a moment when all of us at the table seemed to realise it. The hubbub faded into near-silence.

Henry spoke and everybody listened.

'I'm not going to make a formal speech,' he said. 'I know we shall all miss Dame Alice and Joe.'

There were assenting murmurs.

'We shall miss Dame Alice for the wisdom of her social conscience.'

He smiled at her. Could he mean it? More assenting murmurs.

'And we shall miss Joe for the wisdom of his experience with people.'

More assenting murmurs. I couldn't help glancing down the table. Baz's eyes were glowing, his duelling-scar looking deeper.

'I think everyone knows *I* should have liked to have kept the same team.' He paused. 'Ministers seem to like a change.' He paused again. 'Possibly because they get changed, themselves.'

Everybody smiled. (The incumbent Minister was different from the one who had appointed Alice and me, Jock and the other two.)

'I suppose,' Henry went on, 'this means we shall have two vacancies for some unspecified time. I'm afraid Dame Alice's activities will lapse.' He paused. 'So far as Joe's are concerned, I propose to interest *myself* more in personnel affairs.'

Interest *himself* – oh,oh,oh!

He'd said it blandly and seriously. There was no reason why he shouldn't interest himself more in personnel affairs: there was every reason to believe he'd do it as skilfully as everything else he did. But that wasn't the point.

Henry's glance moved smoothly round the table. Everybody

else's glance moved to one single place at it –

'Does *that* mean,' said Baz loudly, 'in *my* company?'

Blue eyes blazing with high tension.

Henry smiled imperturbably. 'It means, Baz, in the organisation of which I'm Chairman and in the company of which I'm Chairman.'

Lightning leapt the length of the table.

'I must see that *in writing*!'

Henry said, 'I think we could manage that.' His tone of voice was smooth and friendly as ever. But slowly the faintest of pinkening rose up the side of his neck.

Those two! Into the future together, I thought.

So ended my last luncheon in official life.

CHAPTER VI
HELLO TO A FLAT

We moved to our temporary quarters, Viola sleeping on a made-up bed in the living-room, Annie coming to see us and plainly thinking we ought to have made a more comfortable, less expensive arrangement.

Having now done my last day's work in an office, I had the opportunity to do other things. I had the opportunity, I discovered immediately, to take all my own telephone calls, make all my own telephone calls, answer all correspondence in my own hand or on my own typewriter, look up my own train-times, book my own table for lunch at my club.

There was nobody now whom I could tell or ask to do things *for* me.

'You won't *like* it.' It may have been the voice of senile dementia, but it was the voice of truth.

And suppose I'd been Henry, one of the people who had a car standing outside the door all day long . . . Most horrible fate of all – nobody now to *take* me anywhere.

It is not a laughing matter. Whatever you've been used to, you miss. Preach as you may, there are no absolutes.

I had accepted George Bantock's offer, but I was not due to start till the Summer term, which gave me time to prepare a course. Would I make his students read novels? Of course I would! Would I include one of my own novels? What a question! I sat in buses and Underground trains, having ideas.

Most of my sitting in buses and Underground trains was in the course of travelling to and from our new flat, where I was acting as a sort of self-appointed – and unpaid – site-manager.

I'd held a site meeting on the first Monday morning. One of the men I already knew, the electrician, who, after knowing us for fifteen years, counted as a member of the family. And I'd met the painter because he'd already started work on the previous Saturday, a 'little man' so devoted to the paintbrush that he'd be found painting henceforth on seven days to the week, painting everything white – which made sense to me when I discovered he'd been in the Navy. If it doesn't move, paint it!

The heating-engineer turned out to be superior, especially towards the two kitchen-fitters. We'd employed a classy firm of kitchen-designers, who, after satisfactorily designing us a kitchen, disclosed that they didn't have sub-contracted fitters: they could only suggest we made a contract of our own with these men whose work they had previously experienced – once. The plumbers didn't see fit to turn up. The carpenter put in a courteous if token appearance. I managed to collect all the different parties in one room, and then there didn't seem a great deal for anyone to say – other than what the electrician said.

We had got as far as the subject of wiring up the electrical machines in the kitchen.

'I'll do that,' the electrician said with a menacing glance to his left. 'I don't want any cowboys touching the electrics in this place.'

On his left were the two kitchen-fitters. The elder was Irish and had the sort of pasty, grimy complexion that I associated with its possessor's having sojourned rather long as Her Majesty's guest somewhere: the younger, born unusually pretty, seemed intent on living it down by a rabid display of low-grade *machismo*, being tattooed, of course.

I can't say I was surprised when, a few hours later, I was discussing the contract and the Irish senior one conveyed to me that the job would cost 30% less if I paid him in bank-notes; nor when, a few days later and Elspeth being with me, the younger one contrived to signify that he considered both of us were attracted to him but neither was acceptable.

I wondered whether the two of them objected to being thought of as cowboys; alternatively, whether the Irish one was too thick to worry and the pretty one too neurotic. In the kitchen the pair of them spent a lot of time poring over the plans provided by the kitchen-designers. They could be heard discussing technical points, such as That's the door that's got to be shifted, ay? (As the kitchen had only one door I was surprised by the implication of an alternative, but after more sustained thought I concluded they were perhaps giving vent to natural satisfaction upon recognising a door.)

A respite from troubles on the site, I'd discovered – just like everybody else – was in fantasies of interior decorating. Fresh curtains everywhere; all the furniture that was upholstered freshly covered; the walls and ceilings and woodwork all painted white; fresh carpet everywhere coloured greenish-blue for repose. Elspeth had chosen a classy individual firm of interior designers and decorators, where we paid many enjoyable visits, trying out pretty colours together and choosing sumptuous-looking inexpensive textiles. Dreams, dreams, everybody's dreams . . .

I didn't tell Robert what was going on, so as to avoid his giving me one of his characteristic looks which combined incomprehension with censoriousness.

'What for?' he would have said, in a slightly hollow, slightly lofty, slightly horrid tone.

He would find out What for? for himself, I thought, when Veronica got thoroughly under way with renovating Vincent Square. And then it occurred to me that Veronica would find out for *her*self that he was missing from Vincent Square, receiving honorary degrees in America, Russia, Australia . . .

Meanwhile at the new flat it began to seem to my innocent eye that my troubles were diminishing. But I distrusted innocence. Either you need to be trained as a site-manager, I thought, or you have to have an MBA. (I'd become a great believer in a Master's degree in Business Administration for teaching you how to run something you didn't understand – there were so many dazzling examples of it to be seen in all walks of life.)

The heating-engineer had practically finished. The electrician had gone as far as he could before the kitchen machines came in. The cowboys, having moved the door, had got on with building what they called the Breakfast-Bar, installing cupboards, and fitting the sink into what they called the Work-Top . . . The moment I heard those ghastly words, Breakfast-Bar, Work-Top, I realised that we should never get rid of them –

You Can't Stop The Progress Of Illiteracy

Then came the heating-engineer's final day. He came up to me and said:

'I think you ought to know the kitchen-fitters have boxed in my boiler, so that you can't even get at it to light the pilot-light.'

He must have stood superiorly by while they did it.

That evening the unfortunate kitchen-designers came whizzing round in their car after they'd finished work, and gave a rather impressive show of not looking appalled by what they saw. As a start they decided the cupboard that boxed in the central heating boiler should be mounted on castors – you could then get to the boiler to light the pilot-light by rolling the cupboard out. (A bit of resourcefulness that made one proud of being British.) Then they took out their tape-measures and measured how far from the wall the sink had been installed – four inches further than it should be, thus preventing the dish-washer from sliding next to it under the Work-Top.

'Would you mind going outside for a moment, Mr Lunn? While my colleague and I discuss this.'

I went out. I came back.

'They'll have to cut a new Work-Top and let in the sink at the correct place.'

'Who's going to pay for that?'

They gave a rather impressive show of not looking hunted.

'We shall have to consult our managing director, but we shall recommend that the firm pays for it.'

The following morning the cowboys were called to the designers' office. To be sacked, one might have hoped – until one realised that neither we nor the designers had anybody else on hand to replace them.

The cowboys returned to us. I was waiting for them. 'First of all we'll be finishing your hanging cupboards,' the Irish one announced on breath that was like a gale of Irish whiskey. 'Then we'll be putting the rollers under your lower cupboard, see? And then we'll be cutting you your new Work-Top.'

The butch pretty one said: 'Okeydoke?'

So we duly came to *their* last day. The day of the bank-notes. It was quite clear that they expected an additional percentage for themselves, though who the final recipient of the bank-notes was to be was not revealed.

Everything was ready for the arrival of the kitchen machines. The door actually had been moved the correct number of inches for the refrigerator-cum-freezer to stand beside it. The dish-washer actually slid into place without hitting the sink. The laundry machine fitted in. The cupboard rolled out on its castors so that one could light the boiler. The hanging cupboards were all lined up after a fashion.

Then the gas company delivered the cooker.

I was present when the engineers manoeuvred it into place. 'Good God!' I exclaimed facetiously. 'The top's actually flush with the Work-Top.'

The gas engineers weren't listening to me. Their eye was on something else. One of them took out a folding-measure and stood it on top of the stove. He looked at me.

'Your hanging cupboards have been hung five inches too low. It brings your cowling and your extractor-fan five inches too near to the cooker.' He put his hand on the cooker.

I said, 'And that means?'

'When you've got your cooker going full-on, your fan may seize up, and this acrylic hood may fracture.' He gave it further thought. 'Or it might possibly melt.'

A veil over what followed!

CHAPTER VII

MOVING IN

Another veil, more veils – please!
The removers delivered our property to us from store. A veil over the scratches and bashes in the furniture, over the scars and dents in the picture-frames! A veil over the vistas which opened before us of claims on insurance, of framers patching up gold leaf, of restorers appearing with bottles of glutinous french polish!

And the tea, yes, the tea ... Anyone who thought those tea-chests had been emptied of tea was mistaken. A veil over the tea leaves between the pages of the books, inside the sleeves of the gramophone records!

And above all a veil over the chaos that filled our new little home to the brim, in the name of that *Name In Furniture Removal* which will never be erased from our *Household*!

Is that all? It is not.

More veils in readiness for the arrival, a couple of weeks later, of our freshly-made curtains and newly-covered upholstery, especially for our wonderful made-to-measure, ceiling-to-floor curtains, which in two of the rooms mysteriously dangled a foot short of the floor, and for our two large sofas, to be covered in a wonderful soft corn-coloured material, which unwrapped were a dirty mustard yellow!

I'm afraid I hadn't got those veils in readiness, in fact I had simply run out of veils altogether by now.

I telephoned Elspeth at her office and insisted that we should go to a theatre that night, to see an Ayckbourn play. (There was always an Ayckbourn play on.) It would make us *laugh*.

So to the theatre we went, and a surprising coincidence happened. The house was not very full. As we went down one of the aisles, a man already in his seat looked up at us. It was Steve.

'Joe!' He stood up.

'Steve!'

He had a woman beside him. He turned to her with a fond smile, and then to us.

'Meet *ma petite amie*!' And he introduced her. Burke Loeb. 'Actually Burke's not French,' he said with self-deprecating amusement. 'She's American.'

We all smiled, arranged to meet in the interval, and then Elspeth and I found our seats and settled down in them. 'I wonder what's become of Marìa,' she whispered.

'So do I,' I whispered back. 'Do you think this is another lifeline?' 'I shouldn't be surprised.' I had never expected the previous lifeline to last – I believed that becoming less 'free' was one of love's irreversible processes.

The play began. It made us laugh.

At the interval Steve came across to us, alone. 'Instead of fighting for drinks in that awful bar,' he said, 'Burke wonders if you'd join us for a little supper after the show.' We said we'd love it.

The second act made us laugh.

On the way out our party collected together. 'Burke has her car,' Steve told us. We were driven out to a small Italian restaurant in Notting Hill.

'I like to go to some place I know,' Burke explained.

I'd been to the restaurant before: it was known as one of the best Italian restaurants in London. It became apparent that Burke lived somewhere in the vicinity. And that Steve now lived in the same place. (Later it turned out that the place was an attractive house in Campden Hill.)

Elspeth and I, sitting at the back of the car, exchanged glances. We had moved into our own flat: Steve had moved into Burke's. Moving in! . .

At the restaurant Burke was received with the sunniest of Italian smiles from the proprietor, and so began a delightful supper-party. Parma ham with melon, *scallopine alla Perugina*, and so on.

Burke was small, very lively and very attractive. She had dark hair cut into short wisps, a pale complexion with almost no colour in the cheeks, and lustrous eyes so dark that they looked almost black. She was wearing a pretty black skirt that glimmered with lurex thread, a plain black sweater and a small collection of slender gold chains, and one ring only – but that was the largest square-cut emerald I'd ever seen.

The impression made by her personality was piquant. About her liveliness there was something nervous, almost jumpy; but it was overlaid by a slightly stylised relaxed manner. Very piquant. I watched her with interest: it suddenly came into my head that *au fond* she was a very self-conscious person – the sort of woman whose girlhood might have been made truly painful by self-consciousness. But now she had come to this stylised solution. Was I right? I didn't know. I continued to watch her with interest, and attraction . . . I liked her.

'I'm into children's theatre, in New York,' she was saying brightly. 'This is presently my main interest.'

'Very successful children's theatre,' Steve said. 'Peter Brook thinks it's terribly good.'

'Peter's a wonderful person,' Burke said, in the style of an actress, though I was sure she meant it.

'You remember, Joe,' said Steve, 'I've done some work in children's theatre.'

I will content myself with observing that this was the first I'd ever heard of it. I nodded my head acquiescently – after all, I was far from knowing everything Steve had worked in.

Burke said to us: 'I've done a lot of things – I *do* a lot of things. This is the most rewarding thing I ever did. You know?'

Elspeth said to her, 'I envy you.'

(I was not the only one who came from a long line of non-Conformists with a predilection for doing good: Elspeth's present job was with a charitable trust – where, like most people who do good by working for charitable trusts, her reward was to be underpaid.)

'I agree,' said Steve.

'My great joy,' said Burke, 'is audience participation. It's amazing, the things those kids can do.'

Something made me think of Steve's theatre of improvisation.

'I'm sure,' said Elspeth to Burke.

I thought the evening was going very nicely. We were finishing our Parma ham.

'The surprising thing is,' said Steve to Elspeth and me, 'that Burke knows *Tom*.'

'Good gracious!'

'My ex-husband and Tom,' said Burke, 'were Executive Vice-Presidents together at Boyce Peterhouse New York. Tom is still there.'

I thought that explained, and disposed of, Loeb.

'Isn't that amazing?' said Steve.

'Tom,' said Burke, 'gave me Steve's address.'

I could have said Good gracious! again.

'And that,' said Steve, looking at her fondly, 'was great good fortune for me.' I thought that was a very beautiful way of expressing it.

Burke smiled back at him, but said nothing.

The waiter took away our empty plates.

Steve said to me: 'Burke says Tom is rich.'

We all glanced at Burke. Did rich people, I wondered, talk in public about being rich, especially rich people who were *richer* than the rich person under discussion? Burke said blandly, rather as if she were somewhere else:

'I think Tom has a great talent for playing the stock-market. He always seems to know what's going to happen.' She was smiling. 'You know?'

I could only bow my head in agreement with that.

Steve went on. 'And Burke knows Robert, too.'

Burke laughed. 'Robert's often in New York. He loves it. In New York he rates very highly as a novelist. Very highly.' She paused and then looked me in the eye, sharply, amusedly, sceptically – 'How does he rate as a politician in your House of Lords?'

I blinked. A waiter moved between us, the waiter with fresh plates and the *scallopine*. I was saved from answering.

Now what had led her to ask that question? *Who* had led her to ask that question?

Tom.

I had absolutely no evidence that it came from Tom.

Our glasses were being re-filled. Steve spoke to me.

'I've heard again from Tom. He says he's definitely coming to London later this spring. He isn't going to cancel his trip again.'

As I was enjoying the food and the wine I received the news with equanimity, for the moment.

'But you know what Tom's like,' Steve concluded. 'Here, there, everywhere. I should know.' He laughed at me, probably referring to those days long ago when Tom harried him all over Europe. (It was for Tom that Robert coined the term *dromophilia*.) 'Steve has got to be educated', Tom was wont to tell the rest of us. We thought Education was a nice name for it.

'He's one of the most restless men,' Steve said, 'I've ever met.'

'Reminds me of a bluebottle.'

'Now, now . . .'

'What's he coming for?'

'A house. He's coming to find a house.'

'A house? What on earth for?'

'Oh, didn't you know? Robert knows . . . Tom's going to take a house over here for a month in the late summer. We're all going to be invited to go to it.'

I noticed that Elspeth was listening. Robert had *not* told me. I knew that Robert sometimes saw Tom when he was in New York. I always assumed it was because Robert felt safest if he knew what Tom was doing. Burke was listening, too.

'Tom has a beautiful house,' she said, 'on the Hudson River.'

I should have felt happier to know that he was going to it.

'That reminds me,' Steve said. He looked at Elspeth and me with sympathetic interest. 'You two have moved house.'

'Really,' said Burke. 'That's interesting. How was it?'

'Oh, oh, oh.'

'As bad as that?' said Steve.

I explained why we'd come to the theatre tonight.

Burke said: 'Then I'm so much happier we asked you to have supper with us. Isn't that lucky, Steve?'

Steve said to me: 'Do tell us about it – you've left us . . . all agog.'

'Go on!' said Elspeth to me. 'Tell them some of the things that happened!' I could see she thought it might have a therapeutic effect.

In fact it did have a therapeutic effect. I found myself telling

my story as a subject for mirth instead of misery. By the time I'd
covered the removal men and got to the cowboys they were all
amused. Even I was beginning to think it was funny. Granted I
was giving a theatrical performance – I thought that Steve and
Burke, as theatre-people, could put up with it. It was being a
help to me.

By the time I'd got to today's last straws we'd all finished our
scallopine. The proprietor came and made up to Burke. We
ordered coffee. Elspeth, having started me talking, now nudged
me under the table to stop.

Steve said: 'I'm sorry, Joe. I really do sympathise.'

I said: 'I gather it's pretty universal – it's the way we live now.
In this country, anyway.'

Burke said: 'It sounds unnecessary to me.'

Steve said mischievously: 'It's all experience, you know. The
stuff of life.'

That was too much for me. 'That's exactly my point. That's
just what I've learnt. And that's just what I complain of. For
weeks this has really been *the stuff of MY life*. And I can tell you
it's damned unnecessary. Worthless, wasteful stuff!'

Burke looked at me, her lustrous black eyes wide open.

'It's experience,' I said, 'that's of no value to man nor beast. I
resent it.'

Burke said smoothly: 'You're going to have a beautiful
apartment. I know it.' She looked at Elspeth.

'Of course we are,' said Elspeth.

Steve said: 'You can't have beauty without a price.'

The others laughed, but I didn't. Steve said:

'If it's been the stuff of your life, you can write a novel about it.
That's what novels are supposed to be about, isn't it? The stuff of
people's lives.'

'There's stuff and stuff!' I cried. 'And nobody wants this stuff.'

'I don't see why not,' said Steve.

'They want, they want . . . ' I realised that I didn't know what
they wanted. 'They want,' I said furiously, 'profound spiritual
experiences, profound psychic suffering, don't you see?' I
paused. 'Not the worthless experience of being crucified on The
Wheel of *Things*!'

Despite my agitation, I was pleased with the metaphor –

mixed *and* misconceived! (I'd recently been re-reading *Kim*, which was constantly going on about The Wheel of Things.)

'Have you had profound spiritual experiences?' Steve asked in evident surprise. 'Or profound psychic suffering? *I* wouldn't know what they are.'

'One man's common woe is another man's profound psychic suffering,' I said. 'It depends on how inflated a view you take of yourself.'

Burke intervened. 'Couldn't you use this experience in a novel? It's so valid.'

I thought Oh dear! And then I noticed the bright lustrous look she was giving me. I hoped Elspeth didn't notice it.

'There you are,' said Steve.

There was a pause.

'There you are,' I echoed.

It was the end of the party. Burke said they would give us a lift home. Steve and I went to the cloakroom. When we were alone he said:

'Joe, you're limping.'

'Yes.'

'Isn't it worse than it was last time I saw you?'

'You don't expect it to be better, do you?'

'Are you doing anything about it? You were having physiotherapy.'

'I gave it up. Physiotherapy made it worse faster.'

'Is it really painful? I'm a terrible coward about pain.'

'I can't say it isn't.' I laughed at him. 'The pain keeps waking me up during the night, and that's a bore.'

He didn't say anything.

I said to him: 'You can't have age without a price, either.'

He didn't laugh. 'Can't anything be done?'

'I suppose when it's thought to be bad enough, I can have the hip-joint replaced, by a stainless steel and plastic one, or something.'

'Another operation.'

'It can't be replaced *without* an operation.' I laughed again. 'Anyway, old age is a succession of operations.'

'*Don't!*'

I glanced sideways at him, struck by the tone of voice.

'Have you started to have to get up in the night to do this?' he asked.

'Yes.'

'Joe,' he cried, 'I don't like it!' And he looked at me.

In his face I saw a flicker of resentment, of fear.

So Steve was having his first desperate intimations of age. Oh dear!

We moved across to the washbasins. Steve said: 'What about your eye?' We looked at each other in the mirrors. 'I never asked you if that was all right.'

'I've got my contact lens. His Majesty says I can see like a hawk.'

'Thank God for that! I'm terribly glad.'

We dried our hands and moved out of the cloakroom. 'By the way,' he said in his more usual, amused, confidential tone of voice, 'Tom is very rich.'

I laughed at the idea, and we joined Elspeth and Burke. Burke said she, rather than Steve, would drive. Clearly an active sort of woman.

Elspeth and I let ourselves into the flat. Our evening out had really had a therapeutic effect. Even my hip was less painful. There, before us, we saw the origin of my crucifixion on The Wheel of Things, such Things as I'd run out of veils for – beastly-coloured sofas that had to be re-covered, dangling curtains that had to be lengthened. At the moment we didn't care. Our spirits were high. *Sod* The Wheel of Things!

'Well,' I said, glancing round while I took off my overcoat, 'if there's anything else that can go wrong, I'd like to know what it is.' And I flopped down on one of the sofas.

With a cracking noise the front sofa-leg nearest to me collapsed and I slid on the floor.

PART III

CHAPTER I

TOM

One bright morning in April Steve rang me up. 'Did you know Tom's actually here?'

I didn't know.

'I thought you mightn't.' Steve paused. 'Robert knows.'

We both paused, both reflecting on Robert's not having told me. I said:

'Have you seen him? Tom?'

'Not yet. We've had a long telephone conversation. Joe, he's got the American habit of holding long conversations on the telephone, as if he were in the room with you.'

'Had he got a lot to say to you?'

I heard Steve laughing. 'It took a long while for him to say it.'

In a lapse of taste I said: 'You can't pretend you're totally unused to being harangued by Tom.' I was thinking of those harangues in the long-distant past, as between patron and protégé, master and apprentice, corporal and private.

'That's true,' said Steve with alacrity.

'What was the gist of it?'

'That's what I couldn't really remember afterwards. I did so get the habit of not listening to Tom. You know. I had to.'

I laughed. I remembered the clarion-call with which such harangues began. *Now, Steve!* Obviously the signal for Steve to switch off. I said:

'You must remember *something*.'

'Well, yes, as a matter of fact I do. It's a bit embarrassing, Joe.'

'Come on, Steve, you've never been embarrassed in your life.'

'I have, Joe. I'm constantly embarrassed. You don't understand me.' He assumed a comically plaintive tone.

121

'All right,' I said. 'Tell me what Tom wanted, that embarrasses you to tell me. Stop! I know what it was. He wanted you to sound me out about whether I'd meet him. He wants to poke his nose into my affairs again, not miss anything.'

'Right.'

'What a nerve!'

'That's what I told him, but it didn't make any difference, Joe.'

I didn't believe that was what Steve had told him, but something else had occurred to me. That might be a reason why Robert kept it from me. If he had the nerve to ask Robert to sound me out, Robert would have turned loftily evasive. And not told me.

'That makes me sound terribly weak.'

'Not at all. Anyway, don't let's argue about it! You've delivered the message and I presume you want an answer.'

'Yes. He *is* going to go on telephoning me till he gets an answer, you can see that.'

'I can see it. Poor old Steve!'

'Yes.' There was a pause. 'Well? . .'

'I'll see what Elspeth says about it.'

'And you'll let me know? He *will* keep on at me. I can't take the 'phone off the hook all the time.'

'I'll let you know.'

'Thank you, Joe.'

'When are you seeing him, yourself?'

'Next Tuesday. He fixed it up with Burke – he talked to *her* for hours. We're invited to dinner with him at his hotel.'

I said, 'Which hotel's he staying at?'

'The Carlos.'

'Very nice, too.'

'Trust Tom, to stay at the best hotel.'

'I'd trust Tom to do *that*,' I said in such a tone of voice as to imply that my trust mightn't extend much further.

'It's terribly expensive. Do you know how much a night he's paying? £137!' (I imagined a malicious smile on Steve's face.) 'He couldn't resist telling me.'

'I'm sure he couldn't.'

'He loves having a lot of money.'

'I'm sure he does.' I thought about it. 'It'll give him another platform from which to chuck his weight about.'

'How right you are!'

'Never mind! You survived it in the past: you will in the future.'

'Hopefully . . .'

'You will. So let's have no nonsense, Steve!'

'Joe, you tear away my façade.'

I began to laugh. I heard him begin to laugh. It was the end of our conversation.

I broached the subject with Elspeth.

'What are you going to do?' she asked.

'Consult you. That's what I'm doing now.'

'Surely you're not expecting *me* . . .' Her voice trailed off.

'I'd like to know how you feel about it.'

'Darling, I haven't really got any basis on which to feel anything.' She paused. 'I scarcely know the man – I mean, personally. I only know him personally through you. I really do feel it's for you to decide – if you feel inclined to meet him again, I'll come with you; and if you don't, it doesn't matter to me in the least.'

That seemed clear enough. I was thoughtful. It struck me that she had not come out with a rousing No. I continued thoughtful. Was I making too much of it? Did Robert think I made too much of it? Did everybody?

I made an effort to make less of it. I said: 'I must say Steve was rather funny.'

Elspeth smiled. 'I expect he was.' In closer acquaintance with Steve her disapproval of his worthlessness seemed to have melted – it's not easy to keep up a high level of disapproval in the presence of somebody whose company constantly beguiles you in one way or another. Also I thought she liked Burke, a good woman who was going to make Steve a better man.

'He and Burke are going to have dinner with Tom at Tom's hotel. And where do you think Tom's staying? The Carlos!'

'Oh!'

I was touched to see the slight pinkening of her cheeks. Her eyes shone. It was to the Carlos that I had taken her out to dinner the very first time I ever took her out to dinner.

'My darling,' I said.

'Do you remember?'

'Of course I remember.'

'I was terrified.'

'Not terrified – just a bit shy.'

'That's what you think. I'd never been anywhere as grand as that before – '

'There isn't anywhere grander,' I interrupted.

'And I'd never been out with anyone – '

'As grand as me?'

She laughed. 'Well, you were trying to impress – admit it!'

'What man wouldn't?'

'You didn't have to work very hard to impress me.'

'Well, I didn't know that.'

'You ought to have.' She looked at me steadily, as a woman looks at a man she knows inside out. She was telling me what I knew, but knowing it seemed to make no difference at all, that perhaps I should not be unconfident about my powers.

We'd been over this conversation many a time before, but it never failed to give us pleasure. Elspeth began to smile with recollection.

'You were sitting in that chair opposite the revolving door,' she said.

That was in 1949. The Carlos entrance in those days had a fine mock-Tudor chair with square arms and a high back, simply inviting one to sit in it looking like Hamlet. I realise it must be obvious that my temperamental resemblance to Hamlet is nil. I have to disclose that my physical resemblance was nil also – Hamlet a pale, slender, intellectual-looking, melancholy fellow; I a short, healthy-looking, over-lively, dapper chap. Did that deter me, sitting in the chair, from trying to look like Hamlet while I was waiting for Elspeth? If we all had to *be* like Hamlet, to sit in a chair looking like him while we were waiting for our girl, none of us would stand much of a chance.

'And that delicious *lobster bisque* we began with,' I said.

'We didn't. We began with *hors d'oeuvres*.'

'I could have sworn it was *lobster bisque*.' I couldn't help laughing.

Elspeth laughed.

'It's the past, the past . . .' I said romantically.

'It would be if you got it right.'

I said sadly, 'We've scarcely been to the Carlos since.'

'You might have taken me sometimes.'

'Have you been holding that against me for all these years?' Elspeth assumed an unconcerned tone of voice. 'Yes.'

There was a long pause.

I said, 'Oh, let's give in! Let's let Tom give us dinner there!'

'Do you really mean it?' Elspeth had stopped smiling. 'Are you sure that's what you want to do?'

She was giving me a chance to back out, alternatively making me recognise that it was my decision, not hers.

'Why not?' I said. 'I've probably been rather silly about it. It's time to stop.'

'What will you do?'

'I'll ring Steve and tell him to tell Tom we gracefully consent to dine with him.'

And that was what I did, there and then.

Steve was glad to be relieved of his task. He expected we should hear from Tom very soon. I expected that, too.

'And Joe,' Steve concluded, 'when you do see him, don't forget to ask him how he came here!'

'How he came here? Oh, you mean by what mode of transport. I can guess – the Concorde.' The flights had just started about six months ago: it was the height of chic – and expense – to travel on them.

'Right.'

We had a call from Tom that night. 'My dear Joe, I was so pleased to get your message.' For such social occasions Tom had a specially silky tone of voice – Tom, the diplomat. 'I was slightly diffident about asking you, but I thought, Why not? I'm delighted that you thought the same.'

How did Tom know I'd said to Elspeth, Why not? Ah! that empathy, that understanding, that second sight . . .

He went on. 'I called you straight away, but I'll have to call you again to make a date for our dinner, because my secretary's out for the evening. *He* keeps my schedule of appointments I always travel with a secretary. *Invaluable* . . .'

Elspeth had her head close to mine so that she could hear what he was saying. At the word 'secretary' we exchanged ribald glances.

So that was that. Three days later Elspeth and I, dressed in our most up-to-date clothes, made our way to the Carlos. 'Don't dress!' Tom had told us. 'Old friends don't stand on ceremony.' We were going to find him in a very stately, gentlemanly mood, that was clear.

He was waiting for us at the entrance of the Carlos.

I thought that in appearance he'd aged less than I was expecting. He was about my height and sturdily built, with a somewhat plump, pneumatic look. I'd been expecting him to be much fatter – he loved food and drink. My first impression, though, was of his looking neither as much fatter nor as much older as I'd been expecting. He had never looked anything but Jewish when he was young, and he didn't look any less so now. However his rich, thick, carroty curls had turned grey and he was wearing them clipped very short – they had already begun to recede from his forehead when I first knew him, and they were distinctly sparse now. But his bulging greenish eyes were bulging as ever behind his spectacles.

'How nice to see you both!'

A silky smile lingered round his wide, pouting mouth. He was dressed in a dark, very gentlemanly suit, which looked as if it had been made for him in London. I'd been right: we were in for a very gentlemanly time – to begin with, anyway. That amused me. Tom's social origins, like mine, were petit bourgeois; and no one English could have mistaken his physiognomy for anything but petit bourgeois – a cause to him for more than fleeting misery when he was a young man, aspiring. But seeing him now, I concluded that it had not held him back after all.

He shook hands and he smiled with egregious silkiness at Elspeth.

'I thought perhaps you might come up to my suite for an *apéritif*? If that suits you?'

His *suite*! I liked the idea of that.

'Lovely,' said Elspeth.

Tom laughed at her. 'I thought you would.'

He began to lead us across the foyer towards the staircase. I was glancing briefly around me – the high-backed Tudor armchair in which I'd looked like Hamlet had been replaced by a high-backed Tudor chair without arms. You can't, I thought, look like Hamlet if your chair has no arms. Alas, alas!

Tom's sitting-room was decorated with flowers. We sat down. Tom rang for room-service. He said to Elspeth, 'Would you like a cocktail?'

Elspeth looked slightly flummoxed. Cocktails had come after sixty years into fashion again – for instance, a small hamburger restaurant in our High Street was now advertising a Cocktail Hour, when cocktails were a pound apiece – but she and I had not thought of drinking them. Tom was watching her. She asked for a gin-and-tonic. He looked at me.

'Oh,' I said, in as gentlemanly a tone as it was within my powers to muster, 'I think I should like a glass of sherry.' I guessed that was what he would choose for himself, so I'd got in first.

'I take it you'd like it dry but not too dry?'

'Exactly.'

Two men of perfect taste together. I was very happy about that.

After the order had been given, we settled down to conversation, Tom addressing himself mainly to Elspeth. I noticed that despite his having lived in the United States for thirty-odd years he had not assumed an American accent. It didn't surprise me. When Tom wanted to please he knew how to please; but below the surface flummery he was a stiff-necked, obstinate little man. (He said he inherited his obstinacy from his mother, who had insisted on his being called Tom, though it was not a Jewish name.)

He and Elspeth were sitting on a sofa together. First of all he asked her about our daughters – all very nice, I thought. But it was not long – and I can't say I was surprised – before he was sounding her, his inquisitiveness having got the better of his gentlemanliness, about her job and how much she earned. When she told him she worked for a charity, he said with his friendly pouting smile:

'Then I expect you're underpaid, my dear.'

Elspeth said, 'Yes . . .'

He'd made a score there. He said:

'Is yours a charity that's endowed, or one that lives from hand to mouth on subscriptions?'

Elspeth told him its name. 'Oh really?' he said. 'That must be more than comfortably endowed. Probably very comfortably indeed.'

'It is. Very comfortably indeed.'

He leaned closer to her. 'What *is* the endowment?'

Elspeth hesitated, bullied into telling him. 'About five millions.'

'Then they've no excuse for underpaying you.' His silky tone was entirely dissipated by the intrusion of irascibility. Tom's silkiness was beautiful but it was liable not to last. He leaned still closer to her, his eyes seeming to bulge with sympathy.

'How much *do* they pay you?'

Elspeth was surprised. I could have told her, being fair to Tom, that I would not have expected his becoming rich to have made him prudish about money – or prudish about anything for that matter. (After all, we had been close friends in that distant past.)

Elspeth said, '£5,000.'

'And what was their income surplus to expenditure last year?'

'About £60,000.'

Tom's complexion went purplish-red. 'Then it's disgraceful they don't pay you another £1,000!' His cheeks were swelling. 'At least!'

Elspeth was becoming roused. 'All charities are the same. They take advantage of their staff. It's like the way nurses are taken advantage of – they can safely be underpaid, because they have the reward of knowing they're doing good.'

'My dear, how wise you are!'

I wouldn't have thought he'd have the nerve to say it; but, having been said, it did him nothing but good. Rapport between them was visible. The times I'd seen him do it in the past!

We nished our drinks. Tom paused, while the simmering of his own and Elspeth's emotions subsided. I glanced idly round the room. The flowers were florist's roses and carnations. It was all very pleasant.

Tom, having cooled down, asked us if we would like another *apéritif*. We decided not, and chose to go down to dinner straight away.

In the doorway of the restaurant Tom and the *chef de restaurant* engaged in some typical flouncing. Meanwhile I noticed that the elderly man in charge of the booking-list was smiling at me – in recognition. I was stunned. After God knows how many years! Tom and the *chef de restaurant* were momentarily stopped – not with enormous signs of pleasure – in their flouncing. Then we passed on into the dining-room.

Elspeth and I looked round with pleasure, nostalgia, delight – the dining-room hadn't changed! The mahogany panelling was as ever, the chandeliers and the pink-shaded wall-lights . . . It had *not* been transmogrified by Time.

We settled down at our table with a flourish of table-napkins by the waiters and the subduedly enthusiastic receipt of the menus by us. We saw Tom, the *bon vivant*. (The nearer we got to the food, the more French everything became.)

Elspeth spotted *saumon coulibiac*, which instantly brought choosing to an end for her. As I too liked it very much, I chose it. Then Tom chose it. Our party was united. A little asparagus to precede the salmon –

'I have to be circumspect about my eating,' Tom said to Elspeth. 'I can see that *you* are.' Then he looked at me. 'And about my drinking, too. Gout, Joe. I'm having signs of gout. I hope you're avoiding it.'

I said I was, but that I was succumbing to arthritis.

'Ah yes,' he said sympathetically. 'When you came into the hotel I noticed you were lame.' He smiled. 'I hope it doesn't mean that you have to forgo wine?'

I said it didn't.

The wine waiter came up and Tom ordered. (When the bottle arrived I had to admit that he'd done us proud.)

We enjoyed the food. It was obvious that amity and reconciliation were prevailing. We all began to relax from our task of making them prevail. We became friendly and gossipy. When we were half-way through the salmon, the name of Robert came into the conversation.

Tom looked at me. 'Have you seen Robert during the last few days?'

I said I hadn't.

'Then you don't know?'

'Don't know what?'

Tom paused. 'I'm sure he'll tell you when he sees you, so there's no harm in my telling you now. It had better be in confidence, of course. A startling piece of news, a disastrous piece of news –'

'What on earth?' I interrupted.

'His accountant has not seen to it that his Income Tax was paid for the last two years.' He looked at me hot-eyedly. 'I discovered it. Thank God I did discover it!'

Elspeth and I were astounded.

'The Old Boy was going on,' Tom said, 'thinking he was all right, because his accountant didn't tell him about it.'

I said: 'He's been earning a lot of money in that last few years. He must owe the Inland Revenue a colossal amount.'

'By his standards, yes.' He smiled smoothly, and with an elegant gesture appropriate to a graceful turn of phrase, said: 'By *my* client's standards, chickenfeed.'

There was a pause. I recalled my determination not to be prudish about money. I managed to ask, 'How much?'

'That isn't completely worked out at the present moment. I'd say in the region of £50,000.'

'Good God!' To me that was truly a colossal amount. 'What happened?'

'The man who was handling his account appears to have been grossly incompetent – he's been sacked, of course – and dotty as well. I've never come across anything quite so dotty before. He wasn't being fraudulent in any specific sense.' Tom paused. 'If I hadn't discovered it, it's possible the state of affairs would have gone on longer. Not indefinitely – even in the most incompetent of firms there are checks and balances that come into operation in the end. Actually this particular firm was taken over last April by Pettinger's, who are pretty well organised.' (I'd heard of Pettinger's.) 'Pettinger's would have discovered it in some months.'

'That doesn't relieve Robert of finding he's in debt to the tune of £50,000. What can he do?'

'I'm acting for him.' Tom smiled blandly. 'In a purely personal way, of course. As an old friend . . . Pettinger's will pay the interest on the £50,000 he'll have to raise to pay the debt.' His silky smile came back. 'And I think I may be able to persuade them to contribute towards the capital sum.' Tom looked at Elspeth and me in turn. His pop-eyes shone with a fresh gleam through his spectacles, and his voice became quieter, liquider. 'You see, Sir Abe Pettinger, the head of the firm, wants to cultivate Robert's goodwill . . . Sir Abe wants to get into the House of Lords, and he thinks Robert can help him.'

'But Robert couldn't!' I cried.

'Sir Abe doesn't seem to know that.' Tom shrugged his shoulders elegantly. 'It's astonishing how *naif* some of these City men are.' He was enjoying himself. 'You may assume, Joe, that I shall take no steps to reduce Sir Abe's *naiveté*. Least of all before he's made good his desire to help Robert.'

I couldn't resist laughing. 'Oh goodness!' Then I looked at Elspeth: she appeared not to be enjoying it quite so much – she might have been thinking about how many thousands Robert had still got to find after receiving Sir Abe Pettinger's help. (I rather liked its being called help.)

Our laughter subsided. I realised with regret that I'd finished my salmon almost without noticing it. Tom and Elspeth had finished theirs. Somehow the talk had been too dramatic – splendid meals should be eaten with the lightest of conversation.

Tom, the hero of the hour, turned his glance upon Elspeth again.

'What can I tempt you to have now, my dear? The puddings here are delectable. I remember Joe's weakness for them. Do you share it?'

'I simply couldn't, Tom.'

'Just a little sorbet? Just made with water and lemon juice.'

'Not to mention sugar,' I said, 'and white of egg.'

Tom said to Elspeth: 'You hear? Joe hasn't lost his touch.'

I said: '*I* will have a lemon sorbet, thank you, Tom.'

So we came to the end of the meal. I felt pleased and happy on the whole. We hadn't taken the bloom off a grand occasion by eating and drinking too much. As Tom had been wont to say when he was young, to the amusement of the rest of us – 'Everything was in perfect taste'. I was amused now: the exercising of our perfect taste was due to age.

We let Tom order brandy, which Elspeth liked after dinner.
'How nice it all is,' I said, glancing round the room at the other
people.

Elspeth was still thinking about Robert. She said to Tom:
'How did you come to discover Robert's tax-position, Tom?'

'I suppose I have a nose for these things.' Smiling, he paused
while the waiter poured coffee for us. Then he said to her
seriously: 'And the fact that one has experience of handling, say,
a Rockefeller account, doesn't mean that one isn't ready to cast
an eye over the financial affairs of one's oldest friends.'

I thought I'd never heard bustling interference described in
such poignant terms. On the other hand I had to ask myself,
suppose Tom hadn't interfered? My ill-will towards him had
simply been proved wrong.

A waiter poured Rémy Martin into our glasses – Elspeth's
favourite among brandies.

'I should be happy, my dear,' Tom said to her, 'to be of any
help whatsoever to you and Joe. I gather from Robert that you
and Joe are staying afloat after Joe's retirement.'

'Oh, yes,' said Elspeth.

Tom looked at her admiringly. 'It must be entirely due to
you,' he said.

'No, it isn't, you know.'

Tom gave her one of his I-understand-you-better-than-you-
understand-yourself looks. 'I can imagine what it's like to be in
your position, with Joe unfortunately having no pension, and
your other resources limited. I take it that you have *some*
investments?'

Elspeth reluctantly signified that such was the case.

'About how much are they worth? Robert didn't seem to
know.'

Elspeth glanced at me and hesitated.

I drank some brandy.

'That's all right,' said Tom, not missing the glance. 'Don't
let's go into the detail here and now! Some other time,' he went
on, his eyes bulging again with sympathy, 'we'll study the figures
together.' He explained to her: 'I've made a lot of money. You
see, I can *think* about money.' And he glanced at *me*.

I said nothing.

Elspeth drank a little of her brandy. Tom drank a little of his. I drank some coffee.

Tom said to Elspeth: 'I expect *you* have to think about money for the two of you . . . I shall be very happy to think *for* you . . . if you'll allow me.' He added in a slightly different tone of voice, clearly intended for me: 'I haven't done so badly for Robert.'

Elspeth just smiled.

Tom said: 'Have you got a good stock-broker?'

Elspeth said: 'We had one who did quite well for us, but he died last year, and since then . . .'

'Ah,' said Tom. 'What you need is a financial adviser. There's been quite a development, in recent years, in financial advisory services, even for *small* investors . . . Sometimes coupled with brokerage services.' He paused. 'I know of one such that would suit you perfectly.'

I couldn't help listening to him. Had he come to London to save us all?

Tom went on addressing himself to Elspeth. 'I have in mind a youngish man I know in a very reputable firm . . . He'd be interested in you as people, not merely as investors. Able, thoroughly competent in his job. To be recommended. Will you think about it? And you, too, Joe?'

Elspeth and I looked at each other. I said:

'We *will* think about it.'

I admitted to myself a piercing sense of relief at the prospect. I knew that I couldn't really think about money and that Elspeth was forced to do it for both of us. Of course Tom was right. The prospect of his finding someone for us whose professional skill was in thinking about money was enhanced by Tom's gloss that the man would be interested in us as people. Tom would be right about that, too. I have to admit that a base thought crossed my mind – about how Tom had come to be struck by the young man. I dismissed it. Nobody's ear could be closer to the ground in this part of the financial world than Tom's, I didn't doubt. If only it weren't for the limitations of physiology, Tom would have *both* ears to the ground.

Tom saw that we had taken the bait. He said, 'Let's drink to this!'

We all drank a sip of brandy. I felt happier. I saw that Elspeth was feeling happier.

'I think some of your anxieties can be relieved, Joe,' Tom said. 'It's only a question of finding someone to think about money for you.'

I grinned wryly.

He turned to Elspeth again. 'I hope the future looks a shade easier, my dear. I'm sure it will be.' He paused. 'And that's pretty wonderful' – he paused again – 'when you think that once upon a time I should never have been surprised if Joe ended up on the breadline.'

CHAPTER II

'I THINK SHE'S LOVELY'

I rang up the convalescent home – before nine in the morning: we had to watch the telephone bills now – to say I proposed coming down to see my mother. I got the Matron at the other end of the line.

'Perfectly all right, Mr Lunn. Will you be coming at the usual time?'

I said I would.

'I should like to see you, just for a few minutes.'

Oh dear – what now? 'I'll look in at the kitchen on my way up to her. How is she?' I felt my recurrent fear that they were going to ask me to find somewhere else for her.

'That's what I want to see you about. She hasn't been so well, these last few days, and yesterday we had the doctor to see her.' She went on rapidly to lessen my anxiety. 'There hasn't been any sudden change but I think I should tell you what the doctor said.'

I took it that she was speaking from the telephone in the hall, where conversations were audible to some of the other patients. I said:

'I'll wait to hear it.'

I thought of travelling down by an earlier train, but decided against it. I arrived at the convalescent home just after tea-time and found the Matron in the kitchen, beginning the preparations for supper. For the moment there was no one else in the room. She said:

'We called the doctor in because we were having a bit of trouble over clearing up a sore place on your mother's back.'

I said nothing. Elspeth would have something to say about that. She considered there was no excuse for letting patients get bed-sores. (Suddenly I thought of the night nurse in the eye-ward, going the rounds rubbing baby-powder on every-body's rear-end – excepting the handsome Sikh's!)

'Your mother had been complaining about her back. And about her breast . . .'

I realised that I was being led up to the point. 'What's the matter with her breast?' I asked.

'He's afraid she has cancer.'

I knew it must be so. A cancer, at the age of ninety-two – no escape, even then . . .

'He's coming again, to give her a more thorough examination, but I thought I ought to tell you now, Mr Lunn.'

'Oh yes, of course.' I thought about it. I said, 'I suppose she's too old for very much to be done about it?'

'I'm afraid so.'

'At this age a cancer develops pretty slowly, doesn't it?'

'Usually.'

'Is it causing her pain?' As I said it I thought how she already suffered with aches and pains all over the place from arthritis.

There was silence. The young girl who'd let me in at the front-door came into the kitchen with a tray.

The Matron said: 'Would you like me to send up your usual cup of tea, Mr Lunn, and a cake?'

I said, 'Yes please.' I noticed on the dresser beside me a wire tray with freshly-baked little cakes on it – I could smell them.

I went up to my mother's room. The window was open and the sunlight was shining on the carpet, the huge fawn and brown roses on the dazzling turquoise ground.

My mother looked much the same, half-propped up in bed and lying as usual askew.(She sat out in a chair during the mornings and complained that it tired her.) I noticed that the movement of her mouth, as if she were chewing, had ceased – perhaps the doctor had changed the drugs she was being treated with.

'I'm glad to see you,' she said. 'If you'd come a few minutes earlier you'd have found the doctor here.'

'Oh,' I said. 'That's interesting.'

'I don't know what they sent for him for.'

'It's right that you should be seen by a doctor at regular

intervals.' I'd said it before I realised that Elspeth had told me it was necessary, for the issue of a normal death certificate – were my mother 'to go at any moment' – for her to have been seen by a doctor within the previous two weeks.

'I don't know about that,' my mother said. 'I could scarcely tell a word he was saying.'

Yet so far as I knew this was the first time they'd called in the doctor for many weeks. I said to my mother, 'Why not?'

'He mumbled. These doctors ought to be trained to speak properly.'

'Perhaps – ' I drew back, on the brink of casting aspersions on her hearing.

'Perhaps what?'

'Perhaps he was tired.'

'Possibly.'

I thought a change of conversational topic was to be recommended. I noticed a fresh air-letter from America – from my sister – on the dressing-table. I volunteered to read it to my mother.

'Yes,' she said, 'you can do that.'

I said, 'I suppose somebody here read it to you when it arrived.'

'Yes. But you can read it again. These people here can't read properly.'

'Oh dear.'

'You never heard such a mess as they make of it.' She paused. 'If they can't read better than that, they oughtn't to get the money.'

I began reading the letter. My mother seemed to find my reading and my sister's news relatively satisfactory. (Having a huge family to bring up in the USA, my sister never came to England; my mother followed reports of the children's activities with an affection that survived from the days when she had tried emigration to America.)

'You can read it again,' my mother said.

So I read it again.

Relief appeared – the young girl helper brought in my tea. I thought she seemed a nice girl. When she'd set the bedside table in place before me, she looked at my mother and said to me:

'I should like to make Mrs Lunn a bit more comfortable.'

'Yes – she always seems to lie askew.' A cause for the skewness now crossed my mind.

The girl bent over my mother. 'Mrs Lunn, I'm going to make you a bit more comfortable.' She lifted my mother with one arm – easily, because my mother was so shrunken and frail – and straightened the pillows with the other arm. Then she gently laid her back again.

'There you go,' she said.

'Thank you, my dear.'

The girl stood looking at my mother.

'It's very good of you,' I said to her.

Still looking at my mother, she said: 'Isn't she lovely?'

My mother, *lovely*?

'We all think she's lovely. She's very popular. She entertains us all.'

I felt stunned. Lovely, entertaining, popular! Could she really mean *my mother*?

'This morning,' said the girl, 'she was singing to us.'

'Singing?'

'Yes.' Pause. 'I think she's lovely.' She patted my mother on the head – 'There you go, Mrs Lunn' – and went away.

So I was left to join in private conversation with my mother, beginning with the usual catechism. 'How's Elspeth?' 'How's Viola?' 'How's Virginia?'

No sign, I'm happy to say, of senile dementia-born questions about the Matron and divorce. All that appeared to be totally forgotten.

There was a passing lapse in the catechism and I was wondering what to say next, when my mother asked earlier than usual –

'What about Robert?'

'What do you mean?' I said. She couldn't possibly know anything of Robert's financial tribulations. 'What about Robert?'

'About his lumbago, of course. I always want to know about his lumbago. I know what it's like, myself, to have lumbago. Year in, year out. If you haven't got it, you're lucky.'

I rejected the impulse to mention arthritis in the hip-joint. I said, 'About the same.'

Actually he seemed to me to be worse in health. Both Elspeth and I were worried about it, and Elspeth was suspicious – could it be only lumbago?

'And that poor girl? What's her name? My memory's suddenly gone.'

'Annette.' (That poor girl, I thought, must now be in her mid-fifties.)

'Yes, Annette.'

'I think she's about the same.'

'Don't you know?'

'Robert doesn't like to talk about it.'

'Does *he* go to see *her*?'

'Yes.'

'That's good. Regularly?'

'Yes.'

'How often?'

'I think about once a month.'

There was a pause. Then she said: 'Poor girl, I'm sorry for her.'

I realised that she genuinely was sorry for Annette. If only, I thought, she could make it sound like that!

There was another long pause. A cloud must have passed in front of the sun – the fearsome glow of the carpet was muted. The open window let in a loud zooming of cars and lorries going by. I was thinking about Robert.

I was sure that Robert went to see Annette regularly, but long ago he had quelled my asking him about it. Quite often he asked me, Had I been down to see my mother? and How was she? But I'd learnt that I wasn't to make similar enquiries of him. After always being told either About the same, or She's all right, in a tone of voice that, despite its friendliness, was brusque and dismissive, I'd given up. (It struck me now that her being in a private institution must be costing him a lot of money.)

Once he'd told me that they were trying a new treatment, but soon after that we were back again at About the same. Mere acquaintances, hearing the brusqueness and dismissiveness of his tone, might have thought that he didn't care about her, perhaps wanted to put her out of his mind. Yet the opposite was true. It was constantly painful and constantly hopeless – why should he be constantly asked about it? One lives with things without constantly examining them.

'You haven't got so much to say for yourself today,' said my mother.

'I'm sorry about that.'

'There's no need to be sorry. All that music, going on in the background, doesn't make it any easier to talk.'

'What music?'

'That choir singing. They're always singing. They can't get much work done. They're always at choir-practice.'

'*I* can't hear them.'

'*I* can. Listen!'

For a moment I listened; and then she began to sing, as if with them. Slowly, and for her age quite tunefully –

'There . . . was . . . no . . . other . . . good . . . enough,
To . . . pay . . . the . . . price . . . of . . . sin.
He . . . on-ly . . . could . . . un-lock . . . the . . . gates . . .
Of . . . Heav'n . . . and . . . let . . . us . . . in.'

There was, of course, no choir singing anywhere. She went on.

'Oh . . . dear-ly . . . dear-ly . . . has . . . He . . . loved,
And . . . we . . . must . . . love . . . Him . . . too . . .'

It was a tune I knew from my childhood.

'And . . . trust . . . in . . . His . . . re-deem-ing . . . blood . . .
And . . . try . . . His . . . works . . . to . . . do.'

Then silence. 'They've stopped now,' she said.

'I see,' said I.

'Do you still say you can't hear it?'

'I'm afraid so. I think you're dreaming it.'

She was not listening to me. She said:

'My eyesight's no good any more. But I can hear better than most folk.'

Most folk included me.

She recited now: '*Oh, dearly, dearly, has He loved, and we must love Him too . . .*' She paused. 'I was always fond of poetry when I was a girl.'

'I'm sure you were.'

'But nobody else was.' She was thinking of the stepmother's family, in which she was brought up alone, after her father had disappeared, her mother having died in giving birth to her. She went on.

'I was very fond of Wordsworth. I suppose nobody reads Wordsworth nowadays.'

'No, lots of people do.'

She was not listening to me. 'I wrote about Wordsworth in my scholarship examination, my scholarship to Owen's College.'

I was familiar with the story from its re-telling over a lifetime. She had won a scholarship to what was then Owen's College and later Manchester University. But her stepmother's family couldn't or wouldn't find the money wherewith she could take up the scholarship.

'If I'd been able to go to Owen's College I should have had a very different life.'

I couldn't bring myself to speak.

'But I was trapped.'

'Yes . . . '

'I suppose we're all trapped in one way or another.'

'You could say that.' Trapped by our genes: trapped by our circumstances . . . It was enough to make one weep – weep for one's genes, weep for one's circumstances!

'There they go again,' she said.

'*Oh . . . dear-ly . . . dear-ly . . . has . . . He . . . loved,*
And . . . we . . . must . . . love . . . Him . . . too.'

She went on singing but my thoughts drifted away to I don't know where.

Suddenly she said: 'How is your book getting on?'

'What do you mean?'

'Is it selling well?'

'It hasn't come out yet.'

'When does it come out?'

'Next month?'

'What month's that? Not that it makes any difference to me.'

'May.'

'What does Robert think about it?'

'He thinks it's one of my best.'

'That's good.' She paused. 'I've asked you all this before, haven't I?'

'I think so.'

And then I heard the doorbell ring. 'Oh!' I exclaimed.

'What's that?'

'My taxi.'

'Then you must go.'

I felt disinclined to go, I couldn't understand why. 'In a minute,' I said. 'There's no hurry.'

'You mustn't miss your train.'

'I suppose so.' I stood up and collected my impedimenta.

I went up to the bed. She was humming, *'Oh . . . dear-ly . . . dear-ly . . .'*

I bent down and kissed her forehead. 'I must go now. I'll come and see you again, soon.'

'It's good of you to come.'

'I have to come. I want to come.' Suddenly I said: 'Because I love you.'

She said: 'I love you, too.'

It struck me that this was the first time in my life that that exchange between us had taken place – it must have happened when I was a child but I couldn't remember it.

'Don't keep that taxi-man waiting!'

Half-laughing at her I said, 'Oh, all right.' And I went out of the room and down the stairs.

CHAPTER III

RUNNING LATE IN A PUB

I met Robert on the following Saturday evening, in a pub round the corner from his house – at six o'clock: for the time being we'd given up the struggle to find one open at five-thirty. It had been a fine day and he must have been sitting in the sun somewhere – I didn't know if there'd been any cricket for him to watch. His forehead was pink. I thought he looked altogether better in health.

I put our pints of beer on the table and sat down opposite him. We drank.

'Well, what have *you* been doing?' he asked.

'Nothing of note. A lot of domestic chores that wouldn't interest you. But that have to be done.' I expected him to say gloomily, *Why* do they have to be done? He said:

'Oh.' He drank some of his beer gloomily.

I decided to tease him by making him listen to what they were. 'Such as cleaning bathrooms, using the laundry-machine, shopping at Sainsbury's' – he hated shopping, and he had never been in a Sainsbury's – 'answering business correspondence, paying bills.'

They had to be done by me, I felt, because I went out to work, teaching for George Bantock, on only two days a week; whereas Elspeth and Viola went out to work on five. Oh, those happy years when I had an office to go to, every day! What man in his right mind, I asked myself, would choose to go to Sainsbury's? Pushing a trolley up and down aisle upon aisle of serried merchandise, and, having made his choice, queuing up for twenty minutes to pay for it. (Actually I'd discovered that supermarket shopping induced a sort of cameraderie among the shoppers, especially the middle-aged to elderly – the young never having known any different. I was always having sympathetic chats with women waiting next to me in the queue: it sometimes went as far as our guarding one another's place while we went back for something we'd forgotten. Suffering does indeed make fellows of us all. In Sainsbury's I was often reminded of the cameraderie of life in London during the Blitz.)

I drank some of my beer.

'I've discovered,' I said, 'what woman's work is like. And *I don't like it.*'

'No,' said Robert gloomily.

I said: 'I think our GP – she was a bit worried over my retiring – was afraid my having to do woman's work might upset my virility.'

Not for an instant gloomily now, Robert said, 'Did it?'

I laughed. 'That's for Elspeth to say. Hers is the opinion that matters.' (It was age, not woman's work, which caused me any lapses from what I regarded as my usual form.)

With an innocent, distant expression, Robert drank some more of his beer while looking away from me. 'Elspeth seems relatively cheerful.'

I was astonished. By the normal standard of Robert's prudishness in conversation, the present atmosphere was tinged, to say the least of it, with lubricity. I didn't miss an opening – I said:

'Veronica seems relatively cheerful, too.'

He nodded his head gravely, and said in a hollow, lofty tone of voice: 'She doesn't seem to have much trouble . . .' And then he drank some more beer.

I burst into laughter. Robert pretended not to notice.

We sat drinking for a little while. After all, we had something to think about.

Robert said, 'I think I should like another beer.'

'Going the pace, aren't you?'

He felt in his pocket for money, and gave it to me. I went up to the bar, which was as yet fairly deserted.

'How's the teaching?' he said when I came back.

'I'm enjoying it.' I sat down. 'And so are my pupils, apparently. They're quite a decent lot.'

'Wouldn't you expect them to be?'

'On second thoughts, yes.'

My first thoughts about them, when I took the job on, had been coloured by recollections of 1968 – the Sorbonne! Ten years had wrought a change.

'They're decent enough by nature,' I said, 'as you'd expect scientists and engineers to be. And they're very decent in behaviour.' I was reflecting on the riots of the Sixties having been in the province of 'Arts students'. (I thought of the 'Social Sciences' as 'Arts'.) 'They're not at loggerheads with post-industrial society. Nor with me.'

Robert laughed. I went on.

'They're prepared to read all the novels on my list, and to listen to me talking about them. What would you expect me to find more enjoyable than that, I should like to know?' I was laughing, myself.

'Nothing, I should say. Absolutely nothing.'

I paid no attention to his sarcasm. After all, I thought, the sort of things I told them seemed to me fun. To start off with –

There Is No Word Of God In Literary Criticism

(The fun of the aphorism was enhanced for me, I have to admit, by hearing in my imagination Leavisite screams.) And it wasn't my only aphorism, as a matter of fact. I'd never thought of aphorisms before; but finding myself in front of a class of young people seemed to provoke me to invent them one after another. Later on in the course –

Technique Is Like A Lady's Slip – It Must Be There, But
It Should Never, Never Show

Or the same in shortened form –

It's Vulgar To Show Your Technique

(Let Henry James put that in his pipe and smoke it! I thought surreptitiously.)

And when I came down to the present-day academic priesthood of structuralists, post-structuralists, post-post-structuralists, their arcane and impenetrable writings seemed like a gift to me –

There's Nothing So Up-To-Date In EngLit As Ancient Alexandria

(The fact that in France, where it came from in the first place, structuralism was by now somewhat less than up-to-date, only added to the ironic beauty of the situation.)

145

I was having a high old time. Was I getting above myself? It was all very well to say these things to youthful scientists and engineers: if these things came to the ears of certain other less youthful persons, I might be rapidly precipitated below myself.

Robert went on grinning at me sarcastically. 'I'm glad you're enjoying yourself. And that your students are enjoying themselves.'

'How could I help it,' I said, 'reading a series of novels that begins with Jane Austen, Trollope and George Eliot, and ends with you and me?'

He drank some beer without saying anything.

I thought I'd better stop being playful. I said: 'It's possible that I'm at a bit of an advantage with my pupils, having gone through a scientific education myself. I suppose that was part of George Bantock's calculation.'

'Yes, it was.'

'How do *you* know?'

Robert pretended he was drinking some more beer. Keeping his head down, he said, 'I think he consulted me about it.'

'What do you mean, you think? You must know.'

Robert did not deign to reply.

'Really! The things that go on at the H of L! And anyway, why does everybody ask you about things, before they ask me?'

'I told him I thought it was a good idea. You approve of that, don't you?'

This time it was I who didn't deign to reply. I left a suitable pause and then said in more cosmic vein:

'It's a very pleasing turn of Fate, after all we used to say about EngLit. I mean for one of us, of all people, to end up teaching it.'

In our Oxford days, when Robert was a science don and I a science undergraduate (both of us intent on becoming novelists), we had gone about saying that EngLit ought to be abolished – because it stopped people writing.

Since then we had actually come across people whom reading EngLit had put off writing for three or four years, others, put off altogether. For one thing through making them feel that everything worth being written had been written already; for another through cluttering their minds and their time with stuff that had been fabricated in order to make something that was not properly an academic subject look as if it was.

However we had mellowed. We had gradually come to change our minds for an unforeseen reason. After decades of EngLit's being what was nowadays called 'a growth industry', there were so many dons in it that we couldn't face proposing its abolition because of the disastrous effect that would have on full-employment.

I was suddenly thrown out of my cosmic vein. A young man in jeans had come up behind us and put a coin in the juke-box. Music broke out. As he was passing us – we were the only people sitting at a table – on his way back to the bar, he gave us the most civil and unexpected of smiles and said:

'I hope you like Country-and-Western?'

Robert looked as if he'd been addressed in Swahili or Urdu. The interruption brought us back again to conversation.

'What else has been going on at the H of L?' I asked, knowing that he wouldn't want to be bothered to tell me.

'Nothing of note . . . It's all pretty tiresome.' He paused. 'This Government hangs on.' He drank some of his beer as if to mark the conversation with a full-stop.

For months, now, the country had endured a 'hung Parliament', which couldn't be expected to make life less tiresome for anyone, apart from the Prime Minister and various colleagues who were hanging on to office.

'I wasn't thinking about government. I was thinking about people.'

Robert said nothing.

'What's my friend the Noble Lord Albert-Smith doing?'

'I told you about him.'

'You never did.'

'I'm sure I did. You've forgotten '

'Nothing of the kind. Tell me now – or tell me again, if that's the way you see it!'

Robert drank first, and then said:

'You remember that committee of Lord Grimley's he'd been asked to go on?'

' "No Way. No Way",' I quoted happily.

'After six months the wretched Grimley had got nowhere. So your friend Bert agreed to be "drafted" – as he inimitably expressed it – on to the committee.'

'And then?'

'Grimley was effectively elbowed out of "the driving-seat" and Bert installed in it.'

' "The ropes are the same everywhere",' I quoted even more happily.

'Grimley stays nominally the Chairman, but it's generally accepted as Bert's committee.'

'Excellent!' I said. 'That's just the kind of story I like to hear: it has a moral to it.'

Robert looked at his glass.

I looked at my glass.

Robert said: 'Look here, do you mind if we have another beer?'

I was astonished. We had already consumed our statutory two pints. 'You really are going the pace tonight.'

'Veronica won't have the supper ready quite so early.' He didn't tell me why.

I stood up to go and buy another round. I thought I'd better let Elspeth know I was going to be late, and that reminded me of one of the insoluble problems of married life. There was a case for saying that when I went out for a drink with one of my friends, I had two other courses that were to be preferred over the one I was taking. The first was to get home at whatever time I'd said I'd get home. How simple! If only Time didn't pass, *without one's noticing it,* twice as fast when one was out drinking with one of one's friends as in any other circumstances! The other was to say I didn't know what time I'd get home. I simply couldn't take that one: it seemed to me tantamount to admitting, before I ever set out, that I was going to put up no fight against *the temptation of drink.*

Coming away from the telephone I glanced at the clock on the wall and wondered if I'd been right to say another hour would see me home.

The pub was beginning to waken up. There were more people at the bar; the young man who spoke to us had gone – to be replaced by someone who chose music with a deafeningly invigorating THUD-THUD-THUD-THUD. I noticed that the daylight coming from the windows was beginning to lose its intensity. Night was on its way.

I bought our drinks and went back to Robert. He was looking

miserable, because of the deafening THUD-THUD-THUD-THUD. I said, 'I'll ask them to turn it down.'

'It's all right,' he said, stoic as ever. (Actually, while we were speaking, somebody else had it turned down.)

We drank for a little while. I realised that neither of us had mentioned Tom. I suspected that if I didn't mention Tom, Robert was not going to. I said:

'When you asked me what I'd been doing, I didn't tell you we'd been having a famous dinner at the Carlos with Tom. I suppose you knew?'

'Yes, he did say something about it.'

'You've seen him since then?'

'Yes.'

There was a pause. Robert looked up from his glass.

'You'll be pleased to know,' he said, 'that Tom expressed the highest approval of Elspeth.'

'That's nice of him, I must say.'

'He thinks she's sympathetic, and wise . . . '

Though Robert disclosed nothing from his tone of voice, I knew what he was up to. I said:

'By contrast with me.'

Robert ignored the remark and went on enjoying himself. The pinkness of his forehead seemed, either from the effects of earlier sunshine or present alcohol, to be spreading to his cheeks.

'He thinks that Elspeth could learn to think about money – under suitable tuition, of course.'

The provocation was so blatant that I forced myself to ignore it. I was being paid out for introducing the subject of Tom. All right – so be it. I said:

'That's all very satisfactory.'

'He enjoyed the evening.'

'He enjoyed having me there?'

'Oh yes. He thinks you've become much more sensible with the years. More ready to listen to reason.'

I couldn't contain myself. 'Insolent little bastard!'

'I think you must agree that he doesn't lose his touch.' Robert was laughing now.

'And *you* should agree that, too,' I said, preparing to take the war into the enemy's camp.

But Robert was much too cagey to ask what Tom said about him. He drank some beer and said mildly:

'He didn't say anything about you that wasn't more or less flattering.'

In that case Tom couldn't have reported that bit about my ending up 'On the breadline'. (Tasteful use of the English language, as well!) I said:

'Nor did he about you.'

That was true – if I excepted Tom's inference that if Robert had been more capable with his money, he'd have known whether or not his accountant was seeing to it that he paid his Income Tax for two years. A sum of about £50,000! (I bet Robert didn't know Tom had told us how much it was.)

Not, I may say perhaps unnecessarily, that my own knowledge of the state of our Income Tax payment, even though our accountant was neither fraudulent nor dotty, was much different from Robert's. The delays introduced by the machinery of the Board of Inland Revenue into dealing with Claims were, in my opinion, enough to ensure that any taxpayer could scarcely know whether he was coming or going. I regularly asked Elspeth, who read the letters from our accountant, where we stood. And when as a consequence of my income being reduced to goodness knows what, our accountant started to get money *back* for us from the Inland Revenue, I was stunned.

Robert was thoughtful. The music had stopped.

I said: 'Tom told us about the activities of your accountant.'

'Yes, of course.' His tone was dismissive. He'd asked Tom not to tell anybody, but he must have known that Tom would.

'I'm terribly sorry,' I said. 'It must be disastrous.'

'It's bad luck,' said Robert, with a short, hollow-sounding laugh.

I felt I was taking the plunge when I said: 'Elspeth and I were upset – to think this happened to you just after you'd laid out the money for the Trust, for me . . . and the rest of us.'

It was the first time I'd mentioned the Trust since the night Robert told me he'd set it up. I knew that he would never have mentioned it again, and I wondered if I'd done wrong by mentioning it, myself, now.

He said easily, 'You had the good luck, old boy.'

I felt relieved and pleased. I thought he was a wonderful man. I raised my glass to his health.

'Here's some good luck for you!'

He lifted his glass, and said in a tone of voice that I hadn't expected:

'And here's to more good luck for you!'

Suddenly I realised what he was thinking of. *Happier Days* was due out next month. I said:

'To *Happier Days!*'

He drank quietly and thoughtfully. I said:

'You still think it's one of my best books?'

'I do.'

'I think my publishers probably think so, too.'

'I think they do.' His tone of voice was still quiet, and curiously flat, as if he were worried.

'Do you actually know?'

He nodded his head to signify yes. I waited.

'I was talking to your publisher the other day. He does think it's one of your best books, just as he's told you. Probably one of your very best books . . .'

There was something else to come. He hesitated a moment. I waited. I felt I could see him make up his mind to tell me.

'The trouble, old boy, is that he doesn't think he can sell it.'

I can only say the night went dark immediately, the night of the soul.

I could understand why he'd been making up his mind whether to tell me. He could either prepare me for disaster or let me wait for it to strike me.

'That's the kiss of death for me.'

'I shouldn't be too hasty, if I were you.'

'It'll mean he'll print 3,000 copies at most, sell half of them at most; and write to me in a couple of years' time saying he's going to remainder the rest.'

'It may not happen . . .' He fiddled with his glass on the table.

I said: 'I've had it.'

'I don't agree.'

I wasn't going to argue with him. Just as we were in agreement that the nature and function of literature had changed during our lifetime, so were we agreed about the nature and function of

151

publishing. In our New Age the fate of a book was more likely than not decided long before it was actually published. For one thing the sums of money involved were such that The Experts were bound to get in with a ruling say, The Experts being accountants, lawyers, MBAs, entrepreneurs of one sort or another – none of them, it scarcely needs to be said, knowing anything much about writing. In fact the writer was relegated.

In a recent speech I'd heard him making, Robert had come out to my astonishment with an aphorism of his own, delivered with great bitterness –

Writers Are The Serfs Of The Publishing Industry

There was no difficulty in seeing the sort of thing that happened. If a book was heading for making its author a fortune, all the things that brought in the money – serial rights, paperback rights, film rights, television rights – had been sold, possibly by auction, months before it reached the bookstalls, in some cases months before it had even been written. (Before the serf was set to work writing it!) And the more money that had been spent on its purchase, the more money was then laid out on its 'promotion' – in order to bring in a comparable return. You couldn't say all that didn't make sense, especially to accountants.

And what did I see happening to me? No book I'd ever written had ever seemed to be thought by anybody to be heading for making me a fortune – it must be that I hadn't written that sort of book. So I saw myself at the opposite end of the scale of fortune-making. And in our New Age of Publishing the two ends of the scale were getting further apart; and, more disturbingly, there was less and less in between. The tendency towards All-Or-Nothing. I saw myself heading for Nothing.

'You can never be certain,' Robert said. 'Odd things can happen.'

'Such as being run over by a bus.' I finished my glass of beer.

Robert drank moodily.

'I'd like to know what else *can* happen,' I said.

Robert said nothing.

I was feeling terribly upset.

Robert said, 'Let me buy you another beer!'

'What – a fourth?' I cried. 'I can't go home to Elspeth after four pints. She'll tell me my eyes aren't focusing straight.'

Robert grinned briefly. 'Well?'

I glanced at the clock. My extension was practically up. I ought to go. I said, 'Suppose we just have halves?'

He felt in his pocket for the money.

While I was waiting at the bar I thought that over our last drink we'd better talk about something else. (I was feeling the effects of the drink.)

Robert must have thought the same thing. His face was now pink all over. He said in a friendly, matter-of-fact tone of voice:

'Been down to see your mother this week?'

I drank some of my half-pint. 'Yes.'

'How is she?'

I put down my glass. I said: 'You haven't done much better, alas! by the change of topic.'

He looked fleetingly hurt and then worried. 'Is she worse?'

I told him the latest news.

'I'm desperately sorry.' His voice was low.

I said: 'You have your troubles . . .'

He said nothing.

Suddenly, in an access of courage and sympathy, I asked him something I hadn't asked him for ages. 'How's Annette? . .'

He drew in a breath. 'I'm afraid she's become diabetic. Apparently it's rather serious.'

I thought, Oh God! I said, 'How long ago?'

'Some months. I didn't tell you because I didn't want to distress you.'

'. . . There's nothing to say.'

He shook his head, looking down at the table.

'I'm afraid not.'

I glanced back at the clock again.

'We ought to be going,' he said.

'Yes,' said I. 'I'm afraid I'm going to be late home.'

CHAPTER IV

AFTERMATH OF A VISIT

We had a telephone call from Veronica. 'Will you and Elspeth come and have supper with me at Vincent Square? Keep me company while the Old Boy's away.'

'While the Old Boy's away?'

'Yes. Didn't he tell you? He's gone to get an Honorary Degree in Minnesota.'

'He didn't tell me.'

'How extraordinary!'

'I suppose there's no reason why he should.' I realised that since I was in the habit of making fun of his appetite for honorary degrees, there was reason why he shouldn't.

'I want to ask your advice about various things.'

'What?' I said suspiciously. Was I going to be called on as an ally in the campaign for capturing Robert?

'Advice about alterations I'm having made to the kitchen, for one thing. Your kitchen is so super.'

'So super!' I cried agonisedly. The result of the cowboys' being sacked was that for our first two months nobody at all had been to raise the hanging-cupboards. Elspeth still had to cook only dishes that didn't require an oven-temperature above Mark 4, and even then she kept feeling the acrylic strip along the front of the hood to see if it appeared to be approaching melting-point. (Actually it didn't – we suspected the gas-engineers of exaggerating the cowboys' crimes.)

'I *know*, Joe. But it *will* be super. And the rest of the flat looks absolutely super already.'

'You don't know what you're saying!'

'Of course you're such a perfectionist.' Veronica was scoring off me: it was normally I who attacked *her* for being a perfectionist (which indeed she was.) Perfectionism I regarded as a manifestation of anxiety neurosis out of control.

'Nonsense! Don't you see? I want to get the place finished so that I can forget about it, and start *living* in it.'

Veronica laughed, and then had the effrontery to play, against me, one of Robert's favourite quotations from College history –

'If that's what you think, Joe, you have a right to say so.'

I'd often quoted it, myself, to great effect. A quotation to be recommended –

If That's What You Think, You Have A Right To Say It

We ended the telephone call, having arranged to meet the following evening at Vincent Square.

Elspeth and I speculated on whether the supper would be cooked by Veronica or Dolores. We thought it possible that Dolores was not accepting with any great equanimity the advent of a new mistress in the establishment, especially as galvanising and efficient a Civil Servant as Veronica. It was hard to imagine anyone less cut out for *mañana* than Veronica. In Veronica the interval between thinking of something and doing it was infinitesimally short.

We found the supper was being cooked by Dolores. Veronica gave us large whiskies, not necessarily to prepare us for it – Veronica didn't drink very much, any more than we did, but she did like a large whisky.

'What do you think of this room?'

We were sitting in the sitting-room which had been completely re-painted by her 'little man'.

'It's an extraordinary transformation,' I said, and Elspeth made sounds of agreement.

'The only trouble is,' said Veronica, 'it shows up the state of the loose covers. They're filthy dirty!' And she gave her laugh, 'Ho-ho-ho!'

I have to say that in her place I should not have laughed. The loose covers had previously looked dowdy: they now answered to her description vociferously.

'I shall cover them myself,' Veronica said. 'I've bought the material in a sale.'

Elspeth and I glanced at each other. In a sale!

I thought of Robert, gone to Minnesota. Next thing he'd be off to Novossibirsk or Tbilisi.

Then it occurred to me that he'd got to pay off £50,000 from somewhere; unless Tom managed to charm a slice of it out of Sir Abe Pettinger, by hinting that Robert might help him to get into the House of Lords – Tom knowing that Robert wouldn't be able to do much about it, even if the Prime Minister hadn't changed to someone whom Robert knew less well than the previous incumbent of No 10. (It was the previous incumbent who had sent Robert to the House of Lords in order to appoint him, without his having to go through being elected to Parliament, as a Junior Minister.)

'I suppose you've heard about the Old Boy's tax situation,' Veronica said.

'We have.'

'I don't know what would have happened if Tom hadn't arrived on the scene.'

I said: 'It would have been picked up when Pettingers' took over – so says Tom.'

'I wish I had that degree of faith. I'm jolly glad he came, that's all I can say. He saved us.'

'I see the force of that remark.'

'And I gather,' said Veronica, 'he's given you and Elspeth some helpful advice. Found somebody to help with your financial affairs.'

'He has. We now have a financial adviser.' I said it mockingly, but could only think of it with relief. I looked at Elspeth for encouragement.

'What's his name – Stewart Something-or-other?' Veronica said. 'Have you met him yet?'

'Yes, of course. We had lunch with him. He struck me as a very able young man; and also, as Tom promised, likely to be interested in us as people, not merely as clients.'

'He and his wife,' said Elspeth, 'do social work in their spare time. I don't understand how they manage it – they've got two children.'

I said: 'I'm very pleased with him. It really is a relief. I'm born with the twin gifts for not being able to think about money and for worrying about it.' I glanced, smiling, at Elspeth. 'So it's more than a relief for my loved one, here.'

'That's marvellous news,' Veronica said. 'All, thanks to Tom!'

I sensed a rebuke to me. Veronica knew my attitude to Tom, and it sounded as if she thought I was wrong. Time will tell, I thought. At the same time I knew my moral position had been temporarily weakened by finding that my base suspicion, about how Stewart had come to Tom's notice, was entirely misjudged.

'All thanks to Tom,' I said sarcastically. And then I corrected myself. 'That's not fair. So far as I can see, Tom's choice for us was extremely knowledgeable, unprejudiced, and sensible.' I couldn't help laughing at my own expense. 'Extremely knowledgeable, unprejudiced, and sensible. Who would ever have thought the day would come when I'd use those words to describe something Tom had done?'

Veronica laughed as well. 'It describes his intervention in the Old Boy's affairs.'

I went on with my own line of thought. 'One's always defeated in the end by the turns of human nature . . .'

There was a pause. Veronica said:

'Did you meet Jim, when you had dinner with Tom at the Carlos?'

'No.' Jim was the name of Tom's secretary. 'Did you?'

'Yes. He wasn't at all what I'd expected.'

'Oh, tell us about him!'

'You'll be meeting him – when we all go down to Tom's country house in August or September.' Veronica stood up. 'You know Tom's rented an eighteenth-century country house in Kent, complete with a chef to do the cooking and the chef's wife to keep house.' She looked at our glasses. 'Another whisky?'

At that moment Dolores came in to say supper was served, so we didn't have another whisky. We followed Veronica down to the dining-room, which presented a rather odd appearance as the 'little man' was half-way through painting it.

'We'll go and look at the kitchen later,' Veronica said, 'after Dolores has finished in it. I really do want your advice.'

I'd already seen enough of Robert's kitchen to know that my only advice to her could be to get rid of everything in it and start again from scratch. I said:

'We had someone to design our kitchen for us.'

We were sitting down at the dining-table.

'Yes,' said Veronica. 'But you and Elspeth have now learnt *so* much about it, I'm sure you could dispense with them if you were doing it again.' By that she meant if we were advising on the design of *her* kitchen.

I didn't risk glancing at Elspeth. We'd had a sort of bet on the subject. What were the odds against preventing Veronica from Doing-it-Herself? Infinite.

Dolores brought in pancakes stuffed with shrimps.

'Good gracious!' I exclaimed with pleasure. 'You don't need any advice on how to begin a supper-party.'

Veronica's cheeks were pink and her eyes were sparkling. 'I like them myself.'

I wondered whether I ought to retract my accusation against Veronica of having a touch of parsimony in her nature. And yet something made me hold back for a while. Mention of Jim had reminded me of how I was given to base suspicions. I had another base suspicion now. Veronica was doing us proud: I remembered that I was an ally in a campaign. Perhaps I ought to wait and see if anything was coming next.

It was quite a long time, however, before something did come next. We had a very good supper. Veronica, an excellent cook as one might expect, had supervised Dolores's preparation of beef *bourguignon*; then there was a delicious meringue-y gateau which Veronica had made herself. The evening began to pass very entertainingly and companionably. We went down and inspected the kitchen, gave our advice. Then we went up again to have a last whisky – 'for the road' said Veronica, although she was not going anywhere. And then we somehow found ourselves talking about Tom again.

'You know,' said Veronica, 'Tom gave his blessing to the Old Boy and me. I thought he'd got a bit of a cheek.'

I laughed. 'Tom wouldn't be Tom if he hadn't got a bit of a cheek. A lot of a cheek, as a matter of fact.' I glanced at Elspeth, who was smiling.

'Yes,' said Veronica. She paused. 'I think he thinks Robert ought to get a divorce.'

So there it was! I got her message.

I looked at Veronica with the expression of an ally. 'Let's

hope,' I said lightly, 'he doesn't tell the Old Boy that!'

Veronica got *my* message – which was that if Tom did tell him, Robert, labyrinthinely sensitive like an elephant, would immediately shy off in a different direction.

Veronica gave me a shrewd, clear-eyed look and said:

'He only said it to *me*, so far as I know.' She paused. 'I'm pretty sure he didn't say it to the Old Boy.' She paused again. 'I agree. Let's hope he didn't!'

All three of us drank some of our whisky – to occupy a rather strange few seconds of silence.

It was time for Elspeth and me to go home. Veronica called a taxi for us and five minutes later we were on our way.

In the taxi, Elspeth said:

'Well, what did you think of that?'

I said: 'You know, my darling, without my telling you.'

'What are you going to do?'

'Absolutely nothing. That is, I'm going to give no sign that I know anything about it. A thing I will not do, I will not do, is take part in manoeuvring.' She took hold of my hand. I went on: 'If I so much as mentioned the word "divorce" in the Old Boy's presence, he'd *know*, and he'd *remember* . . . for the rest of Time.'

CHAPTER V

MORE AFTERMATH OF A VISIT

I can't say I was surprised when I heard from Steve.
   'Are you likely to be dropping in at the pub in Soho?'
   'No, Steve. Now that my days in Whitehall are over I don't
come up to Marshall Street Baths any more. They're shut,
anyway.' They were shut supposedly for re-decoration, but in
my opinion they were shut for ever. All over London public
swimming-baths were being shut, because of the inflated cost of
upkeep. Public swimming-baths were being shut; public
lavatories were being removed; even public clocks were
disappearing from the streets – anything that needed 'service'
was destined to go. And the streets themselves were getting
dirtier and dirtier.
   'You can guess why I want to see you, Joe.'
   'My guess is Tom.'
   'That's right.'
   'Nothing wrong?' I was thinking of Burke, of course.
   'Oh, no . . .'
We agreed to meet in mid-afternoon, one day when I went
shopping for Italian comestibles. A patisserie in Old Compton
Street.
   It was a sunny afternoon and the door of the café was wedged
open. It was just a long room, dimly-lit, cheaply panelled, the
minimum having been spent on meretricious (or any other)
decoration. At the entrance was a counter, presided over by a
big, rosy, business-like Italian and small, sallow, female
members of his family: at the bottom end was a doorway opening
into the kitchen. The point about it all was that the coffee was
good, and the cakes, if not as good as they used to be, still
acceptable.

Steve was already there when I arrived. He was wearing sun-spectacles.

'I've not been to this place for ages,' he said.

'I'm an infrequent sort of regular.'

We looked round the room, which in mid-afternoon was not crowded. The café was frequented by denizens of Wardour Street, talking about making films; by young persons who practised parasitic arts such as graphics, animation; by other young persons who sat sorting large photographs of themselves; and by a few quasi-intellectual old-stagers like me, refugees from a once-upon-a-time Viennese café in Gerrard Street, when the said café disappeared under an avalanche of Chinese non-citizens of the People's Republic, opening restaurants, emporia, and very busy centres of the heroin trade.

Steve and I ordered coffee from an Italian waitress whom I'd known for years; on the other hand there was a new waitress, a pretty girl who seemed to be German. Steve took off his sun-spectacles.

We made our choice of cakes from an old-fashioned, three-tiered cake-stand, such as stood ready on every table, the number of cakes having been previously counted. The coffee came.

'So,' I said, perhaps affected by recollection of the old Viennese café days.

'So,' said Steve.

'Tom?'

'Tom.'

We began to laugh.

'What's he been up to?' I asked.

'You're over-reacting, Joe.'

'Let's see you under-react, then!' I began to eat my cake. 'What was it you wanted to tell me, Steve?'

'Tom was in generous mood.'

I waited.

'He gave his blessing,' said Steve, 'to Burke and me.'

'Oh God!' I began laughing.

'What's the matter?'

'That's precisely what Veronica said. Literally the same words.'

'That's what Tom said to Veronica and Robert?'

'Just to Veronica, I think. Even he wouldn't have the cheek to say it to Robert.'

'He said it to us, Burke and me together, when he was giving us a very super dinner at the Carlos.'

I said: 'How did you and Burke receive the blessing, together?'

'I don't know how to put it.' Steve gave his rueful smile, then dropped it in favour of a shrewd laugh. 'Gratefully, Joe. Gratefully.'

'I'm very glad.'

'He knows Burke quite well, in New York.'

I didn't see what he meant by that. I said, 'One might say he knows you quite well.'

'Did know.' Steve corrected me.

I saw the aptness of the correction. 'Did know,' I repeated.

'You know' – Steve resumed his rueful expression – 'you'll scarcely believe it, but I can't remember a lot of it, you know . . . of the past.'

'I can't either. Perhaps it's as well.' I began to laugh. 'What I *can* remember is the clarion call, "*Now Steve!*" Can you?'

'Don't!' Steve began to laugh. Then he stopped. 'The trouble is, Joe, he hasn't changed.'

'He didn't call "*Now Steve!*" clarionlike, at the Carlos, I hope.'

'No. But I'm not sure, you know, that he won't.'

I wasn't sure, either. I didn't say anything. We ate our cakes. Steve said, 'These are nice. I've always liked cream cakes.'

I said: 'What's the basis for the blessing?'

'He told us we were good for each other. In those words, Joe.'

'How does he know?'

'How does Tom always know these things?' He was thoughtful. 'Actually he spent hours talking to Burke on the telephone.'

'Well, I don't know what you're worried about. By the way, what became of Marìa?'

'She went back to Buenos Aires.'

I said: 'Will Burke go back to New York?'

'That's just the point, Joe. She *will* go back to New York. It's not settled when. Possibly at the end of this summer. She's only taking what she calls a sabbatical half-year from her theatre and all the other things she does in New York.' He was looking at me with a rather soulful expression. 'She's a very busy lady.'

I said: 'As Tom gave you and Burke his blessing, as it were in conjunction, is he thinking of your remaining permanently in conjunction?'

'That's what I don't know.'

'Does Burke know?'

'She hasn't said.'

'Do you want to?'

'Well, yes . . .' He looked at me. 'I'm very devoted to her, Joe.'

One of the things that made Steve engaging was that he always sounded unconvincing: it was his misfortune that he could never sound anything but unconvincing when it was necessary that he should *not* sound so. He repeated –

'Tom thinks we're good for each other.'

'That may well be true.' I could think of a very simple way in which Burke was good for Steve.

Steve might have read my thoughts. 'I *am* good for *her*,' he said. 'She's had a bad time with men in the last few years. She doesn't find life as easy as you think. Being rich isn't everything.'

I couldn't have thought I'd ever live to hear Steve say anything as beautiful as 'Being rich isn't everything'. However I kept quiet about that, and I began to think how perhaps Steve might well be good for her, as Tom said. I could imagine there had been no shortage of men in the New York theatre and its environs who were trying to sleep with Burke to get money and influence out of her. I felt pretty sure that wouldn't be in her line of country at all. How very different a line of country was Steve's unobtrusive need – arising from his sensitive artistic nature – just to be looked after!

I continued to keep quiet. I finished my coffee.

Steve said: 'We get on very well together. Better than I got on with Marìa.'

It was time we came to the point. I said:

'Is there some thought, when Burke goes back to New York, of your going with her?'

'If you mean some thought of Tom's, I think there is.'

I suppressed the impulse to exclaim Good gracious! I remained thoughtful, as well I might.

'I think there is,' said Steve. 'But what I don't see, is – Where do *I* stand?'

As Tom had the gift for making anybody's head spin, I could well understand Steve's quandary. I said, in as cosy a tone of voice as I could muster:

'I think that will become apparent, as time goes by.'

'You think that?'

'I do.'

Steve's mood changed. 'I suppose,' he said, 'as time goes by when Tom's around, things do become apparent.' And then he gave me a grin of amusement. 'As if *I* didn't know that!'

CHAPTER VI

A SHORT CHAPTER ABOUT DISASTER

By the end of three weeks after the book was published, I'd had practically all my reviews. Some of my friends thought that was flattering. Perhaps it was. What they didn't realise was that one's publisher, if he thought the book was not going to sell, tended to regard the reviews as one's advertisement, as 'promotion' gratis; and that was the end of promotion. It was all right for the review-hounds, who didn't miss a review over those particular three weeks. But for the rest, it was silence – it was quite easy to be greeted, after another three weeks, by someone who'd say: 'Oh, Mr Lunn, when are we going to get another novel from you?'

Not that there weren't an encouraging number of review-hounds. I was continually meeting them, when they announced themselves with encouraging candour: 'I haven't read your *novel*, Joe, but I've read the *reviews*.' For myself I have to say that I'd given up reading my reviews several novels back. (It required some fortitude to stick them in a scrap-book for posterity without reading them now.) Reading my reviews, I'd learnt, roused in me little but exasperation. Exasperation is a sterile emotion. I decided not to lay myself open to it.

However I did read two reviews of *Happier Days*, more or less under duress. One evening in my Club a friendly fellow-member held the *Evening Standard* under my nose. 'Have you seen this, Joe?' And he held it there while I had to read it. It was the review I mentioned earlier.

In most reviews there is a sentence which leaps, as poets say, to the eye. You'll remember that the heart of the novel was a love-affair between a sixty-two year old doctor and the twenty-two year old daughter of one of his friends, a love-affair touching and poignant, but nonetheless full-blown. The sentence in this review that leapt to my eye was to the effect that after the age of forty-five all sex is disgusting.

I ask you!

I *ask* you!

While I was speechless with exasperation, my fellow-member said: 'Did you see your review in the TLS last Thursday?' Taking, I suppose, my speechless expression to signify No rather than the lack of presence of mind to say Yes, he went off to the morning-room to fetch it.

I didn't recognise the name of the reviewer and presumed him to be some minor provincial don. The sentence that leapt to my eye in this review was to the effect that after having completed the book I'd sprinkled it with cultural references in order to impress.

I said to my fellow-member: 'Thank you.'

So much for two of my reviews. Elspeth dutifully read them all, as the stuffed manilla envelopes came in from my publisher; and she tactfully withheld her own opinions. Now and then she offered one to me, on the assumption that it ought not to arouse exasperation; but I slid out of reading. On the other hand the information I'd have liked to get from her was whether my story of the love-affair had carried conviction with the reviewers: tact prevented my asking that. (Nor, of course, had I been able to ask her what was even more important to me, myself – if, when she read the book in typescript, it had carried conviction with *her*.)

One of the most serious vocational hazards for the wife of a novelist is having to read his stories about love-affairs that involve women obviously not herself (unless it be having to read those in which the woman obviously *is* herself.) Negotiating it requires great tact on both sides: Elspeth and I managed it by discreet silence on both sides. How could I ask her if my story of a love-affair between a man of my own age and a girl thirty years younger than herself, rang true, true to reality? I asked myself, of course I asked myself, if it embarrassed her. But a novel is a novel. I simply had to get on with it – which, in those terms, Elspeth understood perfectly. She knew that for me a novel had to ring true. If it doesn't ring true, as I've already said – it bears being said again – even the art of it, for me, is wasted.

A Short Chapter about Disaster

Incidentally I may say that even before the book came out there was further evidence for Robert's forewarning and my own predicting. I'd seen fit to write the novel in the form of a private diary – an honourable enough tradition, one would have thought. I'd found, when I told certain literary persons about it, that the temperature of the conversation dropped with a thump. Honourable enough the tradition might be: they signified unhesitatingly that it was dead.

Forewarnings, predictions turned into established fact. It was impossible not to see that the book, one of my best – one of my very best? – had totally failed. My American agent hadn't got me a publisher in the United States. I packed up a copy for my former American publisher who found the book so adorable that she wanted a copy to keep for herself. One copy in the USA? At least it was a copy adored, when there were obviously many copies in the United Kingdom that were unadored – come to that, un-bought.

My London publisher couldn't find anyone who was prepared to publish the book in paperback. Once in a lifetime I'd had a modest best-seller in Penguin; but that was in the days before selling a million copies of *Lady Chatterley's Lover* made all previous Penguin best-selling look, as Tom would say, like chickenfeed – or should it be peanuts? (Perhaps chickens feed on peanuts?) There were no serial rights, no televison rights; I made no bones about accepting that – the book wasn't cut out for either. No translations into other languages: that didn't surprise me, in view of the pretty familiar way in which I normally expressed myself in the English language – imagine a Japanese confronted by, Let Henry James put that in his pipe and smoke it!

So the deadly blow began to fall, the feel of disaster.

The arthritis in my hip had been getting worse: the pain kept waking me up during the night when I turned over in bed. And when I awoke in the night I thought of the book, and felt – arthritis in the soul.

Had I been guilty of a semantic self-deception, I asked myself in the dark hours, a lapse in comparative thought? (I always was the first person to condemn a lapse in comparative thought on the part of somebody else.) The book might be one of *my* best books: that was only by internal comparison among my own books. If one threw open the judgement on it to external comparison among everybody's books, all my books might be at the bottom of the scale, my best merely being at the top of what were the generality's worst.

Elspeth tried to cheer me up. She said:

'You'd better start taking those anti-depressant pills again.'

'How can *they* make my book *sell?*'

We were sitting on one of the sofas in our sitting-room. We were alone. It was evening, a summer evening.

Dark though my mood was, I realised that the room, now it was finished, looked very pretty. In evening light from an open sky such flaws as there were seemed to fade. The curtains, the pictures, the pieces of furniture, the carpet . . . the mild colours among which the pictures shone. We could now start living in the room, forgetting about it now that it pleased us. I could sit in it thinking about disaster – would the book sell even 1,500 copies?

Elspeth said: 'Just look at those clouds!'

Across the blue sky there were three stripes of thin, flocculent clouds, in the sunlight shining pink and gold.

'Yes,' I said glumly.

After a few minutes she tried again. 'Come on,' she said. 'Think how nice the flat looks!'

'It does.'

'You can *live* in it,' she said, making fun of me.

'We can *afford* to live in it,' I said, getting back at her.

'Of course we can.'

'If Stewart says so, it probably is so.' Stewart had made his first appraisal of our finances. Our straits, he told us, were not dire. (They were nearer to what Elspeth had been telling me all along.) Far from dire, he said. In fact he thought I ought to be encouraged by them – we had enough money for holidays! Stewart, it was already apparent, was interested in us as people.

Elspeth didn't take up the argument. I went on.

'It probably is so, provided you go on earning a living for the two of us. As Tom might say, Bringing home the bacon.' (I should never forget, 'On the breadline'.)

'Oh, stop it!'

'You can't expect me to contribute much more than I earn from teaching.'

'There'll be *some* royalties.'

'Chickenfeed!'

'All right – they may be less than you'd hoped for from *this* book – '

'You don't think I'm going to write any more books, do you?'

'I hope you will.'

'What's the point? I'm getting near the end of my literary career. There's nothing really to hope for. I'm not going to go on writing novels, even if *I* think they're good, just for them to plop like this one into . . . the well of nothingness.'

'That's ridiculous.'

'It's an artful use of the title of another book.'

'Let's talk about something else!' She thought. 'If you still insist on being worried about money, you must remember there'll be money coming from other sources. Stewart thinks we've done reasonably well with the money we've put into investments and insurance, and he'll do better with it for us.'

I couldn't bring myself to say Chickenfeed again – or Peanuts. She went on.

'There'll be what you inherit from your mother. Then when you're seventy you'll take your pension.'

She meant my Old Age Pension, which I'd deferred taking on the basis of somebody's dubious actuarial calculations. I said: 'I've no idea how much that will be. I've never seen it printed anywhere.'

'You can write to the DHSS and ask. I think you ought to write straight away – Stewart wants to know. Will you, this evening?'

'All right.'

She went on. 'And then there's Robert's Trust.'

'We've no idea how much that will be and I don't see how I can ask him. I think it's best to leave it out of Stewart's computations – just treat it as a bonus when it comes.'

'All right. But I really did hope you were going to stop worrying about money, now that we've got Stewart. I thought when *he* told you, you'd believe it.'

I changed my tack. 'It's funny,' I said, not in the least

meaning that it was comical. 'Everybody has always thought I didn't need to worry about money. Everybody in the Government Service thought I was making a fortune out of my novels; everybody in the literary world thought I was laying up a fat pension from the Government Service. Both wrong!'

Elspeth was silent.

'Perhaps,' I said, 'it was I who was wrong.'

'What do you mean by that?'

'By having two careers. By not staking everything on one or the other. So ending up as a failure in both.'

Elspeth gave an impatient sigh.

'Though it's probable I couldn't have been a success in either. In the Government Service I was constantly saying sharp, bright things that either maddened people or frightened them . . . Also, because I had a career as a writer, they never felt I was one of them.' I laughed sarcastically. 'Though if I *hadn't* had a career as a writer they still mightn't have felt I was one of them.'

Elspeth murmured something I didn't catch.

I went on. 'And it's been exactly the same on the other side of the fence. If I'd staked everything on my literary career, I should have had to buckle to and show myself, if nobody else, I really believed in my novels enough to live by them . . .' I paused. 'I ought to have written many more novels than I have. To be successful your best novels have to float on a corpus of work. A corpus of work is very important: it carries weight . . . I ought to have written short stories, if only to please people who've been constantly asking me to. And do you realise I've spent half of my life thinking about novels, what they ought to be, and how to write them? And I've scarcely put a word on paper about it. I shall depart as if I'd never been.'

Realising that the last sentence was somewhat ridiculous, I went on quickly.

'Furthermore, if I'd chosen to be only a writer, I should have stood a better chance of literary society feeling I was one of them, instead of always standing outside. There's a great deal to be said, whatever the society you're living in, for that society to feel that you're one of them. If they don't, you pay a price . . . I've never written anything I didn't feel a compulsion inside me to write. I've never taken any notice of other people. I've gone my

own way, regardless.' I repeated it with heart-rending emotion –
at least it rent *my* heart. 'I've gone *my own way!*'

'My darling, this is really getting – '

I was not to be stopped. 'I suspect there's never been a bit of
society that's felt *I* was one of *them*. I haven't been. I'm *not!*'

Elspeth took hold of my hands. 'My darling, please don't go
on! You are what you are.'

'That's the trouble. It isn't that I could have behaved any
differently if I'd not wanted to be a total failure. I should just
have had to be *somebody else.*'

Elspeth said: 'I can only think of one thing to say to you, my
darling, and I don't know how much it means to you.' She leaned
round, so as to look into my face. '*I* love you for what you are. I
love *you* . . .'

And I looked into her face. I turned away so as not to burst
into tears.

There was a very long pause. We were both looking towards
the windows. The stripes of cloud, high and still, went on shining
pink and gold, ineffably pretty.

I stirred, turning to get more comfortable on the sofa.

Elspeth said gently: 'Don't you think it's really time you had
that hip seen to?'

PART IV

CHAPTER I

ONCE MORE INTO THE MAW

I am referring to the maw of the National Health Service; my subject, the hip-joint, replacement of bone by stainless steel and plastic. I decided to go to our GP – I'd now reached the stage when the pain was such that I was avoiding going out.

'It's one of the more successful operations,' she said, with the comparative thought which I regarded as fair encouragement. And then: 'You'll have to decide whether you want to go on taking distalgesic for more years or have the operation now.'

'That seems clear.'

She went on: 'The operation hasn't been going long enough for them to guarantee successful results for more than ten years. 'But that' – she laughed cheerfully – 'should take you into your eighties. Most hospitals have a waiting-list of two years.'

Thinking, Boldness is all, I said promptly, 'I'll go ahead now.'

'Right.'

We got on rather well in a hearty way.

'I'll let you have a list,' she said, 'of three of the best people to go to. Then if I were you, I'd shop around. See what you think of them, and see how long their waiting-lists are.'

I was so struck by the impropriety of 'shopping around' that I just said:

'Thank you.'

A few days later she telephoned me a list of three surgeons and their hospitals.

Mr F R Digby-Waterton
Mr Q Redruth
Mr B J K T Lascelles

I read the names with pleasure – classy names! 'We're obviously at the top of the tree,' I said.

'I suppose Digby-Waterton must be related to Mr Justice Digby-Waterton,' said Elspeth.

I said: 'I rather go for having the solitary initial, Q. That's real class.'

'It must be for Quintin.'

I said, 'It might be Quetzalcoatl.' I tried it over. 'Quetzalcoatl Redruth. An old Aztec Cornish family. It *must* be Quetzalcoatl.'

'Are you going to start with Digby-Waterton?'

'I suppose so.' Digby-Waterton's hospital was one of the largest and most renowned in London. 'But I'm sure "shopping around" is not allowed by the NHS.'

'I don't see why you shouldn't do it.'

'Suppose I'm found out?'

'It'll take so long for your records in the NHS to come together, it'll be too late.'

I saw the force of that remark. 'All right.' I decided, however, to go through all the hoops of each of the processes in series, rather than embark on the hoops of all three processes concurrently. I asked our GP to give me a letter to Mr Digby-Waterton and I set about getting a first appointment – some weeks ahead – with the hospital.

In the meantime there was a film about the operation shown on television – I was in the swim of things! Actually the film was shown on a night when Burke and Steve were giving a party, but if it had been on a different night I'm not sure I should have brought myself to watch it.

The appointed afternoon came and I presented myself at the hospital. There were people everywhere. One of the little girls in the reception found my name on her list and directed me to one of the waiting-rooms down one of the corridors. The name on the door at the other end of the room said –

Mr G E Blenkinsop

That didn't surprise me. I was not expecting to be seen first go by the Great Man himself. (Over my cataract I'd started off with His Majesty in Wimpole Street because I'd gone to him as a private patient.) I sat down as the last-comer to a party of four or five waiting patients. I'd brought a novel to read. Time passed. The patients in front of me in the queue were duly called in to be seen by Mr Blenkinsop. I went on reading. I suddenly realised that patients *behind* me in the queue were being called in to be seen by Mr Blenkinsop. I stood up, preparatory to action. At that moment the little girl from the reception came running in. 'Mr Lunn!' I turned to her. 'Mr Lunn,' she said breathlessly, 'I'm very sorry – we made a mistake. It's Mr Love who's going to see you.'

She hastily conducted me from my first waiting-room to a second one. On the opposite door it said –

Mr T W Love

There were more people in this room. I said, 'I hope I'm not at the bottom of this queue.'

'I'll just find out.' With that she disappeared, never to be seen again. I returned to my novel-reading; till at last my name was called and I entered the room occupied by Mr Love, sitting at a large desk, and a nurse, sitting at a small folding table.

Mr Love was a presentable youngish man, that is to say rising forty, wearing spectacles and dressed in an appropriately dark suit. He had the standard manner for his status. The mantle of greatness had not yet fallen upon him, but I thought there were unmistakable signs now and then of his reaching up to give it a downward tug. At the end of a short interview, obviously standard for this loop in the process, he instructed me to go and be X-rayed, hand in the film at the reception, and return to his waiting-room.

Centralisation being up-to-date – recommended by The Experts – the hospital had one centralised X-Ray Department, into which therefore flowed all the patients from all the Departments. I was reminded of a pre-Bank Holiday afternoon at Paddington Station. I settled down to reading my novel again, waiting and waiting and waiting. Finally, with my film developed and checked and enclosed in a yellow envelope, I went with it to the reception.

Another little girl received the yellow envelope and me. 'I'm afraid,' she said, 'Mr Love has gone . . .' She looked up at the clock for corroboration: it said quarter past six. 'We shall have to make you another appointment to see him.'

As good as her word, she made me another appointment to see him.

In two weeks' time I was back again, safely in the correct

waiting-room – on the door opposite to me, the name of Mr T W
Love. Four or five people were already there. I was now reading
a different novel. It was just coming up to my turn when a little
girl rushed in – I was used to little girls by now – and said:
  'Mr Lunn, have you been X-rayed?'
  I said, 'Yes, I have, the first time I was here. What's more, I
handed in the film at your office.'
  'Thats all right, that's all right,' – she was already rushing out
again – 'we'll *find* it!'
  Three patients later I was called.
  Mr Love was sitting at the large desk, as before. Beside him,
this time, was sitting a slightly junior version of himself – I saw
how the American term 'side-kick' originated. The nurse was at
her little folding table. Mr Love had a few minutes of
question-and-answer, from-the-other-side-of-the-table discussion with me; and then made the remark –
  'You seem very set on this operation. Is it because you
watched the television commercial for it?'
  Stupefaction sent me to the peak of haughtiness.
  'You do me an injustice on two counts. First, I didn't watch
the television film. Second, I'm counter-suggestible to commer-
cials.'
  Stupefaction all round! Mr Love looked at his side-kick: his
side-kick looked at Mr Love. The nurse dropped her biro on the
floor.
  A patient had answered back – had answered back not just on
equal terms, but on *superior terms*!
  For a moment neither of the men knew what to say or do. The
nurse picked up her biro. A delicious moment: I thought.
Insolent young puppy shot down in flames – a delicious
metaphor! Meanwhile I was giving them the opaque, implac-
able stare of which my mother was such a mistress.
  Mr Love began to talk again from an entirely different plane.
A mumbling speech which improved as it reached its point – 'In
this hospital, Mr Lunn, we aim at treating our patients as
individual people.'
  I was relieved to hear that I was not going to be operated on as
a group of people. I was still giving him my mother's stare, but I
began reducing its opacity and implacability.

He said: 'Shall we look at your X-ray?' He put the film in a viewing-machine and switched on the light.

Under the spell of instruction I subsided into normal manners. So did he, though he had further to go. Finally he said:

'I'm willing to put you down on our waiting-list for the operation.'

I didn't feel the speech was warmed with conspicuous enthusiasm. I said, 'Thank you.' He went on.

'But I have to warn you that we have a waiting-list of up to two years.'

I felt it was probably two years for me – two more years of pain. I stood up, preparing to leave. And then devilment inspired me to give his tail a final twist.

'And who,' I asked with utmost innocence, 'will be doing the operation? Mr Digby-Waterton?'

He gave me a cool smile – which I rather respected him for – and said:

'Mr Digby-Waterton. Or myself. Or another colleague of mine.'

Exactly like the Civil Service! Either I myself, or another Under Secretary, will be dealing with your case, Mr Snooks.

'Thank you!' I said.

When I got home Elspeth said, 'Well?' and I said, 'We definitely go to see Mr R. I suspect it's going to be Quetzalcoatl for me.'

She laughed. 'Why are you so pleased with calling him Quetzalcoatl?'

'His initial's Q, isn't it? Also I think one can do with the help of a god in these things.'

'Don't get above yourself!'

Next morning I asked our GP for a letter to Mr Redruth.

So began a career through the hoops of a second process. I was shopping around. I got an appointment at Mr Redruth's hosptial.

Our GP had told me this hospital was small and old-fashioned, but I wasn't prepared for its being quite so Victorian. A small entrance-hall with a crest in the mosaic on the floor; a little old lattice-gated lift – one wouldn't have been surprised to see Florence Nightingale get out of it. To reach the Out-Patients' one had to go down a corridor, then, startlingly, through the oak-panelled foyer of the Board room; then down a flight of stone stairs that must have been terrifying for crocks on crutches. The waiting-room was subterranean and served partly as a thoroughfare. There was a reception office on one wall and along the opposite wall two rows of seats. But at one end there was a large concertina-gated lift; and at the opposite end a pair of double doors above which a screen said in lighted green letters –

OPERATION IN PROGRESS

I settled down to wait. I noticed the name on the door to which we were being called was –

Mr Q Redruth

It looked as if, here, I was going to see the Great Man himself. It turned out that I was.

'My name's Redruth,' he said grandly, and gave me a powerful handshake.

A round head, a strong neck, and biceps that filled the sleeves of his jacket. Clipped grey hair, a very handsome dark suit. Quick on his feet. Another rugger-player, I thought.

'I believe in seeing my patients, myself, on their first visit.'

The room was rather dark and I'd just noticed that there was a nurse there, Indian-looking, pretty.

'Yes,' I said, trying to make the word sound appreciative – which it was. He was very grand but not exactly regal; more like ducal, Duke of Edinburgh ducal.

We sat down for a short preliminary interchange. Then he said, 'Now I should like to examine you.' There was a little annexe to the room, with a bright light and a curtain to pull across. I stripped and climbed on to the bed. He came in and tested my hip in this way and that, compared it with the other hip –

'H'm, I see what you mean.'

He pointed to a dressing-gown, hanging on the wall. 'Now go and be X-rayed and come back!'

I put on the dressing-gown and said politely, 'May I leave my clothes here?' They were neatly piled.

He started. 'Yes. You may.'

When I got outside I saw other people in dressing-gowns, carrying their clothes round with them. Was I the first patient

ever to dump his clothes in the ducal consulting-room? What a
gaffe! It was too late to go back for them. Would he hold it
against me?

When I returned with my photograph his mood was
unchanged. 'Let's have a look at you!' I put on my clothes.

'Yes,' he said as we looked at the film, illuminated. The second
time round, I was beginning to recognise myself.

'Now this – ' he began. In the nick of time I stopped myself
from saying, Yes, I know.

All went well. He pointed out what was wrong and explained
what he did in the operation. Then he went back to his desk and
we sat down for his final speech.

'You've probably heard this is generally a successful
operation. It is. There's only one thing that goes wrong: the
chance of that is about one in a hundred. It's if you get an
infection.' He paused. 'We have to take the prosthesis out. You
can still *walk*. But one leg's two inches shorter than the other.'
He gave me a look that was penetrating, roughly amused,
unchanging.

Boldness is all. I didn't say anything. The speech was succinct
and contained the essential bit of statistical information.

'If you come to me,' he said, 'I'll operate on you in three
months. I don't believe in long waiting-lists. In Hove the
waiting-list is four years.'

I wasn't thinking of going to Hove.

'My rule,' he went on, 'is that if I can't operate on a patient in
three months, I don't take him on.'

He stood up and I stood up. I suspected that I was going to ask
him to take me on. The risk: one in a hundred. But I didn't say
anything. He held out his hand and gave me another powerful
handshake.

'Good morning, Mr Lunn.'

I said, 'Thank you.'

Outside the room, somebody lying under a scarlet blanket was
being wheeled by on a bed, wheeled from the double doors to the
concertina-gated lift by a man in green overalls and a green cap.
Something made me feel it would be unwise to report this to
Elspeth when I was giving her an account of the proceedings.

I'd now gone through the hoops of a second process. I gave

Elspeth my account of it and I reported it to our GP, who said, 'You'll have to think about it, won't you? You see why I recommended you to shop around.'

I did see. I also saw that if you 'shop around' you have to make a choice – that's if you mean to buy at all. I did mean to buy. I'd endured the pain for years. I'd contemplated the operation for months. I'd mobilised myself for the crisis. It would have been intolerable, now, to call it off, and only somewhat less than tolerable to postpone it.

I had already struck off No 1 on the list before our GP got a letter from Mr Love saying he had 'reluctantly' put me on his waiting-list of two years. And she had ascertained for me that Mr Lascelles's waiting-list was scarcely any shorter; and furthermore his was another big hospital where there was no way of telling if I should be operated on by the Great Man himself: I struck off No 3.

That left me with Quetzalcoatl. Elspeth was doubtful, not about Mr Redruth's skill but about the antiquatedness of the hospital. She proposed that we should find the money for me to side-step the NHS and go to Mr Digby-Waterton as a private patient, when I should be more certain of being operated on by himself after a very much shorter wait. I refused. 'Other people have to go on the NHS. I will.'

We enquired among our medical friends. Quetzalcoatl was acknowledged as one of the masters of his trade. (Our GP happened to have one of his successes on her list of patients, 'an old lady of nearly eighty who's jumping about like a flea!') It was the small antiquated hospital to which Elspeth kept returning in her argument. It was a teaching hospital, annexed to another of the largest, most renowned hospitals in London, and destined to be closed down – Centralisation. Elspeth was afraid I'd get less efficient nursing service. On the other hand, because the nursing-staff was small and not constantly being circulated in a huge machine, its members got to know each other and, so it was said, gave the place an atmosphere that was human and friendly.

What to do?

Elspeth said, 'Poor darling,' sympathetically.

I said, 'Think of the thousands of other people who have to . . .' The end of my sentence was lost in a vision of that

Paddington Station of X-raydom. Throngs and throngs of people, all having to think about these disturbing, wearying, frightening things for days on end, weeks on end, months on end. Suffering humanity.

Actually I'd begun to feel that I knew what to do. Boldness is all.

'Unless you're too doubtful, I shall go to Redruth.'

'I'm not *too* doubtful . . .' she said doubtfully.

'One has to remember that the element of chance probably outweighs any of the things *we*'re weighing up.' It was the sort of remark I found sensible but Elspeth didn't find comforting.

So it was decided. I was accepted by Quetzalcoatl. Within three months. It was now the beginning of July. We had received our invitation from Tom to spend the last week in August at his country house in Kent. If I could persuade Quetzalcoatl to do me in the first week of September, that would leave a month before the University teaching term began. ('Don't worry at all, dear boy.')

I wrote a polite letter about dates to Quetzalcoatl and got a friendly, sensible reply – to my astonishment not from a secretary but from him. Elspeth said:

'You really must stop calling him Quetzalcoatl.'

I had to admit that he didn't look at first sight like a plumed serpent. Yet wasn't the Royal Army Medical Corps' symbol the caduceus, that staff with *two* serpents entwining it?

I could see it wasn't going to be easy.

CHAPTER II

BEGINNING OF A HOUSE-PARTY

The white Mercedes we'd been told about was waiting outside the railway station. A young man in his early thirties jumped out of it as Elspeth and I appeared at the exit.

'Hello! Joe and Elspeth? I'm Tom's secretary.' He held out his hand. 'Jim.'

We looked at him. Veronica had told us he wasn't what she expected; nor was he what we might have expected. First of all we observed that he couldn't be more than five foot three inches in height. He was dressed in a close-fitting denim boiler-suit, and nobody could miss the fact that his body was strong and very well-shaped, alert, springy, filled with energy. We shook hands with him.

'Welcome to Hattersley Hall – when we get there!' He glanced round and gave a merry, ringing laugh. 'Welcome to the railroad station – let me take your baggage!'

While he was stowing away our suitcases he went on. 'Tom's waiting to welcome you. Everyone else is here.' He looked up for a moment. 'Robert and Veronica, whom you know. Burke and Steve, whom you know. And two more couples from Boyce Peterhouse New York – Peter and Merrill, and Jack and Barrie. Quite a party.'

Elspeth and I said something, but we were mainly occupied in looking at each other with a question – Merrill, Barrie, were they men or women? If only Americans wouldn't call their children, particularly their girls, by names which gave no clue to what sex they were! Actually I guessed that Merrill was a woman, because Steve had once naughtily told me that Peter was a former 'secretary' of Tom's who had gone off and got married. (Later it transpired that Barrie was Jack's wife, and a strikingly attractive woman to boot.)

'Ready?' Jim looked up from completing his task. He had a very presentable lively face – wide-open bright blue eyes and a firm laughing mouth. His hair was brown, cut shortish and ruffled.

He held the door of the car for Elspeth to get into the front seat. She told him I would sit there as it would be more comfortable for my hip.

'Your hip?' he said. 'I noticed you were limping. Is it arthritis?'

I said it was.

'Then you've just got to have it replaced. It's a great operation – my aunt had it and she's good as new.'

I was settling into the seat. 'Actually I *am* going to have the operation.'

'Oh really?' As he got in beside me he glanced at me with his bright blue eyes and gave his merry, ringing laugh. 'Then you don't need my advice!'

I said, 'I suppose not, but it's reassuring all the same.'

He started the car.

I went on. 'I'm hoping to go into hospital a few days after we leave here.'

'Oh! That's too bad. You won't be able to come back with us all to New York.'

'To New York?' I said. I didn't know how Elspeth, at the back, was taking this.

'Tom will tell you about it.'

I shifted my head so as to see Elspeth's reflection in the mirror. It showed nothing.

Our journey was under way.

In half an hour's time we arrived at Hattersley Hall. We exclaimed with pleasure as it came into view. It was a beautiful, late eighteenth-century country-house, quite small – smaller than I'd expected. The car crunched over a spacious gravelled yard with a coach-house on the opposite side.

The door was opened by Tom himself, our host waiting to welcome us in person. He was looking plump in casual shirt and trousers, his greying red curly hair freshly clipped very short, his pouting smile composed and smooth.

'How nice to see you both!' He turned momentarily from us. 'Now, Jim! If you'll just take the cases up, then we'll all meet for tea in the drawing-room.' A woman-servant quietly disappeared into a doorway. Tom turned back to us. 'I'm sure you'd like to go up to your room. Jim will go with you.'

We looked around us with wonderment and more pleasure. The house was as beautiful inside as it was outside. We went up a broad eighteenth-century oak staircase, where there were bunches of flowers on the window-sills, to a broad landing with a Persian carpet. It appeared that there were two master bedrooms with their own bathrooms; one occupied by Burke and Steve, the other reserved for our host and his secretary. Robert and Veronica were in a bedroom down a few steps at the end of the landing. The two Boyce Peterhouse couples were installed, no doubt in equal comfort, over in the coach-house.

'Tom apologises,' said Jim, as he showed us into our bedroom, 'for your bathroom being next door' – he was amused – 'instead of *en suite*.'

Left alone we looked round our bedroom with more wonderment and pleasure. It was lofty, and the walls were papered in a pattern of dark, sumptuously-coloured leaves and flowers, a pattern which repeated itself at such long intervals that it was barely discernible. There was the same pattern on the material of the curtains. There were two tall sash windows, the lower halves open to let in the warm, sunny, afternoon air. We went to one of them and looked out. Below us was a part of the garden, lawns divided into compartments by clipped yew hedges twenty feet high.

'Coo, what it must be to be rich!' I whispered.

'Tom says he isn't *really* rich,' she whispered back.

'When did he tell you that?'

'That day when he took me out to lunch to talk about our finances.'

I did know about the occasion, but was distinctly inclined to ignore it.

We turned to look at each other. 'I asked him about it.' She went on whispering. 'He says that in America you don't really count as rich unless you're worth tens of millions. And not *very* rich unless you're worth tens of billions.'

'And he hasn't made *that* much?' I was beginning to laugh.

Elspeth began to laugh. 'But he wishes he had!'

I laughed aloud.

'Sh! . .' Her eyes were sparkling. 'I think Burke just counts as rich.' She paused. 'And Tom intends to behave as if he did!'

'What a man!'

Elspeth went on. 'He told me something else that was interesting.' She became serious. 'Burke once confided to him that rich people only feel really at ease with each other. So I don't suppose she feels really at ease with us.'

'Other things must come into feeling really at ease with someone,' I said stuffily. I was thinking again of what I had imagined to be the deeply ingrained self-consciousness in Burke's nature. Self-consciousness to that painful degree didn't seem to me, as I'd ever observed it, to be affected by whether one was born rich or poor, beautiful or plain, intelligent or not.

Elspeth with her thoughts obviously on a different tack, said: 'She seems to feel really at ease with Steve.' A different sparkle was in her eyes now.

'But I'm sure she could never marry him. That somehow just wouldn't be allowed.'

'Poor Burke! . .'

I laughed. 'I don't know about that!'

We turned back to the room. We tried the bed. We thought how pretty the furniture was, and how alluring the selection of bedside books. On one of the little tables there was a small radio set.

'It's a wonder it isn't a television set,' I said.

'Wouldn't that make it seem like a hotel? . .'

'I wonder if we shall get breakfast in bed.'

'I thought you didn't like having breakfast in bed?' She knew perfectly well.

'No. But I love settling down afterwards . . .'

'Darling,' she whispered, eluding me, 'we *must* go and wash our hands – they'll be waiting for us.'

'They won't.'

'Even if they're not, we ought to go down.' She laughed at me. 'We *are* going to be here for a week.'

'All right . . .'

We went down to the drawing-room. With the exception of Robert and Veronica, everyone was there. It was a spacious room, decorated pleasingly and unobtrusively, leading into a smaller room, furnished as a summer-room with white painted furniture and verdant plants.

In the main room Tom was standing with his back to an empty fireplace.

'What a marvellous house you've found!' Elspeth said to him.

I said, 'I didn't know you could rent such places.'

'I'm glad you like it.' He smiled. 'I looked at several houses that were bigger, but this seemed just right – more intimate . . .' For the latter remark he was addressing himself intimately to Elspeth. Then he turned to me and said in a grander tone of voice: 'Also it means one can dispense with having a butler.'

I was delighted – Tom with a butler!

Elspeth said to him: 'It's all so beautifully done.'

'Ah yes,' said Tom to her. 'It's owned by Lord Reresby Willoughby.'

'I'm surprised he can bear to let it.'

'I'm told,' said Tom, 'his agent chooses tenants with exceptional care. They have to be in *Who's Who* if not *Debrett*.'

I continued to be delighted. How could *he* be in either? I wondered. I was reminded of, Everything in perfect taste . . . But I'd forgotten Tom's basic down-to-earthness –

'All the same,' he was saying, 'Lord Reresby Willoughby locks up his best pictures and his oldest silver.'

We were amused. Tom said to Elspeth: 'Now I must introduce you to those of my house-guests whom you don't already know.' We began to move away from the fireplace.

At that moment a good-looking youngish woman came in carrying a big silver-railed tray with the tea on it. 'This is Mrs Birrell,' he said to us, 'who keeps house for me. In tremendous style.' When she had gone he went on. 'Her husband's my chef. The two of them live here permanently and run the place between them. I always want to call him Augustine, of course – his name's Leonard!' And then his silky smile flickered into a private grin for me. 'Actually Len . . .' Unmistakably alluding to his own lower middle-class origin and mine – I grinned back.

'Is he a good cook?'

'Superb! . .' And then he failed to resist adding, 'He'd *better* be!'

The other guests were helping themselves to tea, and Tom took us to meet his entourage from Boyce Peterhouse New York.

They were agreeable people. Peter, intelligent but to my mind slightly softish – I suspected that he must owe his successful career to Tom's dynamism: Merrill, not especially prepossessing but the reverse of softish, and somewhat over-ready to talk about her five children – to whom Tom was most appropriately godfather. Jack, I took to – one of those men who, one gradually comes to realise, are so complex and interesting that one forgets all about their absence of looks and physical charm: Barrie, very satisfied with him. (According to Steve, who told me later, Jack had risen to the entourage as one of Tom's chief lieutenants, not as his 'secretary'. One was pleased to think that Boyce Peterhouse offered two channels for promotion to higher rank.) We all chatted amiably.

Suddenly above the conversation, was to be heard –

'Jim! Where are Robert and Veronica?'

'I guess they went over to watch the cricket game.'

'They're *missing their tea!*'

I tried to catch Steve's eye – he was sitting on a sofa with Burke. Fortunately I failed. I went on talking to Jack.

I gathered that in the previous three weeks the party had included other entouragistes from Boyce Peterhouse New York. It seemed that we, in the final week, when old friends from England had been summoned, represented the pick, the nearest and dearest of the bunch. I have to say that our being there at all was sheerly a manifestation of Tom's personal imperialism. In advance the party had provoked Robert and me to malicious comment. Yet now that we actually were all here, I felt that we were going to enjoy ourselves.

There was a mild bustling disturbance in the company. It was Tom, followed by Jim, leaving for the kitchen, there to discuss with Len the evening meal – we subsequently learnt it was one of the most solemn moments of the day. As the time was six o'clock, most of us promptly went up to our rooms to listen to the BBC News. (In a disgraceful way most of the nation was following salacious references to a leading politician being accused of conspiring to have a male model removed from the scene.)

Afterwards we bathed and changed – our clothes had been laid out for us with exemplary neatness.

When we were coming downstairs again, we met Jim, still in his boiler-suit, running upstairs. He stopped, looking up at us, his blue eyes bright with fun –

'How is it?'

'I think we're going to like it,' I said.

'Don't you think it's real Agatha Christie?'

'I hope not.'

'*How do you know?*' Before we could reply he was on his way upstairs again, leaving a merry, ringing laugh to float down on the air.

The door of the master-bedroom shut. I whispered to Elspeth:

'Do you think he's always in the manic phase?'

She looked amused. 'I like him.'

'So do I.'

We found Tom already down, ready to make the first drinks for his guests with his own hands. The woman-servant we'd seen before, looking like a pleasant middle-aged woman from the village, stood discreetly by while her master performed. Tom handed Elspeth a gin-and-tonic.

'I do hope you'll like a slice of lime in it. We tend to have lime, here; but Josephine will gladly change it for a slice of lemon if you prefer it.'

'I'm sure I shall like lime,' said Elspeth, who had never had lime in it other than when she had been in the USA.

Tom smiled encouragingly at her. He made a drink for me and then, as we were the first down, began a private conversation.

'I hear you've been seeing Stewart.'

I said, 'It doesn't take news long to get around.'

'I make it my business.' He smiled at Elspeth as if the remark were purely social. Purely social, my foot! It contained an element of pure menace. He said to Elspeth and me jointly, 'What did you think of him?'

'Very impressed,' said I.

'And you, my dear?' He made it clear that it was Elspeth's opinion that really mattered to him.

'I agree with Joe.' I wondered if she had intimations of what was going on – it sounded as if she had.

'Furthermore we like him,' I said, 'and I think he likes us.'
'He does like you.' Tom nodded his head grandly. 'I think Stewart will serve you well.'

The conversation was ended by the appearance of Robert and Veronica. Tom turned his attention to Veronica. Robert grinned at me. Tom made a drink for Veronica. Scotch-and-soda.

'Did you enjoy the cricket?' he said to her.

'Yes, Tom.'

'I didn't know *you* were so interested in the game.' He was implying that she was putting up with it because Robert wanted to watch it.

'I don't know what makes you think that, Tom. I was practically brought up on it.' She laughed. 'Ho-ho-ho!'

Tom was taken aback.

'A long time ago,' said Veronica, 'one of my brothers nearly got into the England side.'

'Really, really . . .' Tom's smile was distinctly uncomfortable. 'I hope our local team gave you an enjoyable performance. I should have thought, myself, they were bloody incompetent.' (The local cricket-ground adjoined the garden of the Hall.)

'We enjoyed every minute of it, didn't we, Robert?'

At the cost of missing their tea! I thought. Robert said with lofty amusement:

'It was very nice. Very nice . . .'

More people came into the room, the Boyce Peterhouse contingent, Steve and Burke.

'Now Jim! I think you might take over getting Josephine orders for drinks.'

Veronica, standing beside me, said *sotto voce*: 'What do you think of Jim? I should think he's a little sex-pot, wouldn't you?'

She was waiting for a reply, her narrow grey eyes sparkling with stern amusement. I looked round for help. Making a move towards the small garden-room, I said, 'I don't know.' I was hoping that everybody else would now be out of earshot.

'You must know,' said Veronica.

My technique of saying this was a back-of-a-postcard expression such as I'd never use entirely failed me. Feebly I said: 'Certainly he's got a lot of energy.'

'Energy for everybody, *I* should say. Ho-ho-ho!'

'I should think Tom absorbs quite a lot of it in one way or another.' I was trying to get the conversation on to a broader footing.

Veronica thought about it.

En passant it occurred to me that Jim, with the example of Peter and others before him, must be far from oblivious to the good that Tom's dynamism could do his career in the firm of Boyce Peterhouse New York. (And for my money, Jim was a better man than Peter.) Harking back to the long distant past . . . Tom had done pretty well, for those days, by Steve.

Veronica said: 'Do you think that Jim will go off and get married?'

'I shouldn't be at all surprised, in fact I should think it very likely.'

'Wretched Tom . . .'

We contemplated the fortune of the unhappy man who desired only heterosexual young men. Robert and I had sometimes talked about it, but only on the premise that most of what was to be said about it had already been said by Proust.

Yet there wasn't in *A La Recherche* a character quite like Tom. Through personal magnetism and personal dynamism Tom had managed to live a long life – next month he'd be sixty-seven – without ever lacking the attendance of a clever, personable young man drawn from the same circle in society as himself. One of them had followed another. (To end up with Jim seemed to me pretty triumphant.) When their heterosexuality got the better of them and they went off and got married, Tom's personal imperialism came into force, and they found themselves joining the entourage – themselves, their wives, their children!

Robert pointed out that members of Tom's entourage didn't put up much of a fight against remaining thus. When Tom died he would be leaving a lot of money, a lot of money! He wasn't going to leave it to any of his family, and he wasn't going to leave it to any institution. The future of the special entouragistes was golden – Tom said so, to Robert. Robert and I speculated on how much some of them might get. But alas! alas! not Steve. Steve had got away from Tom when Tom left for the USA – just at the time when Tom took off on his flight to riches. Poor old Steve! . . Steve had lost his chance – Tom said so, to Robert.

I said to Veronica: 'Given the cards Fate dealt him – and some of them were pretty bum cards – Tom has played his hand jolly well. When you come to think of it, consummately!'

Veronica said, 'I suppose he has.'

'That sounds a bit too grudging. He's a very intelligent, gifted man, you know.'

Veronica thought about it. While she was thinking, a gong sounded softly. Tom announced that it was time for us to go into dinner.

On the way to the dining-room we passed one of the small wonders of the house – an alcove-room turned into a library. As we went by I glanced round the shelves and saw book after book that I should like to read. (We discovered later that they'd been assembled not by Lord Reresby Willoughby but by the Birrells.)

We sat down to dinner at a long Regency table on which stood two handsome Sheffield plate candelabra, the candles burning stilly in the faded summer light. Tom sat at the head of the table; on his right, the first evening, Burke, and on his left Veronica.

The serving of the dinner – in the absence of a butler! – was overseen by Len in person. It had better be superb – it *was*. The voice of our host acquired a purring sound. I was too far away to hear what he was saying to the two women, but it was clear from the soapy, pop-eyed looks he was giving them that he was making up to them. I had a presentiment that during the week we were going to see a fair amount of Tom's making up to the women members of the party – suborning *them* into his personal empire while he had the chance.

I imagined Veronica being admired for being so clever and so effective. I thought with distaste of the evening when Elspeth would be sitting up there, being admired for being so sympathetic and so *wise*, my dear . . . I wondered what Tom was admiring in Burke. Her riches, I hoped; her artistic flair in the theatre; her desire to do good with her riches – and I wondered what he was saying to her about Steve. From their facial expressions I could see that, whatever he was saying, both women were lapping it up as readily as the superb dinner, at that stage Romney lamb fresh from the Marshes. Especially the candle light suited Burke: her pale complexion looked warmer and her black eyes gleamed more softly, as did the square-cut emerald. And Veronica looked more blooming, more at ease: I saw Robert eyeing her from his end of the table, where Jim presided.

If I knew anything about it, Tom's ploy with Burke – though of course the words would never be spoken – would be to the effect that 'We rich people, my dear, *know* each other . . .' If it hadn't been that she was upper class in origin and Tom lower middle class, she Irish in origin and he Jewish (a standard New York juxtaposition), I might have found it easier to judge how he was faring – or what Burke happened to be thinking about it. The fact that Burke's inherited riches were doubtless by several orders of magnitude greater than those Tom had made for himself – according to him, her grandfather had built railroads, 'relatively small railroads, I believe' – only made the ploy more appealing to contemplate.

I was always entertained by the spectacle of rich people together. The quotation from Scott Fitzgerald about the rich being 'different' struck me as wrong. All human beings, rich or poor, are made of the same stuff. On the other hand, in the way the very rich behave, the way they comport themselves . . . there, there is the difference. A slight air of apartness, of truly belonging elsewhere than with the not-rich, their antennae sensitised to recognise each other; of feeling really at ease only with each other, (I recalled Tom's transmission of Burke's confidences to Elspeth). Seeing them, the very rich, pair off with each other in America was, I thought, very like seeing members of the high upper class pair off with each other in England – or, come to that, members of the Party hierarchy's top layers in the Soviet Union. As long as that went on, the human comedy was in no danger of petering out – nor was the grip of people who were in power.

Meanwhile I was trying to fend off questions from Merrill about my views on Northern Ireland, needling questions. (Was she, too, Irish in origin?) As it happened I knew something about Northern Ireland, through belonging to an independent association of people of good-will, mostly Irish in origin though I was not, which devoted its energies to searching for any moves whatsoever that might be made towards composing the conflict. Regrettably I found the current views of many Irish-Americans as ignorant as they were vociferous: they didn't want to *listen* to anybody – Merrill didn't want to listen to me, really – and that puzzled me. I had my work cut out to hold my tongue. I stalled. And Merrill was not the woman to take stall for an answer. The conversation became tense.

I was saved by Steve, who was sitting next to me. (There were two spare men, and Steve had found himself next to Jim, with whom he appeared to be getting on hilariously.)

'Do we overhear the makings of an Agatha Christie situation?' Steve enquired. (A merry, ringing laugh from his left.)

Nothing I might have said or not said about Ireland could have had the same effect. Giving them her most stunning high-and-mighty glance, Merrill ostentatiously turned the other way and started to talk to Jack. Horrid woman!

Steve gave his mock-rueful smile, which was patently appreciated by Jim.

I was saved.

'Quite a party,' I said to Jim.

'*I* said it first!' A merry, ringing laugh again.

CHAPTER III

END OF A HOUSE-PARTY

The days passed very swiftly. The weather was fine and I should have been content to do nothing but hang about in the garden – reading (I was on the panel of judges for a book prize); writing (I had to do a review); or even thinking . . . The garden, being divided into compartments by the tall yew hedges, was made for such pursuits; or rather, it would have been made for them if Tom had not seen fit to revive a tennis court in one of the compartments, install a croquet lawn in another, and designate a third place where we could play a sort of *boules* with stainless steel balls.

Tom didn't exactly command, but we found ourselves kept on the move by *dromophilia* most of the time. There were some very pretty walks in the countryside, trips by car to local places of literary interest. One evening – the evening being on Len's day off – we were transported to a very grand country restaurant. Another evening we went to a nearby town to a repertory theatre, one of the recent generation of repertory theatres named after celebrated actors and actresses, and created, when the old reps were dying out, to put on interesting and mildly superior lists of plays. (Steve had once directed a play in one of them.)

Robert discovered urgent affairs which called him up to London for a couple of days. Nobody was less given, I thought, to being a captive, least of all a captive kept whizzing about like a bluebottle by Tom.

But then I thought that perhaps I was being unfair to him. I had a feeling that this might be a week when he went down to see Annette – he'd never tell anybody about that. And I wondered how her treatment for diabetes was going. (He'd never mentioned it from that day to this.) I thought they would probably be finding it difficult to treat her for diabetes on top of all the other treatments. Robert must be more worried than ever before.

From time to time I myself managed to escape the company for a few hours at least. Along one of the boundaries of the garden there ran a delightful brook, beside which I could lie peacefully in my swimming-trunks, even if the water was too shallow to swim in. Also there was a small secluded pond, too stagnant to swim in, at the edge of which there was a sweet little tumbledown pavilion. It was a few days before my hiding-places were discovered.

One afternoon, a 'free' afternoon before we all were due to dine at the country restaurant, I was lying reading by the brook when Burke came upon me.

'I'm discovered!'

She laughed. 'I knew where you were. We all know where you are.' She stood before me, looking small and trim in carmine slacks and a multicoloured top – very elegant, very American.

'Don't get up! . .'

I was by now standing up, facing her. She wavered.

I said, 'Let's both sit down!'

'Intelligent proposition.' She smiled, with a piquantly stylised turn of the head.

We both sat down on the grass.

'I wanted to talk with you, Joe.'

The unease, the jumpiness I had noticed the first time we met, were back in force.

'Yes,' I said as gently as I could.

She began.

'I love England so much, Joe. I have so many friends here . . . I've already stayed beyond my schedule. I really have to get back – for my theatre. I stayed on to come to this party of Tom's, but I can't stay any longer. I just have to get back to New York as soon as the party's over. You know?'

I said – feeling slightly jumpy myself – that it had been fun having her here. I hated that word 'fun' as we all used it – it always sounded to me vulgar and trivial.

'It's been fun, being here.' She paused an instant, flickeringly. Then: 'It's been fun, having Steve around.' The more nervous

197

she was, the more she sounded like an actress.

Steve was what she was wanting to talk about.

I said: 'I can believe that.'

'I know you can. Joe, I've had more fun with Steve around than I'd have imagined possible.'

Irrelevantly I was visited by the image of Steve around with her at grand ambassadorial parties up in Regent's Park. Steve! . . Delightful image.

I dismissed the image and looked at her.

'Not just fun.' She glanced at me and then away. 'What I really mean,' she said, 'is happiness.'

I said, 'Steve's a very easy person to feel . . . at ease with.'

'How right that is! How well you know him!'

I wondered if perhaps I was beginning to know her, too. I said quietly:

'Long may the happiness last!'

Too quick on her cue – '*Quien sabe?*'

I said, 'I think you probably know . . .' As I watched her I thought I saw for the first time a faint colour come into her pale complexion – I might have imagined it. Her eyes were very bright.

We stopped talking. Only the brook went on making its watery noise on the pebbles.

Her mood changed. As if getting down to business, she said:

'I suppose you know Tom suggested I ask Steve to come back to New York with me?'

'I guessed.' I grinned.

She laughed with amusement. '*I* don't collect scads of people to take around with me.'

I laughed too.

'There's a lot of things for Steve to do, *independently*, in New York. In my theatre. He was into children's theatre in your country five years back. You know?'

I nodded my head as if I did know.

There was another pause.

'What is the trouble, then?' I asked.

'No trouble. It's just Steve seems uncertain.'

'Do you want me to speak to him?' The minute I'd said it I realised it was stupidly crude.

'No, no.'

'I didn't mean that – '

She interrupted me, not worried by my gaffe. 'It's just he's uncertain of himself.'

I said, 'He always has needed someone at hand.'

'That's right. But I want him to understand I'm offering him something independent. Work in my theatre.' She looked at me directly. 'I know he can do it. You know?'

I looked directly back at her, sitting there in her carmine slacks, pale-complexioned, brightly black-eyed. A clever woman, rich and influential no doubt; and a very nice, good woman. I wanted her to be happy.

'I know he's going to talk with you about it,' she said.

'Tom has talked to him?'

We exchanged a glance, agreed in making no comment on Tom's interventions.

'That's all,' she said, and got up. 'I'm grateful to you for this. . .' And then suddenly, surprisingly, as if her self-consciousness and diffidence had suddenly melted, she said, 'I like you, Joe.'

Before I had time to find a reply she was walking away.

I lay back on the ground and stayed there for a while.

I began to think about the pursuit of happiness. Was ever a pursuit more ill-advised? Happiness is one of the random gifts of Fate; you just happen to find you *are* happy . . . And that's all. It can't be predicted or commanded or caught – pursuing it is about as well-advised as pursuing the end of the rainbow. The most you can do is put yourself in a position where it seems to you a shade more likely that you'll happen to find you're happy. I thought Burke would probably agree with me.

I remained by the brook, expecting Steve to put in an appearance. He didn't.

Finally I went up to our room to change for the evening's expedition. Elspeth was already there. Suddenly there was a knock on the door. Saying, 'What on earth?' I went to open it.

'It's me, Veronica. Can I come in?'

I opened the door and she came in.

'I'm sorry to disturb you just when you're going to change.' She looked at us and we saw that her eyes were darting with light.

'I'm spitting mad!' she cried. 'I can't contain myself. I've got to tell somebody. Positively spitting!'

I moved a chair for her to sit down. She refused it. The colour in her cheeks was brilliant.

'Tom,' she said. 'What do you think Tom's said to me.'

Elspeth and I sat down side by side on the bed.

'He's given me his advice. He thinks Robert ought to marry me. His advice to me is to threaten Robert, that if he doesn't get a divorce I'll leave him. Can you believe it?'

Elspeth and I glanced at each other. I said, 'I'm afraid I can.'

'Did you ever hear such ridiculous advice? The man's a fool!'

'No, he's not a fool,' I murmured.

'*I* think he is. Do you know any advice less likely to achieve the desired result?' She looked at us furiously. 'I know you think I don't know Robert as well as you do, as well as Tom does. Perhaps I don't. You've known him for more than forty years. But in two years I've learnt *this* – I've never met a man less susceptible to blackmail. He'd positively hate it. And he'd hate *me*.'

We were silent in agreement.

'Do you wonder I'm spitting mad?'

'*I* don't,' said Elspeth.

There was a pause.

'I hope to God he doesn't hint something of the kind to Robert.'

I said, 'I don't suppose he will.' Knowing Tom's mania for interfering, I didn't feel that the remark carried unlimited conviction.

'I told him pretty forcibly not to,' Veronica said. 'He's a monster!'

'No,' I said, hoping to calm her down. I smiled at her. 'You could say he's a Force of Nature. You have to take him as he comes.'

'*You* can say that!' She looked at Elspeth as well as me. 'He hasn't tried to break up you two.' She laughed harshly. 'Yet!'

I said, 'In a way he's seeing it from your point of view. He knows you want Robert to marry you. And he thinks that's a good thing – just as we all do. So he goes all-out for the desired result.'

Veronica paused to think about it.

I went on. 'He's rash, impetuous. What his mother used to call "mad-headed". He probably thought he was doing his best for you.' Knowing Tom's natural capacity for breaking things up, I didn't feel that this remark carried unlimited conviction, either.

Veronica sat down on the chair.

'The important thing now,' she said, 'is to make sure not a word of this reaches Robert's ears.' She was struck by a fresh idea. 'It's interesting – Tom took the opportunity to do this while Robert's away. I hope you noticed that.'

I said, 'I'm not so sure he wouldn't have done it while Robert was here, if Robert hadn't gone away.'

'Stop! You'll make me spit again.'

I laughed. 'I don't want to make you do that, Veronica.'

Veronica showed signs of grinning. 'I feel a bit better now . . . Good God, look at the time! We've all got to change.' She stood up. 'Thank you, both of you!' And she went quickly to the door.

When the door shut behind her, Elspeth and I looked at each other in consternation, but there was no time for discussion. We began changing our clothes. At one stage in it Elspeth said:

'Do you think Robert will get a divorce?'

I shook my head. 'I don't really think so.'

A little later Elspeth said:

'If Annette were to die, do you think Robert would marry Veronica?'

I felt I was not giving the expected answer – I said, 'I haven't the faintest idea.'

After that we completed our changing and went downstairs to join the party for the restaurant.

I found myself sitting next to Tom in the back of the white Mercedes. He was not in silky, soapy mood: on the contrary, irascibility was unconcealed. His face looked red and puffy. I thought it must be the after-effects of a row with Veronica.

I was wrong. He said bullyingly:

'Have you been talking to Steve?'

I said No.

'I suppose you heard Burke's offered to take him back with her to New York?'

I said Yes.

'I hope he won't be such a fool as to turn it down.'

The brutal tone of voice made me look again at him. His eyes were glaring.

I said peaceably, 'I don't think he will.'

'You know Burke means to keep him? *And* he'll have a job in her theatre. *For as long as he wants*!' Tom's voice rose, as at the thought of that length of time.

'That sounds good.'

Tom hadn't finished. '*And*, he'll have *me* to take care of his future.'

I was silent, digesting that information.

'Jim! You should have turned left there.'

There ensued an altercation about the A this and the A that. Jim was obviously on the right road. I was glad when the journey was over.

It was the following afternoon when Steve approached me. I had changed my site to the little pavilion beside the pond. The bushes around it were undisturbed by the breeze, and there were a few leaves floating on the water. I looked up – Steve was carrying a copy of *Happier Days*, one of the two "house copies", as Tom called them. He settled down beside me. I put down the book I was reading.

'I've just finished this,' he said. 'It's terribly good.'

I laughed.

'Honestly, Joe, it is.'

I didn't propose to renew my paranoiac argument about there being only ten other people who thought so.

He opened the book and began to laugh. 'This scene is terribly funny.' It was one of the scenes in which a patient came to ask the GP's advice about a quaint intimate difficulty, quaint, to say the least of it. The doctor told him not to worry – it happened to other men . . . Steve finished reading the scene again. Then he said:

'I think the doctor and the girl are terribly good.'

'I'm quite pleased about that.'

Steve said, 'What does Elspeth say about it? The doctor's obviously you.'

'She expressed general approval of the book.'

'Wasn't she embarrassed?'

I said, 'I think – I hope, she puts art before embarrassment. She tries to, I know.'

'What a marvellous wife!'

'You can say that again!' I thought about her. 'She was my greatest stroke of good fortune.'

We were silent for a moment. I contemplated the still reflection of the clouds in the water.

Steve said:

'Joe, what am I to do about New York?'

I said, 'So far I've only heard Burke's side of it. And Tom's.'

'And Tom's!' He laughed. 'Can I bear being drawn into . . . the circle?'

I said, 'I take it you've realised there are certain practical advantages in being drawn into the circle, as you call it.'

'What?'

'One day Tom's going to leave a lot of money, certain members of the circle are going to do pretty well. He's said as much, to Robert.'

'*Joe!* . .'

I grinned at him – innocently he had *not* realised it. 'It's something to be taken account of,' I said.

Steve said, 'You may not understand it, Joe – one of the reasons for going to New York is that I should have *work* . . . Having work is more important to me than you think.'

I nodded my head to indicate my being convinced.

'The other reason is Burke, of course. Joe' – he looked me in the eye – 'Joe, I'm *devoted* to her.'

'Yes,' I said, respecting his manifest struggle against the flaw of sounding unconvincing. He actually was telling the truth, as he had been over wanting work in the theatre – and also over not having realised that if he went to live in New York some of Tom's money might ultimately come his way.

Suddenly he said, 'I envy you being settled, here.'

I could have made some horrid quip about being settled in failure, but I didn't. Anyway he was probably thinking about Elspeth. I said:

'Yes.'

We were both thoughtful. Finally he stood up.

'You're waiting to go on reading,' he said. He went away.
And so we came to the last evening.

Tom saw to it that this last dinner was the most superb of all.
We dined a little later than usual, and there was in the
atmosphere that warmth of mutual affection, bonhomie, high
spirits at prospective liberation, which characterises the end of a
school term. We really did all like each other. (In fact Tom's
personal empire comprised likeable people – with the exception
of Merrill!) The house-party had been a success.

Towards the end of the meal we started to drink toasts. Tom,
sitting at the head of the table, had Burke on his right and
Elspeth on his left. (Veronica had been demoted.) Tom, I could
see from his gestures, was taking the last opportunity to butter
up Elspeth. Robert was now with us again, and Veronica had
broken the rules of etiquette by planting herself determinedly
next to him. The contingent from Boyce Peterhouse were doing
well on the alcohol. Jim had the expression of a man whose
staff-work has come off perfectly. We were all happy.

The last of the toasts was of course kept for Tom. We all drank
to him with feeling.

And Tom replied:

'There's nothing more heart-warming than to be surrounded
by one's friends. I'm deeply honoured by you all, for coming.
And I'm deeply grateful . . .'

We made appreciative murmurings. He went on.

'My friends from New York have no option in going back to
New York – they've got to get back to Boyce Peterhouse.' He
smiled dominatingly at them. 'And I can tell you now that Steve
is going to come with Burke.'

There was modest hand-clapping.

'I know that Robert is in the throes of important discussions
with his publisher about a new book.' (Nobody else knew.) 'And
I know that Joe is going into hospital quite soon. But I make
them this offer . . .' He smiled seductively at us. 'Just for the hell
of it – a quick return trip to New York, out by one Concorde and
back by the next Concorde. Come back with us! Just for the hell
of it.' His smiling went on. 'And to give me pleasure.'

Elspeth and I were glancing at each other: so were Robert and
Veronica.

Tom said, 'Jim has already made our reservations for the day after tomorrow. If you, Robert and Veronica and Joe and Elspeth, think it's fun, Jim will get reservations for you – we know how to do these things. How do you feel about it?'

In exchanging glances I had observed that Elspeth's was totally non-committal. Robert appeared to be shaking his head.

'Just let Jim know first thing in the morning.'

There were encouraging sounds from the others. 'Do come!' and '*All* go to New York.'

I imagined that Concorde flights were about three days apart. It would be nice to see New York again. Money no object!

The dinner-party ended with warmth, bonhomie – and afterwards, slight signs of drama.

When Elspeth and I got to our room, our room with the dark leaves and flowers on the wallpaper endlessly entwined, I said:

'Well, what about it?'

Elspeth shrugged her shoulders.

'Shall we go?' I said. 'We can just make it before I go into hospital.'

'You can go, if you like. I shan't.'

I was surprised by the remark and the tone of voice in which she made it. I said: 'I shouldn't go without you.'

'I don't see why not.' She was making preparations for going to bed, not looking at me.

I drew back. 'I suppose it wouldn't be a very good idea to cross the Atlantic twice in the week before I go into hospital.'

'I should have thought it would be a very bad idea.'

There was a silence. A long silence. I was sitting on the bed, watching her.

'What's the matter, my darling?'

She said, 'What do you mean, what's the matter?'

'You seem . . .'

She was putting on her dressing-gown. 'Oh.'

I stood up and went towards her. 'What *is* the matter, my darling?'

'I've got a headache.' She was not looking at me.

I stepped backwards. 'I'm sorry.'

She fastened the dressing-gown and went out of the room.
I told myself it must be the effects of alcohol. I began to make
my own preparations for going to bed.

CHAPTER IV

'THERE MUST HAVE BEEN SOMEONE'

Afterwards I couldn't think how I'd missed something
seriously the matter with Elspeth. The following day we
were occupied with travelling back to London, and then, as
Viola was away, with getting the flat into working-order again.
Elspeth was distant, tired, unwell.

'What's the matter, my darling?'

In a slow, uninflected tone of voice, 'Nothing.'

The day after that was the day when Tom and his entourage,
an entourage augmented by Steve and Burke, took off in the
Concorde. Robert and Veronica had turned down Tom's
invitation. (Veronica had privately told me she was still spitting
mad.) Elspeth went back to work. It would have been exciting to
see New York again, but foolish for me to go, on the brink of
going into hospital for a major operation.

Was Elspeth desperately worried about the operation? I asked
myself. How could she be anything else?

At the height of insensitiveness I accepted an invitation from
one of my friends to spend the evening with him at his club,
leaving Elspeth to come home from work and spend the evening
alone.

At least, I thought when I was letting myself into the flat, I
was not over-late coming home. The flat was in darkness.
Elspeth had gone to bed. The flat was silent. I crept about as
quietly as possible and finally opened the door of her room.

I could tell in the darkness that she was awake.

She was lying on her side, facing outwards, and I knelt beside
the bed and kissed her.

Her face was wet, wet with tears.

'My darling, what *is* the matter?'

She began to sob.

'You *must* tell me.' I felt a terrible apprehension.

She shook her head.

I began to stoke her forehead and her hair, waiting for the sobs to quieten. At last I said, 'Now? . .'

The bedside clock was ticking. She said:

'Tom told me . . . you didn't invent it.' She burst into tears again. 'There *was* someone . . .'

I suddenly felt rage, fear, despair. 'No!' I cried.

She was weeping without restraint. I said:

'*It isn't true*! My darling, it isn't true! . . He was lying.' I couldn't believe it. 'Did he actually say that? In those words? Or did he somehow make you believe it, by one of his innuendoes?'

She did not answer.

I went on. I scarcely knew what I was saying. 'How could Tom know, anyway? He wasn't even in the country!'

Between sobs she said:

'He got it from Steve – Tom said Steve . . . thought there was someone.'

'*Steve!*' I was appalled. 'Steve couldn't have said that. He knows there wasn't.'

Elspeth said nothing.

'Tom could make anything sound true,' I said. 'But Steve wouldn't lie about a thing like that. Steve will tell you. Steve will tell you it was Tom's idea.'

I suddenly realised that Steve was gone, not there to tell her. And Tom was gone, so I couldn't beat the destructive lights out of him. 'This is horrible!'

She moved her forehead away from my touch.

'Robert knows I invented it,' I said. 'He will tell you.'

'Everyone who reads the book thinks there *was* someone.'

The book. My novel! I couldn't speak.

'Everyone thinks it rings true,' she said.

Art must ring true or it's wasted. 'They don't,' I cried. 'They can't.'

'There must have been someone . . .'

'There *wasn't*!' Suddenly I found myself bursting into tears. I touched my forehead against her. 'There wasn't anyone. There

208

never has been anyone. Since I married you I've never been in love with anyone but you.'

She sobbed uncontrollably. So did I. 'You're my only love,' I cried. 'I couldn't live without you. You're *my life!*'

For a long time we remained still, silent, waiting for the tension to go. I was still kneeling down beside her. I kissed her on the lips: she allowed me to kiss her. Could this ever be repaired? I was wondering, bereft of confidence. I had never been in love with anyone but her since I married her. It was a nightmare sort of night. I couldn't possibly lose her trust, her love . . . She *was* my life.

And so it went on.

Elspeth was the first to recover a little. She said:

'You'd better get off your knees, my darling. They'll be terribly stiff in the morning. And it isn't good for your hip, either.'

I said, 'I'll come to bed.'

She didn't move.

CHAPTER V

HOW CAN PEOPLE SAY SUCH THINGS?

I thought Elspeth had had a restless night: I knew I had. We sat down to breakfast, at the Breakfast-Bar, with perfunctory exchanges of conversation that might have passed between strangers – only we weren't strangers: we kept eyeing each other.

I could think of nothing more to say than I had said the night before.

I had cooked the breakfast: Elspeth was dressed, ready to go out to work. A radio voice was reading us the News above the whirring of the extractor-fan – something about the Prime Minister deciding to call or not to call a General Election. Between our places lay a picture postcard just arrived from Viola.

What else could I say? What could I do? I realised that I had no idea what Elspeth was thinking – we *were* strangers . . .

'Was that a fresh packet of bacon you opened?'

'Yes. I'm sorry it's so salty.'

'Yes.'

'Sainsbury's.'

For a minute or so we both self-consciously listened to the News. We heard tips on which horses to back in today's races.

'My darling,' I began.

'Yes?'

I hadn't prepared what to say next. I said, 'I hadn't thought what I was going to say.'

'Is there anything *to* say?'

We looked at each other.

'I suppose,' she said, 'it's for *me* to think . . .'

'My love.' I took hold of her hand, on the Breakfast-Bar. She withdrew it, to get on with her breakfast. Then she offered her hand back again.

'My love,' I said again.

The radio told us the time. 'I must go,' she said. 'I'm going to be late for the office and I wanted to be early.' She finished her breakfast.

The telephone rang. It was on the wall beside the door. As I stretched out my arm, I caught Elspeth's glance – we knew it was going to be bad news.

It was the Matron of the convalescent home, ringing to say that the doctor had been to see my mother yesterday and had arranged for her to be transferred to hospital today, in fact now.

'Is she worse?' I was holding the receiver where Elspeth could catch what we were saying.

'Not really, Mr Lunn. But the doctor thought she needed more care than we're able to give her here. It's a new hospital with all the latest things. He didn't know till this morning if he'd be able to get her in. It's only temporary. I'll give you the address and the 'phone number.'

Elspeth handed me a pencil and a slip of paper. I wrote.

'I know she'll be all right, Mr Lunn. We're only sorry to lose her for the time being as a patient here.'

'That's kind of you.'

The conversation ended. 'So,' I said. Elspeth waited. 'I'll go straight down and see her this afternoon.' I'd been intending to go down and see her tomorrow, as it was her birthday.

'Yes, of course.'

A few minutes later I was seeing Elspeth off to work. I held the door of the flat open for her. She hesitated, wanting to say something – not, I knew, about my mother. She said:

'I don't want you to say anything to Robert.'

'All right.'

We kissed each other dryly on the lips. I caught hold of her hand. I simply had to ask her –

'Do you want me *not* to say anything to him because you take *my* word; or only because it would embarrass you too much, in any case?'

She turned back and looked at me.

'I don't know.'

I said nothing. She took her hand from mine. 'I really must go, darling.'

At that she went towards the lift, and I waved to her – it was an old-fashioned lift with side-panels of bevelled glass – as it took her down.

Somehow the hours passed till it was time to go and see my mother. My sister had sent me a cheque to buy flowers for my mother's birthday. At Victoria I decided to spend it all on bunches of freesias. (Freesias seemed to be on the flower-stalls all the year round, nowadays – those stunted chrysanthemums in pots actually were there all the year round.) The train, in mid-afternoon, was empty. I tried to read.

My taxi-driver from the station knew the hospital-entrance which was nearest to the ward I wanted. It was a side-entrance. As I went through it I saw that it was the entrance for the mortuary. Really! . .

The hospital was brand-new, mostly only one storey high and consequently extensive. I made my way along a series of well-labelled corridors, some of them having full-length windows opening on to squares of grass. When I reached my mother's ward I was astonished. Relatively small and divided into compartments like an open-plan office, it was close-carpeted everywhere in a pleasing tobacco-colour; the wood of the new furniture was light maple-coloured; the chromium-plated fittings sparkled freshly; and the air-conditioning was above reproach. There were old people sitting around, quietly; nurses, subduedly busy, moving to and fro. A nurse from the reception showed me where my mother was, in a partially glassed-off compartment by herself.

'How is she?'

'She's taken the move very well. We've just given her some treatment, you may find her a bit sleepy. Otherwise she's quite good – we think she's remarkable for her age.'

My mother was dozing. She was lying on a couple of high pillows and not leaning askew. The nurse roused her.

'Who is it? My son?' She opened her eyes. 'Is that you?'

'Yes, it's Joe.' I kissed her on the forehead as usual. 'I've come to see you.'

'I'm glad you've come.'

'I thought I'd come and see you straight away, in your new place. How do you find it?'

The question seemed to rouse her. 'Comfortable.'

I pulled up a chair and sat down close to her. 'It seems a super hospital to me.'

She spoke muzzily. 'They didn't seem to be able to get that sore place on my back better. And they weren't very good at dressing my breast, either.' She paused. 'I suppose they were doing their best.'

'I think it'll be much better here.'

'Time will tell that.'

'I'm sure it will.'

'Possibly.'

'And I shall keep on coming to see you.'

There was another pause. She closed her eyes.

I said, 'Good gracious! I've forgotten your flowers. It's your birthday tomorrow and I've brought you a great bunch of flowers from my sister.'

'What's that, flowers?'

'I've brought you some. They're from your daughter – it's your birthday tomorrow. They're from *her* – for your birthday.'

'What sort of flowers?'

'Freesias.'

'My favourite flowers.'

'That's why I chose them.'

I got up and carried them across from a small table I'd put them on, by the door. I undid the paper and held the flowers close to her nose. She sniffed them slowly and deeply.

'What a glorious smell!' She sniffed again. 'Hold them there a bit longer, my dear!'

I held them there.

'That's all right, now.' Then she said, 'Please write and thank her for them. She knows I can't write. Tell her how much I enjoyed them!'

'We'll put them beside the bed and you'll be able to smell them from where you are.' (There were half a dozen bunches of them.)

On the window-sill there was an empty vase, waiting. (The hospital that had everything!) I filled the vase from the tap over a wash-basin and dried the bottom of it with a paper towel. I went back to the bedside and put the flowers on the locker.

My mother said, 'I'm thirsty. Have they left me a drink?'

There was the usual plastic drinking-cup with serrated spout on the bedside table. I said, 'I'll give you a drink.'

I held the cup for her and she tried to grasp it with her arthritic hands. 'There you are,' I said. She clutched at the cup strongly as I tried to guide it.

'You'd make a good nurse.'

'You've told me that before.' I laughed.

'I'll tell it you again.'

I wondered how often that would be.

The drinking was over and I sat down. There was a long silence. I wondered if she was asleep.

'I can smell those freesias from here.'

'I'm glad – that's what I hoped.'

'They smell glorious.'

And then she said:

'If *only* I could have a peep at them! Just one little peep.'

I could say nothing. I suddenly recalled the moment when they took the bandages off my own eye – the impenetrable milky veil, gone. The pink cheek of the nurse, the darkness of her eye, the white oblong of her cap – an unforgettable *sight* . . .

'Oh well, it's not to be,' said my mother.

I nodded my head in agreement, acceptance. My mother was quiet again.

At last I was beginning to think it was time for me to leave when a nurse came in, wanting to give my mother some sort of attention. I said, 'I'll go now.'

I stood up and said goodbye to my mother, touched her forehead, and told her I'd come again. 'It's your birthday, tomorrow,' I said. 'Here's a big kiss for your birthday.' How could I wish her many returns, or even a happy birthday? I kissed her forehead.

To the nurse I said, 'Perhaps I might see the Sister before I go?'

She said the Sister was not available. 'You'll find the Charge Nurse in his office, just next to the reception.'

I went to the office. The door was open and a man in a white coat was sitting at the table, writing. He asked me to come in and sit down, and he went on writing.

I waited for him. He was a toughish-looking man, well-barbered and closely-shaven like a Regular Service-man. There was a framed photograph of a wife and three children on the table in front of him, on the wall behind him a collection of notices, including one roster showing nurses' duties and their time off, and another showing their leaves – rosters that couldn't be missed. He went on writing, and I speculated about him. Ex-Royal Navy, medical orderly? Efficient, male, the sort of man to keep those nurses to their rosters, I was ready to bet.

'Now, sir.' He looked at me. In the manner of a petty official he'd kept me waiting, but his facial expression was not unamiable. I told him who I was.

'Your mother was only admitted this morning,' he said. 'I've still got her file on my desk.' He took it out of a tray and opened it. 'Ninety-three tomorrow.' He looked at me. 'She's a remarkable woman, your mother.'

The atmosphere began to change. I found – and he found, too – that we were beginning to chat. He was interested in my mother; and then in me, especially when I told him how impressed I was by the hospital.

He explained: 'This is what's classified as a short-term hospital.'

'Well, the convalescent home gave me the impression that she was here temporarily.'

He shook his head. 'I don't think she'll go back to the convalescent home.'

I said, 'It obviously got a bit beyond the convalescent home to look after her. They oughtn't to have let her get a bed-sore.'

'Oh, we'll clear that up.'

'What about the cancer?'

'We'll make her comfortable.' He gave me a friendly glance. I said, 'I presume that means morphia?'

'Something that will make her comfortable.'

'How long will she be able to stay here, then?'

'I'll keep her as long as I can.' He gave me a matey, tipping-the-wink sort of look. 'If I were you, I shouldn't worry about it.' The formal decision about her staying was no doubt to be made by a doctor. I imagined the impeccable NCO's manner in which he might double-cross that doctor.

I said, 'I was struck by the shape she was in, even this afternoon after having had to be moved. She didn't say a thing that wasn't rational. Her voice was strong. And I was surprised by her physical strength when I was trying to give her a drink and she was grasping the cup.'

'You're right, there. There's still a lot of strength left in her.' He looked at me and said:

'It's the cancer that'll get her in the end.'

I nodded my head, suddenly too shocked to speak.

The telphone on his desk rang and he spoke into it. When he finished I stood up to go. He held out his hand. 'Cheers, Mr Lunn. I expect I shall see you again.'

I went away with his words haunting me, 'It'll be the cancer that'll get her in the end . . .' Oblivious to the effect they would have on me – just a natural thing to say in the circumstances.

In the train I attempted to read an evening newspaper. I was longing to get home to Elspeth. And then I began to wonder what *her* thoughts and reflections had been during the day.

Elspeth was already home from work, sitting on one of the sofas, reading. I kissed her and sat down beside her.

'You didn't stop at Victoria for a beer?' she asked, not smelling beer on my breath. 'Why not?'

'I was too reduced. I just wanted to get home to you.'

'Was it such an awful day?'

'It began reassuringly,' I said. And then I recounted the whole story, ending with the *coup de grâce*.

We sat for a moment silently. I said, 'I suppose I'll have to ring up my sister and tell her.'

Then we sat for a longer time, silently, haunted by the *coup de grâce*. Finally I said:

'How *can* people say these things to one?'

She put her arms round me. 'Poor darling . . .'

I put my arms round her – and then, remembering Tom, realised that I could well be saying, Poor darling . . . to *her*.

How *can* people say such things to one?

PART V

CHAPTER I
GOODBYE TO A HIP-JOINT

The remaining days of the week passed. I went on finding myself trying indirectly, because I hadn't the heart to ask her, to take the sense of Elspeth's feelings. I thought it wasn't as if she hadn't been previously warned about Tom's propensity for the warm, gossipy, oh!-so-human remark that was really at core destructive. It was his way. How right my first instinct had been to keep her out of his way! I recalled the moment when I'd given in to the idea of our meeting – seduced, that's what it was, by an invitation to dine at the Carlos. The Carlos. If he'd suggested the Dorchester or the Savoy, Elspeth and I would never have set eyes on him.

There were the questions I still wanted to ask – what did Tom actually say? what words did he utter about me? and about Steve? I tormented myself with imagining oozy, empathising remarks. 'The book is so good, we all know it must be taken from life.' And then, 'But you're so wise, my dear, I know you won't let it affect your happy marriage.' I had the idea that his words might have upset her so deeply that she hadn't registered them exactly; for instance, hearing as direct statement what was his typical half-suggesting, half-exploring innuendo. And the same went for whatever he said Steve had told him. I remembered my conversation with Steve in the little pavilion beside the pond at Hattersley Hall, when he asked me what Elspeth thought of *Happier Days* – he simply couldn't have gone in for immediate perfidy after that.

Where did all this take me? I asked myself. The answer was nowhere. The time one spends on thinking about things that get one nowhere!

However there weren't many more days to pass. I was

commanded to go into hospital on the Saturday, to be operated on by Quetzalcoatl on the following Tuesday.

Elspeth went with me, went up to the ward and waited with me in the waiting-room, which seemed to double with recreation-room – dilapidated armchairs, other people's left-behind magazines, and a noisy television set. The patients waiting, all men, were a very mixed lot. Elderly men, only to be expected; middle-aged men who looked as if they might be ailing; young men, some of them hobbling about after accidents – probably having fallen off their motorbikes. (There was one healthy young man who looked as if he hadn't got anything at all the matter with him. 'Wonder what *he*'s in for?' we speculated. I later discovered he was in to be circumcised, poor fellow.)

Elspeth waited while I underwent the first preliminaries and was put to bed – Quetzalcoatl ordered the week-end's bed-rest – and then she sat with me through the afternoon, a sunny Saturday afternoon when we might have been strolling beside the river, watching the sailing-boats tacking from side to side and the power-boats being driven round in circles, and perhaps ending with the delectable spectacle of cars parked on the slipways by owners too gormless to know the Thames had tides that came up.

Mine was a large ward, with one half divided into compartment wards, then a broad aisle, and then a single row of beds against the wall. Very Victorian. It looked moderately clean and well-kept. I was tucked away in one of the compartments, my bed beside a tall window outside of which there was a little iron-railed balcony overlooking a square – where the gardens were still prettily in flower. Actually there was another smaller part of the ward that one had to go through to get to the lavatories and to the staircase and lift, compartments for beds on one side, the Sister's office and so on on the other. When I paid my first visit to the lavatories, I thought they looked like a Victorian 'conversion'. Below a ceiling that must have been about fifteen feet high, there was one tiny shower-room with a door that didn't fit; one bathroom, with a large cast-iron bath in the middle of the floor and behind it a jungle of pipes rising to disappear in the darkness and dust above; three shaving-cubicles, three WCs with chains that didn't look particularly reliable; and a doorway to the room into which nurses were carrying bottles and bedpans. I thought it wisest, on my return to Elspeth, not to describe the lavatories. I'd made my choice: I knew the place was Victorian.

On the following afternoon Elspeth came to see me again, and later on Viola and Virginia. I noticed the girls having a sharp look round, but nothing was said.

By this time I'd done a first survey of the ward-population. Most of the beds against the opposite wall were occupied by athletic young men who'd had cartilage operations: they were noisy and vigorous, lying on their beds in strange postures, playing their radios loudly, organising games of cards, shouting jokes to each other. (Viola and Virginia didn't pass unnoticed by them. We ignored low wolf-whistles and loud guffaws – there are occasions when it's brought home to one inexorably that Humankind is part of Animal Creation.)

The rest of the patients seemed to be mainly divided between sufferers from hernias and from haemorrhoids: they were mostly older and quieter, especially the latter were quieter. There was one elderly man who'd had a knee-joint replacement – interesting to me. One bed contained a hatchet-faced man who was so emaciated and so yellow that I felt he wouldn't be there for long. And there was a strange stumpy little man, near-dwarf, with some kind of breathing obstruction that caused him to make a continuous blowing noise – having his mouth open all the time, he was inclined to slobber.

As it was a teaching hospital there were quite a few student nurses in the ward, young girls, some of them carrying text-books with them: I saw two of them in a corner, coaching each other. My first impression of all the staff was that they were in amiable mood and on good terms with each other – one of the advantages of the hospital's being small, I'd been told in the first place.

On Monday morning I was visited by Mr Redruth, looking large and powerful, treading lightly. (At Elspeth's insistence I was trying to stop calling him Quetzalcoatl.) He was in bashing form, spruce and handsomely dressed – scales flat and glistening, plume erect – and he brought a small retinue composed of the House Physician, who was a tall, lightly-built,

221

fresh-complexioned man with beautiful thick blond hair (he was called Carroll); the senior of the two Sisters, an oldish, experienced, motherly woman (she was called Holmes); and a couple of nurses whom I hadn't seen on the previous day, one of them carrying the patients' files. The new characters in my life!

'I gather you're in good form,' Q said in a loud cheerful voice.

'So far as *I* know,' I said. I noticed his eyes were a dark grey, making his glance seem slightly opaque. His hair was stiff and straight and plastered down flat.

'So far as *you* know? Is that good enough for us, Sister Holmes?' He glanced at the Sister, grinning ironically at my expense.

'We are satisfied, Mr Redruth.'

'Right. Then what is it we say? All systems go!'

He turned to the blond young doctor – whom I now saw to be in his late thirties – and said to him, 'We've got the two of them. I propose to do this patient first.'

'Yes, Mr Redruth.'

He turned to me, 'You heard that? We'll do you first. Nine-thirty, sharp.'

'Good.'

He took a step nearer, and said in a quieter, though equally cheerful tone of voice:

'When you come round you'll find we're giving you some blood. Don't be alarmed! It's standard procedure. This is a rather bloody operation. OK?'

'Yes.'

He grinned. 'I'll see you, Mr Lunn.'

I couldn't help grinning, myself, recognising that I asked for this kind of cheerful, bashing treatment – after my own fashion I bashed back.

Throughout the day there were more preliminaries. Sister Holmes came and gave me a knowledgeable, motherly talk about the operation. She was followed by one of the nurses I'd seen in the morning, a nice girl who talked to me animatedly. She said something about the prosthesis –

'Haven't you seen one?' she asked. 'Haven't they ever shown you one?'

'No,' I said. I didn't know that I should have been able to look at it, if they had shown me one.

'It looks like a pork chop,' she said.

'Oh!'

From what I'd imagined, I could see that was what it might well look like. Like a pork chop. Exquisite simile!

Later on a bearded young man in a white coat came to see me.

'You'll have to be shaved, Mr Lunn,' he said. 'Shall I do it, or would you rather do it yourself?'

I said, '*You* do it, please! You're the expert. I should be terrified of nicking myself.'

He came back a little later to do it. He surveyed the area thoughtfully.

'I think I shall take it off here.' He traced the boundary with his forefinger.

'What?' I cried. 'You're not going to do it asymmetrically, are you? It'd look ridiculous – not being the same on both sides.'

'All right. I'll take it all off.'

I was surprised by how easily he did it. He really was an expert.

So, after Elspeth had been and I'd been given nothing to eat, I ended with the standard notice, illiterate but comprehensible, hanging over my bed –

NIL BY MOUTH

Next morning I made that journey, though I was too far gone under premedication to observe it properly, being wheeled across from the wide, concertina-gated lift to the double-doors above which the lighted sign said

OPERATION IN PROGRESS

I was talked to by the anaesthetist, in green cap and mask, who had one of the deepest, cosiest voices I'd ever heard. (I thought it was a man – it was only when she came to see me next morning that I saw it was a tall, good-looking woman.) And after that . . .

After that x hours must have passed. (I'd been told how many x was but I hadn't bothered to register it.) And then I suppose I must have been wheeled back, under a scarlet blanket, past a row of waiting patients.

y hours passed and I began to come round to a strangely euphoric state, produced by two thoughts that were going slowly

223

and re-iteratively through my returning mind. Euphoric, triumphant –

'*I've not got an infection* – I took a risk and the gamble's come off!' And 'I shan't have to wake up again to realise I've got to have this operation!'

I began to wake up, know where I was, still savouring the two thoughts as they spaced out and disappeared. The lights in the ward were on. I saw Elspeth coming to see me.

'How are you feeling?' she whispered.

'Fine.'

She smiled at me. 'You don't look so bad.'

I looked up at her. 'If there's nobody looking, please kiss me!'

She bent over me.

'Well . . .' I said.

She sat down. I held out one of my hands to her – the other hand was impeded, and I remembered that I was connected up to a blood-supply. She took hold of my hand, and we remained quiet.

Two nurses came up, one youngish, the other very young. 'We want to take your temperature and blood-pressure, Mr Lunn.' They told Elspeth she needn't go away, as she'd only just come. They performed their task. While the very young one was packing up the sphygmometer, the other one said to me: 'We shall want to take your temperature and blood-pressure every hour. Through the night.' She smiled at me. 'We'll wake you up.'

When they'd gone I said to Elspeth: 'Am I in a different bed?'

'They've put you in the bed nearest to the desk where the two nurses on duty sit.'

She kissed me again, and then she went away.

And so I began a long night of being roused hourly. When I was awake I could hear, in the silence of the ward, the two nurses whispering to each other while they measured my blood-pressure and my temperature. I couldn't always catch what they said.

At one hour I thought I heard one of them saying, 'His temperature keeps on going up,' and the other saying, 'It shouldn't . . .'

Well into the night the whispered colloquy was longer. 'His temperature's still going up.' 'It shouldn't be . . .' 'Then *why* is it going up? . . .' I didn't catch the reply, or the remarks that followed. 'She . . .'

At the next awakening there was somebody else there. 'His temperature's still going up, Sister.' (Was the third person the Night Sister from somewhere?) 'Have you checked everything?' 'Yes, Sister.' 'Have you checked his blood-supply? If you're giving it him too fast, that will send his temperature up.'

I missed the next bit. It was hard to listen – was I half-asleep, or partially anaesthetized, or rather ill?

I was aware of one of the nurses moving about at the head of the bed, where the blood-supply was. Her clothes rustled. Then they all went away.

At the next hour I was more alert – I had reason to be. The whispering began while my blood pressure was being measured. 'His temperature's still up.' A few moments later the two of them were rustling near the head of the bed. 'Have you checked the regulator?'

'It doesn't seem to have changed.'

'Are you sure you adjusted it?'

'Yes . . . It doesn't seem to work.' Pause. '*How* does it work? . .'

'It shows you in the diagram.'

'Shall I go and get the diagram?'

'Sh . . . *I* know how it works. I'll have a go at it.' There was a brief pause.

'Is the valve all right?'

Another pause. I could almost hear her fiddling with the controls. Then –

'There! I think I've done it!' Pause. 'Yes . . . That's OK now.'

'Are you sure it's all right?'

'Better stay and keep an eye on it for a few minutes.'

'Yes . . .'

I didn't get straight off to sleep again. After the few minutes, the other nurse came back. 'Is it all right now?' 'Yes.'

At the next hour. 'Has his temperature stopped going up?' 'Yes.'

'Thank God for that! . .'

I went off to sleep.

First thing in the morning I saw that early colloguings were going on at the desk. Sister Holmes was there. I realised that of the two nurses who'd been in charge of the whole ward all night, the older one was qualified, while the younger was only a student.

The blood-supply was in working order. My temperature was now giving no cause for alarm. (Only the chart at the bottom of my bed would give away the vicissitudes of the night.) My blood-pressure had been satisfactory from the start.

Quetzalcoatl came to see me, Dr Carroll in attendance, and Sister Holmes. He asked me how I was. I said, not untruthfully, 'Very well.'

'You look reasonably well.' He turned to the Sister. 'A surprisingly good colour, isn't he?' I appreciated that. I was a bit surprised, too.

He turned back to me, with opaque grey eyes and unchanging cheerful expression –

'The operation went very well. I'm very pleased. We shall get you out of bed tomorrow. And as soon as we're able to stop draining the wound, you've got to try and *walk*!'

At that he went away, giving me a fine example, I thought, of how to walk with a boxer's quick-footed tread.

I couldn't wait for the day when the draining-tubes came out – a nasty sensation, but worth it.

Sister Holmes was there and the physiotherapist handed me the crutches I'd practised with before the operation. I felt a bit odd, to be standing up, staggered nervously, and then made a start –

I could walk *without pain*!

A nurse was walking beside me. I didn't need her. Dr Carroll appeared, to watch me, and he discussed my efforts with the Sister.

'I think that in a day or two, Mr Lunn, you'll be able to try it with two sticks,' he said afterwards. I was beginning to like him.

I was suddenly taken with the idea that I might become a star pupil if I tried.

When I broached it with Elspeth that evening, she said, 'Not too fast . . .'

So I got on to two walking-sticks. I thought I was managing pretty well.

Then came the day for Quetzalcoatl's regular state visit; with Dr Carroll; Dr Carroll's assistant, a bright little Pakistani doctor called Zia; Sister Holmes; the other Sister, who was called Lewell; the male Staff Nurse; and a collection of other nurses.

When he got to my bed, Mr R said, 'I want to see you walk.'

I managed to get out of bed, was handed my sticks, and set off down the broad aisle, diffidently at first and steadily with more confidence. When I thought I'd gone far enough I turned round, to see him with his whole army lined up, watching me.

'Now,' he said. 'I want you to try it with one stick.'

Before I'd properly taken the news in a little nurse came up and relieved me of a stick. I was left with one. I had to try it. I began. I could do it!

Q turned to his cohorts and said, 'If only they were all as easy as that!'

When I reached him, he said, 'You'd better get back to bed. I'm very pleased with you.' There was a pause and then he said to all of us, 'Now I'm going on my holidays for a month.'

CHAPTER II

SOME TURNS OF FATE

The next thing was the removal of the stitches. I felt I was in sight of leaving the hospital. I was walking well with one stick and free from pain. The removal was entrusted to a little student girl under the supervision of a qualified nurse. I noticed, to my surprise, that a couple of small drops of blood appeared: the nurses didn't seem to be surprised.

On the following day Elspeth was spending an hour with me in the afternoon. I found it necessary to go to the lavatory. I kept away from the lavatories, since they were practically always unspeakably awash. The cleaning of the ward, apart from a weekly floor-polishing by external contractors, was in the hands of a party of Jamaican women, by my standards as insolent as they were slatternly: they swabbed the lavatories out, after a fashion, first thing in the morning, and then refused to touch them again – one sometimes came upon a nurse cleaning up the mess, but not often. Anyway I was there, washing my hands at a washbasin, when I felt a trickle of something down my leg. I looked down, saw blood running down my leg, dripping on the floor.

I called out for a nurse. At the end of the passage appeared Elspeth and Sister Holmes. Nurses appeared with a wheel-chair in no time, and I was taken back to the ward. Dressings were put on to staunch the flow of blood – brownish blood, I noticed, not bright red. Elspeth looked pale. What is it? we wanted to know. What does it mean?

The Sister explained and reassured us – it was nothing new to her. After the operation, serous fluid and old blood had collected in the wound: instead of being absorbed internally, it had ruptured externally. It was called a haematoma. (The student nurses wrote the word down and then went away to read up the details in their medical dictionaries.)

I now had to wait for the blood to drain away externally.

'How long is that going to take?'

'It's impossible to say. Perhaps a week. Perhaps a few days.' (That was the first time I heard, A few days.)

Later, after Elspeth had gone away, miserably to break the news to the girls, the Sister told me she had two private rooms vacant at the moment. 'We keep them for emergencies. I could let you have one of them, if you'd like it. You'd have a bit more privacy.'

I said I'd jump at it, thinking of how I could listen to concerts on my radio without distraction.

'You won't feel lonely, Mr Lunn?'

I didn't think so. After all, I spent quite a lot of time practising my walking, up and down the ward. The star pupil. (I was determined to eradicate my limp.) The haematoma wasn't going to interfere with that. And in the course of my walking I got to know some of the other patients. The young man who'd come in to be circumcised was still with us, looking rather sorry for himself. He was having a painful time – he must have had an adhesion. One day, though, he showed a glimmer of amusement. 'Yesterday one of the student nurses did my dressing,' he confided. 'She put it on *over the end* . . .' I laughed, even if it was unkind. Anyway I thought he had something to look forward to. He was visited every evening by a very glamorous West Indian girl who embraced him passionately before she left – I saw how his operation had become an urgent necessity.

I had to wait for the haematoma to drain itself away into the dressings. 'A few more days.' One morning I heard Carroll say to Zia, as they were going out of the room, 'Imagine having a pint bottle of milk on your hip!'

To make me more comfortable I was given a new way of keeping my dressing in place. A little nurse came in holding a roll of white, woven elastic tubing. She looked thoughtfully at my hip – my left hip, it was – then thoughtfully unrolled a length of this sort-of body-stocking, took up the pair of scissors that hung from her belt, saying, 'I haven't done this before . . .'

To tell the story I shall have to explain – what I then didn't

229

know – how the thing worked. The idea was to cut off a piece of tube of appropriate length; then to make, part way down it, a lateral cut half-way across: one began by thrusting both feet down the tube till they came to the cut; then one thrust the right foot through the cut and went on pushing the left foot down the rest of the tube: one ended up with the lower part of the tube round one's left thigh, holding the dressing; and the upper part round one's loins, thus leaving one's right leg and the lower part of one's anatomy free.

Now for the story. She cut off a piece of tubing and diffidently snipped a very small cut across it half way down. The process began. When my feet came to the cut it was too small for my right foot to go through it, so that *both* feet went *down* the tube. As she hauled the tube up my legs I had intimations of what was supposed to be going on. 'That won't do,' I said. 'If you go on like that you'll have me like a mermaid.'

She giggled and blushed. 'I shall have to make the cut wider,' she opined. She pulled the thing off and lifted her scissors, then extended the cut till it went three-quarters of the way across.

This time the process went quite differently. The opening in the tube for my left foot was too small for me to get my left foot into it, and inevitably *both* feet went *through* the cut. As she hauled the tube up, the piece intended for my left thigh dangled at the side.

She stared at it, and for minutes we were both too helpless with laughter to go on. Then I said:

'I think we'll start all over again and you'd better let *me* do the cutting.'

So began my regime of regularly doing it myself. A fresh dressing was put on the wound every night: every morning I looked at it to see if any more blood had seeped out. (Imagine a pint bottle! . .) It took me back to those long-lost days when the children were babies in nappies, when we looked hopefully each morning to see if the nappy was dry.

A few more days. And a few more days. 'Not more than a week, now,' said Sister Lewell.

My friends got into the way of sick-visiting me regularly.

Robert came with books for me. Veronica came and disapproved of my having a haematoma. It was no use my telling her it was fortuitous: Veronica's temperament was not given to recognising the fortuitous – that was not the way of the Civil Service. '*Somebody* must be responsible,' she said.

George Bantock turned up, to tell me not to worry about my classes. That was comforting.

The girls came together, one day, to consult me.

'We think we ought to go and see Granny,' said Virginia.

'It's ages since we saw her,' said Viola.

'It might be,' said Virginia, 'the last time we can.'

'If we didn't go,' said Viola, 'we might always regret it . . .'

They were fond of my mother, but Elspeth and I hadn't suggested that they should go and see her because it was so daunting. Viola had of course heard the reports of my own visits, (with the *coup de grâce* excised.)

As my mother was now in the least daunting hospital I'd ever seen, I didn't discourage them as I'd discouraged my sister from coming over from America to see my mother for the last time – in my sister's case my mother would have realised it must be for the last time; and that, it seemed to me, would have been too heart-rending for both of them. I said to the girls, 'I think you might go.' They began making their plans.

Elspeth, trying to look bright and cheerful, came to see me day after day.

Day after day I went for my walking practice, up and down the wards, learning now to go up and down the stairs by the lift, sometimes merely carrying the stick. Otherwise I stayed in my room, reading my way – like the Noble Lord Balderstoke in similar circumstances – through the Palliser novels; and listening to concerts on my radio.

I was getting onto friendly terms with the two doctors and the two Sisters. I was seeing more of Sister Lewell – oval face, long nose, high colour in her cheeks, dark hair; and a subtle, fluid smile . . . Who did she remind me of? Answer: that early love of mine, forty years ago, who wanted me to marry her and whom Tom, in the midst of passionately pursuing Steve, had thought of proposing marriage to, out of sympathy with her ill-treatment at my hands. *Myrtle*! . . A very strange coincidence. I didn't mention it to Elspeth. When I speculated on why she was not married, Elspeth pointed out that she was wearing an engagement ring. Sister Lewell . . .

Sister Holmes became confidential. One day she told me, 'In your operation and the other one,' – the other patient was a woman – 'Mr Redruth used a new spray they've brought out. It inhibits the flow of blood, so that the surgeons can see much better what they're doing.' She paused. 'Both patients got haematomas. I don't think he'll use it again.'

I thought, Two-out-of-two may strike into the feeling heart but it doesn't go very far with the statistical head. (What you want to know is, How many out of two hundred?) I resolved not to start a row by telling Veronica.

Meanwhile I began to see what Sister Holmes had said about my feeling lonely. In my private room it was easy not to go out and join in ward-activities, for instance not to join the team of ambulant patients who helped with the trolleys of morning-tea and the day's meals. (They thought I was a snob.) I began to notice the symptoms of hospital anxiety-neurosis – 'Have they missed me with the morning coffee?' 'When are they coming to change my dressing?' 'How late are they going to be with the last drug-round? I'm waiting to go to sleep.'

One day the little dwarf came in, blowing and slobbering – I was pretty sure he was one of the causes of the WCs being awash. He had a pack of cards and was obviously going to show me a trick. 'Oh no!' I cried, 'I hate card-tricks!' I felt very ashamed, afterwards.

I became friendly with two men near the aisle, whom I constantly passed and re-passed. They were down from Birmingham, where there were immense waiting-lists for admission, to have hernia operations. They were in their early forties, intelligent, sensible, fathers of families, called Chris and Geoff. Chris, being the nearer one to the aisle, was spokesman for the two. When I asked them what they did, he said:

'Oh, we're only engineers . . . with British Leyland.'

'*Only* engineers,' I said. 'You shouldn't think that.' I told them I'd spent most of my official career among scientists and engineers – the backbone of an industrial nation. 'What sort of engineers?' I asked.

'We're the lowest of the low.' He smiled at me. 'We're on the production line.'

Perhaps he was teasing me, yet his self-deprecation was genuine. I was pretty speechless – that the anti-technology element in our culture could bring men like this to such a pass! Insane.

On the other hand Geoff's sixteen year old son had gone into BL – that very morning, in fact: Geoff had telephoned him at 6.30 am to wish him Good Luck. I was touched. The sort of men they were, the sort of lives they lived, rarely found its way into current novels. So much the worse for current novels!

They had their operations and I saw them sitting up in bed the morning after they recovered. 'How now?' I asked.

As usual Chris replied for the two. 'We're OK. But they didn't tell us . . . after a hernia operation your thing swells up and turns black.'

'How alarming!'

'It was. I called the nurse. But she said it was all right.'

'What about Geoff's?'

'The same,' said Geoff.

'He called the nurse, too,' said Chris.

'What did she say to him?'

'She said, "Oh God! Have I got to look at another one?"'

I burst into laughter and glanced at Geoff. With momentarily lowered eyelids he had an unconcerned look. I went on laughing. On the evening before their operation, I'd come upon Geoff drying himself unconcernedly outside the door of the shower-room. He had something to look unconcerned about.

I left them to go on with my walking-practice, but I smiled every time I thought about it. However when I recounted the incident to Elspeth, she took a high line. 'Men in hospital,' she said haughtily, 'always think the nurses want to look at their you-know-whats.' I didn't enquire how she knew.

Nearly dry, my dressing in the morning. 'Two more days,' said the youthful orderly whom I could sometimes catch, as he was passing my open doorway, to change the dressing. 'Only two more days, I promise you.'

Dry enough for Dr Carroll to tell me I could have a bath, my first bath.

The shower was now out of order; so it had to be the big cast-iron Victorian bath, in the room which towered upwards into darkness and dust. (It would need scaffolding for anybody to get rid of all that grime.) Two nurses were filling the bath for me. Had the bath been cleaned? It didn't look like it. 'That's all right,' they said, showing me that they were emptying into it two sachets of Savlon, to which I already knew I was allergic.

'First of all, think! Mr Lunn, how you're going to get into the bath. And then you'll get out the same way.'

'In reverse,' I said.

'Yes.'

So I was bathed by two nurses. A few hours later the allergic irritation began in exactly the zones where it might have been expected.

However the bath was considered a success, and in a couple of days' time Carroll permitted me another. As a result of my protests, the sachets of Savlon were replaced by sachets of salt. 'Just as effective,' said the senior of the two nurses.

I think it must have been a day or so after that – I'd now been in hospital for five weeks instead of two – when Elspeth was sitting with me in the evening. We were both looking forward to my coming out. Suddenly the door slid across.

Who should be standing there but Steve!

'*Steve!* . .'

He came in, smiling. 'It's all right. I haven't come back!'

I glanced at Elspeth, wondering if she would go straight out of the room. She stood up, saying, 'I'll leave you, now.'

'Oh no!' said Steve. 'Please don't go away! I can only stay a few minutes, and I haven't got anything to say that I can't say to both of you.'

Elspeth reluctantly sat down again.

Steve was wearing a pin-striped suit instead of denims, and he was carrying an up-to-date flat brief-case. He looked well, if a little tired. There was no trace of embarrassment in his manner.

He began to draw up a spare chair. 'You must wonder why on earth I'm here.' He sat down. 'As soon as I left the country, my dear wife decided we should have a divorce. Can you believe it? So I've had to come back to see lawyers.' He looked at Elspeth and me. 'Have you ever had to see lawyers? It's terrible . . . They go on and on. And one's paying for their *time*.'

I was smiling at him, but I saw that Elspeth, though she had stayed, was not smiling at him.

'I found out where you were from Veronica,' he said. 'Robert wasn't to be found.'

'What did Veronica say?' I said.

'She gave me the address of the hospital.' He paused, and smiled in recollection. 'She told me she hates Tom, but she wouldn't tell me why. As if I couldn't work that out!' He laughed. 'He must have interfered between her and Robert. He tries to do it with all of us. You're lucky if he didn't have a go at you two . . . It feeds his lust for power over people.'

I glanced at Elspeth, trying to signal with my eyes, *Steve doesn't know what Tom said to you.* I was sure he didn't. Nor could I square his present manner, easy and careless and honest, with his having deliberately done harm to Elspeth and me. I hoped Elspeth was beginning to feel the same – thank goodness! she was showing no signs of leaving now. I must say I thought it was a test of her amazing spirit.

Steve chattered on. As he wanted to hear, half-wanted to hear, about my operation, I demonstrated to him how I could now walk easily *without* a stick. 'Marvellous, Joe.'

Then we returned to his divorce, which, after so many years, seemed as remarkable to me as it obviously did to him.

'Do you *want* a divorce?' I asked.

Steve laughed with his rueful expression. 'Not much.'

'Does she?'

'She's told her lawyers she does.'

There was a pause. 'Lawyers!' said Steve. And then, 'But I mustn't go on about them. I'm just waiting to get back to New York.'

'How're things going?'

'Burke's theatre is smashing. And with a bit of luck I shall carve myself a niche in it – which is what Burke wants me to do. Think of that, Joe!'

'I think of it with pleasure and satisfaction, Steve. And *hope!*'

Steve laughed and picked up his brief-case. 'I must go. But first of all I want Joe to sign something for me.' And out of the brief-case he took a copy of *Happier Days*.

'It's super, Joe,' he said, and handed it to me to sign with his biro.

I took it from him. While I was opening the pages, he spoke to Elspeth in a quiet tone.

'I think you've been super over it all . . . I mean, the way you've gone calmly on, when you must have guessed what snide people must be saying about Joe behind your back. What *Tom* was saying behind your back.'

Elspeth said coolly, 'Was he?'

Steve smiled at her. 'You don't know Tom as well as we do. He tried to get Robert and me to say that we knew that Joe had been –' Her expression made him stop. 'I'm terribly sorry, I've embarrassed you, Elspeth . . .'

I intervened. I looked up from the book. 'You and *Robert*?' I said. 'When was that?'

'On the last morning at Hattersley Hall. You two had gone. Tom opened a bottle of champagne – he opened a lot of bottles of champagne. It got him into a lascivious mood – lascivious isn't the word, but you know what I mean. When he started to talk about *you* again, Robert put him down in a way I've never heard Robert put anybody down in before. Elspeth will forgive the schoolboy language' – he smiled at her – 'Robert shat on him from a great height. Gave him to understand that he was being a fool, a knave and a liar.' He looked at me. 'I agreed.'

I couldn't speak. I didn't trust myself to look at Elspeth. I finally managed to say:

'Well, here's your copy of *Happier Days*, now increased in value out of all recognition.'

'Thank you, Joe.' He playfully held it up as if he were going to kiss it, then put it into his brief-case and stood up to go.

'Get well soon, Joe! Don't limp any more!' He turned to Elspeth. I wondered if he was going to attempt to kiss her – he did – and if she would allow him. She did.

When he had gone I held out my arms to her, and she came to the bedside and rested her face on my shoulder.

'My darling . . .' she said.

I closed my arms round her. 'My love.'

We didn't discuss it any more.

People clattered about in the doorway, serving the supper.

Elspeth said, 'I must go home and prepare some supper, I suppose. What are you going to do?'

I thought I might well just lie on my bed, thinking of what we had been through. I said:

'There's a lovely concert tonight. I shall listen to that.'

And that was what I did. The concert was in two parts and I listened all night to it. I switched off the light and listened, lost in emotion.

When the concert was over I had to get out of bed. I pushed back the sheets – I still slept with a cradle over my feet – and swung my legs round.

As I swung my legs round I felt a riveting pain. I tried to stand up and couldn't bear to put my foot on the ground. In my leg, my hip, my groin, pain of an intensity I'd never experienced before.

Standing there in the darkness, holding on to the bed, I felt terror. I *knew* what was the matter.

CHAPTER III

THE DARK SIDE

For a minute I held on to the bed in the darkness. Then I managed somehow to find my stick and I set off, half-hopping in a few steps at a time, for the Sister's office. In the corridor everything seemed unusually silent. To my relief when I got to the office door I saw both Sister Lewell and Doctor Zia.

'I can't walk.'

They came out instantly. 'You must go back to bed.' They supported me on the way back to my room. 'Where's Doctor Carroll?' I asked. 'He's in the operating-theatre,' said the Sister. At this time of night! I was not surprised, though: he was unmarried and worked all hours. 'He often operates at night,' she said. (The two of them were friends: I'd heard them call each other by their Christian names – I'd even wondered, at one stage, if it was Carroll she was engaged to.)

In my room Zia said, 'I want you to try and stand up as straight as you can, with both feet on the ground. I want to look at your two legs together.'

The Sister stood beside me while he walked a few paces away and I hitched up the operating-gown that I persuaded the nurses to let me wear in lieu of pyjamas. (It did up at the back – sometimes, to Elspeth's disapproval, it undid without my noticing.) 'Please hurry up!' I begged. 'Please! . .'

'Now lying down on the bed.'

He and the Sister eyed my legs carefully, as it were measuring. They glanced at each other.

He delicately tried to test my hip. He was small and clever and sensitive – sometimes over-sensitive. 'The pain's terrific,' I said agitatedly.

He went back to the bottom of the bed. 'There is no difference in the length of your legs,' he said. 'I think I can tell you, Mr Lunn, that it is nothing dramatic.'

Nothing dramatic! He must mean no displacement of the prosthesis –

'But haven't I got an *infection*?' I could hardly utter the word.

Sister Lewell was about to take my temperature.

'That is possible.'

'Is my temperature up?' I asked when she took the thermometer out of my mouth.

'Yes.'

I said to Zia:

'What happens next?'

'Dr Carroll will see you first thing in the morning, and decide.'

'Aren't you going to start treating it now?' I was near to hysteria.

'I will make sure it is OK to give you some distalgesics. That will help you to get some sleep.' He went out of the room.

What I needed was antibiotics, not distalgesics. Sister Lewell followed him.

A minute or two later she came back with two distalgesics and held up my head while I washed them down with a drink of water.

'When is Mr Redruth coming back?'

'Not till next week, I'm afraid.'

She settled my pillow, for a moment laid her hand on my forehead. And then she went away finally.

I spent the night in pain and sleeplessness and agitation. I was convinced they were not treating me with antibiotics now because they couldn't get me any. This hospital drew its supply of drugs from the main hospital – centralised for efficiency – and I'd come to the conclusion earlier, from watching ward-activities, that after a certain hour at night our hospital couldn't draw any fresh drugs till first thing next morning. Sister Holmes had told me that was not so. I supposed it couldn't be so. Yet in the night I was sure it could.

First thing in the morning Dr Carroll came in. After operating till midnight he looked tired. His eyes looked tired – he had what Robert and I called cerebrotonic eyes; smallish and transparent, eyes that seem to perceive and apprehend instantly. But his golden hair was gleaming and his complexion looked as fresh as ever. Dr Zia was with him.

He examined me, discussed me with Zia, ordered me to be X-rayed – and prescribed antibiotics.

'Have I got an infection?'

'It may be, but you shouldn't react over-hastily.'

'When I'm in riveting pain?' I thought of Quetzalcoatl's, One case in a hundred.

'We shall do something about that.' He closed my file and handed it to Zia. 'I will come in and see you again this evening.'

This evening! That meant a day to pass. Actually a fair slice of it passed in my being carried down to the basement and being X-rayed. The radiographer wanted to repeat one of her photographs: through an open doorway I saw her studying the negative.

'Does anything *show* in them?' I asked, as she handed the envelope to the orderly who'd wheeled me down.

'I don't see anything. The prosthesis looks all right.'

I wondered if Carroll would see anything. What were the things that might be seen? I was so ignorant. The only things I could imagine them seeing were facts about whether anything had gone wrong with the prosthesis – whether anything had happened to the pork chop.

In the late afternoon Elspeth came to see me. Having only just been told, on her way in, she hadn't had time to cover up her distress. She sat down beside my bed and simply held my hand. As luck would have it, or perhaps wouldn't have it, the antibiotics arrived while she was there. After I'd taken my first dose I lay back on my pillow –

'Thank God for that!' I'd now made a start.

'Twenty-four hours late,' said Elspeth.

I thought, Twenty, but felt too ill to say it. She must be wanting to remove me from this hospital forthwith. (When I came to think about it, much later and without hysteria, I realised that it was the bureaucratic machine that had absorbed the time, not an ineffective hospital staff.)

Elspeth just remained holding my hand for a long time.

So I passed another night, and next morning felt worse. Carroll came and examined me, carefully round my groin, but he had nothing more to say. I asked how long it took for the antibiotics to take effect.

'It varies.' He glanced at me obliquely. 'We shall see.'

That morning I had two visitors, not knowing of the change in my state. George Bantock and his Administrative Dean.

I was lying still, with the sheets drawn up to my chin, feeling iller than I'd felt before.

'We've come to say,' George began, 'how welcome back you'll be, dear – ' The word 'boy' disappeared from his lips before he uttered it. He and the other man looked at each other.

I managed to say something; they remained motionless with embarrassment for a second or two, then made a rapid exit. Embarrassment or shock?

When one's ill, time seems to pass in a sort of haze. Nurses came and went. Carroll and Sister Lewell seemed to be in the offing: I felt the better for their being in the offing. Elspeth came. It would have been bad enough to be in pain, if only through the haze I had not kept recalling, 'You'll still be able to *walk*, but one leg will be two inches shorter than the other'.

Next day the antibiotics had definitely begun to take effect. The haze dissipated and I began to feel compos mentis – if one can be said to be compos mentis when still near-hysterical with anxiety and depression. Anyway I was in a sane enough state to begin asking Carroll medical questions, questions buzzing like bees round the central topic in my imagination, infection.

He answered my questions. For one thing I asked them so directly, no patient's inferiority about it, that he'd have had a job not to answer them. For another he was – to me, anyway – beginning to seem an interesting man. And for yet another, he saw that I was able to comprehend his answers.

I learnt some central facts. You could have an infection of the wound – I'd got one. It could be treated with antibiotics – I was being treated. You could have an infection of the bone: that could not be treated without taking out the prosthesis – leaving the leg two inches shorter.

'Can the infection get from the wound into the bone?'

'Sometimes it appears to do so.'

'How often?'

'I can't say. Occasionally.'

(I wanted to ask him to go and look up the statistics, some-where.) I said:

'If it does, how long does it take?'

He closed the file he was holding. 'I don't know who could answer that, Mr Lunn.'

'Mr Redruth?'

A distant look came into his eye. Then he smiled. 'I'll come and see you tomorrow morning.'

That left me with another twenty-four hours before I could ask more questions. I reflected on his patience, and then on his nature. He was a man of quick nervous apprehensions, I was sure; yet there was a smoothing-out layer over them, a layer that made for equanimity, optimism, which might have been professionally assumed but seemed to me genuine.

I had a bad day. Elspeth came and gave up trying to converse. I just wanted her to hold my hand, indefinitely.

Last thing at night, when I was still wakeful, Sister Lewell brought me an unexpected cup of tea. She helped me to lift my shoulders from the pillow while I drank. She said:

'I do wish you didn't get so depressed, Mr Lunn.'

I finished the tea and gave her the cup to put down. 'Wouldn't *you* feel depressed?' I looked up at her. 'I keep thinking over and over again, *Is it going to be all right?*'

Impulsively she held my head against her body. 'Oh! Mr Lunn, I don't know what we're going to do with you.'

Later I went off to sleep, thinking, If only Elspeth were here!

In the light of the next day I realised that I had changed over from being a star pupil to a problem-patient.

Carroll seemed to be spending a lot of care on exploring my groin, where I felt the pain was most intense, on prodding gently in one place after another.

'What are you looking for?' I asked him.

He answered with equanimity and patience, while getting on with the job.

So I was introduced to the subject of lymph nodes; their function – or absence of function – their liability to infection; the possibility of their treatment. Under the spell of instruction, I felt eased. (How to treat a problem patient!) He ended my catechism when he thought it had gone on long enough, and assured me that the antibiotics really were taking effect. Consoling.

When I reported it all to Elspeth in the evening, she said thoughtfully: 'H'm. . . I think he's a bit of an Aunt Martha, myself. Sunshine Sally . . .'

I was indignant, but not well enough to argue. I asked her to read to me, and it was in reading *The Duke's Children* to me that she spent her visiting-time during the next week.

The following day Quetzalcoatl was back from his holidays. He came in with retinue, stepped up to my bedside and said, with his opaque look – but with something less than his former bashing manner:

'I'm sorry about this.'

I murmured something.

'Your X-ray looks good.' Back in louder, more cheerful form. (The X-ray showed that the prosthesis was all right – the main part of *his* business.)

I murmured something else.

'The pain seems worst in the groin? I should like to have a look at you.' He drew back the sheets – with special care, because of the audience, for my modesty – and repeated Carroll's exploration. (Not the occasion for asking questions about lymph nodes.) He demonstrated to the audience that the haematoma was healed. Then he put back the sheets without comment.

As he stepped powerfully and lightly away from the bed, he said, 'We shall keep you on the antibiotics.' And he led his retinue out.

He had not been quite as he used to be, I thought. Something told me I was going to see rather less of him. It occurred to me now that behind the loud, cheerful bashing, there was something sensitive. Professional pride, perhaps, I thought ungraciously.

So I felt I was from now on really in the hands of Carroll and Zia and the two Sisters. I had to concede that the antibiotics were reducing the pain, and after a few more days I was allowed to get out of bed and walk across the room. (I took the opportunity to sneak a glance at my record-chart and see that my temperature was subsiding.)

I found it hard to believe that I could be out of the mire until there was evidence that the infection had been killed off completely, but Carroll and Sister Lewell were steadily more hopeful. (Aunt Martha, Carroll might be – I liked him.) I began to be able to walk up and down the wards. I was X-rayed again. I came to the end of the course of antibiotics. They assured me that the danger was over. I could scarcely believe it, still.

I was walking down the passage-way outside the Sister's office – it was a Saturday afternoon and there were empty beds where patients had been discharged before the weekend. I came upon Sister Lewell and Dr Carroll, chatting outside the office-door.

Sister Lewell looked at me with a happy smile. 'You're walking well again.'

I wasn't totally free from pain and stiffness, as I'd been before, but, I supposed, near enough.

'At the beginning of next week,' she said, 'I think we shall have to discharge you.'

'Really!' I looked at Carroll, who nodded his head in agreement – they must have been discussing me.

'Yes, really!' She gave me a fluid, subtle smile.

'Oh!' I cried, flung my arms round her neck – after all, she did remind me of someone else – and kissed her enthusiastically.

I stood back – we were laughing at each other.

'And now,' she said, 'aren't you going to kiss *him*?' And she glanced at Carroll.

For once my wits deserted me. I couldn't think what to say – to say No would sound beastly. He was standing, looking at the ground. I muttered something unintelligible – 'I don't know' or 'I don't think so' or something. (I thought of really witty answers *afterwards*.) I turned to Sister Lewell – she was laughing at me with subtle enjoyment.

I felt I came out of the incident badly.

CHAPTER IV

IS IT GOING TO BE ALL RIGHT?

Home again! It was marvellous, even if my hip was not quite as perfect as I'd hoped – I was still needing a stick, after having once been able to do without it. But I should be able to do without it again in a little while. I began to pick up my life. I telephoned George Bantock to say I'd be back – perhaps my class could come to the flat? 'What a splendid idea, dear boy!' And I arranged to resume meeting Robert in the pub. And so on.

The weather was awful but I decided I must go out every day. On the fourth day I crossed the road, to walk by the river. As I stepped up a pavement, I felt a sharp pain in the groin –

It was back: the infection hadn't been killed: it was still there.

I telephoned the hospital and was able to get Carroll. Come in straight away! Forty eight hours' observation.

I telephoned Elspeth at her office and told her. 'I'm back at Square One.'

And then I got a taxi back to the hospital.

Is it going to be all right, or isn't it? Who could say that it was?

At the hospital Sister Holmes found me a bed – it was one of the beds the two engineers had occupied. She sent me to be X-rayed. 'Dr Carroll will be in to see you later.'

It was late when Carroll arrived. He drew the curtains and examined me, and he looked at the X-ray photographs. The pain was mostly in the groin and I felt him exploring the lymph nodes – I knew about *them*.

He said, 'Your X-ray looks all right.'

I said, 'If the bone becomes infected, does that show in the X-ray photograph?'

'It does ultimately.'

'How long's that?'

'It takes some time to show.'

I paused. My agitation was surging up. I said:

'I hope to God you'll *tell* me, if and when it does.'

'Oh yes.'

'Because if it does,' I said, 'I'm for the high jump, aren't I?' I meant another operation, permanent lameness.

He suddenly stood up straight, leaning backwards away from me.

'Look here! Mr Lunn, you must *stop* looking on the black side all the time.'

He'd never spoken to me like that before – it hadn't occurred to me that he had it in him, Aunt Martha.

I stared at him. He did have it in him. He was *not* an Aunt Martha . . . My agitation was dismissed: I felt I ought to apologise. He went on.

'I'm prescribing you different antibiotics.' He produced two bottles from his white coat-pocket. (I immediately suspected that it was because they couldn't be procured through our hospital at this time of night that he'd brought them with him.) 'It's a three-week course,' he said. 'I'll finish my round and come back – I want to do a tissue test.'

When he came back the curtains were drawn again round my bed; Sister Lewell held my left foot and a nurse held my left shoulder, while he inserted a series of hyper-fine needles into my hip. At one point he said, 'That's got down to the steel.' I didn't know why the other two were holding on to me, as it didn't hurt.

So I spent forty-eight hours during which the pain began to subside. This time it was nothing new. I tried to think about my plight sanely. If I had to have another operation and was permanently lame, it was not the end of the world – what had become of my courage? I should still have my loved ones, and they would have me. There were lots of things I could go on doing. I could go on writing. (I had momentarily forgotten that the fate of *Happier Days* had made me threaten never to write again.) I could go on teaching if I wanted to. There were some physical activities from which I should be debarred: there were others from which I shouldn't – very definitely shouldn't!

It was Carroll's opening words that had done the trick. 'Look here! Mr Lunn.' His patience had come to an end, and who was I to say it shouldn't have? So far I'd only thought about myself being independent as a man. Well, *he* was independent as a man, too. In this bizarre medical situation we were getting to know each other.

After the forty-eight hours I was discharged again, this time with a three-week supply of antibiotics. I set about resuming my lawful occupations.

I held some classes in the flat. My pupils much preferred it to their classroom, and my teaching went with a swing. In one class I was inspired – though not by anything that had anything to do with my pupils. I was enthusiastically repeating to them Wilkie Collins's advice on novel-writing to Charles Dickens –

Make 'em laugh! Make 'em cry! Make 'em wait!

What better advice could one have? And then suddenly I realised that time after time in my own novels I'd made 'em laugh: it had never occurred to me to set about making 'em cry.

For a moment I was carried away – that's what I mean by inspired. That's what I'm going to do! I thought. If ever I write another novel I'll make 'em cry as well as laugh. I'll make 'em laugh and make 'em cry in the same chapter, on the same page! (You see how inspiration makes a novelist get above himself.)

I went on with my class. *They* didn't notice anything.

I resumed other lawful occupations. I went down to see my mother. I met Robert, who, apart from being pleased to see me out, was in low spirits that I didn't understand – it seemed that all was well with Veronica. Viola got us some tickets for Carreras and Sass in *Un Ballo In Maschera* at Covent Garden. I watched Elspeth preparing our suppers – a very lawful occupation.

I came to the end of the pills. The state of my hip was just about what it had been when I was discharged the first time. What happens now? Is it going to be all right or isn't it? The first day passed, the second, the third . . . I was awakened in the night –

The pain in the same place.

I let Elspeth sleep on while I waited for the morning, to telephone the hospital.

The routine was the same. Come in immediately, for forty-eight hours' observation! This time I was received by Dr Zia, who drew the curtains and examined me himself, incorporating, before I realised what was happening, a new test of his own – I thought it would serve him right if *I* felt *his* . . . I was X-rayed again. And late at night, as usual, Carroll appeared.

'Your X-ray's all right,' he said.

'What about the results of the tissue-test?'

'They haven't come in yet.'

'After three weeks?'

'They often take longer than that.'

I thought, in that case a patient could have died in the meantime. But I was resolute in behaving myself. I said nothing.

'This time,' he said, 'I shall try another pair of antibiotics. And I want you to take a course of three months.'

'Good Lord! That'll take me to the New Year.'

'Yes.'

I looked at him: he looked at me. Neither needed to say anything.

The new antibiotics were huge capsules, bi-coloured as usual – the size of horse-pills.

In the following forty-eight hours they took effect. I was discharged for the third time. Sister Holmes saw me off and we chatted about my antibiotics. She was in her sensible, motherly, confidential form.

'Antibiotics are a marvellous discovery,' she said, 'but there's still an element of hit-or-miss.' She looked at me. 'But *you* will be able to understand that.'

(I supposed the news of my medical catechising had spread round.) I said:

'Please God this is a hit!'

She said, 'I've seen what he's prescribed for you, one general and one specific. The general's a very good one. The specific one has come out under test with flying colours.' She paused an instant. 'I think you stand a good chance.'

I said, 'Thank you,' and kissed her motherly cheek.

'We shall miss you,' she said.

Such a thought had never occurred to me. I kissed her again on the strength of it. I said:

'Goodbye. You've all been very good to me.'

And so I embarked on a three months' course of continued

wondering, *Is it going to be all right or isn't it?* But I found that in the passing of three months, some of the steam goes out of wondering. I returned to comparative thought. So obsessed with myself, I'd never thought of other people being lame and surviving. They had to put up with it, and they lived their lives all the same. I felt ashamed of having let my courage desert me.

After a few weeks I was free from pain or discomfort, walking without a stick again, forgetting that I might really be under sentence. I kept renewing my supplies of the multicoloured horse-pills – it was only occasionally that I thought, when I woke up in the mornings, *What's going to happen when I stop taking them?*

Then one day came the news that the fine new hospital, where my mother was, could keep her no longer. She was to be transferred to a cottage hospital not far from the convalescent home. My spirits sank. 'I'll go and see her straight away,' I said to Elspeth.

It was a horrible December afternoon, with a dark sky and rain beating against the window of the railway carriage. I had a taxi out to the cottage hospital, which looked to me like a collection of wartime huts. As a nurse showed me in one direction down a narrow passage-way, I glanced back in the opposite direction and saw a large common-room in which nurses were entertaining geriatric patients sitting smiling in chairs.

My mother was in an equally large room. It was bare – a few ancient hospital-beds round the wall, half of them empty; some vases of fading flowers on the window-sills.

During the last weeks I'd seen my mother deteriorating. Her voice was no longer resonant, her grasp on the drinking-cup had disappeared.

Now, as I looked down at her, I saw that she had gone further. The nurse had difficulty in rousing her. Her mouth moved but she was not speaking. I said, 'It's Joe.'

I sat down beside the bed. I thought, Thank God! she can't *see* this place. I watched her breathing. Her mouth was still moving.

Without having thought about it, I'd always taken it that you were either living or you weren't. It seemed to me now that my mother was somewhere between the two.

A nurse came back to give my mother a dose of medicine out of what resembled an eye-dropper. Morphia? This time my mother looked as if she might understand that I was there. I bent over her. 'It's Joe. I'm here.'

'Joe? . .' Her lips formed the word.

'Yes, my dear. Joe. *I*'m here.'

I could scarcely catch any sound from her, yet I knew what she said. *'That's good . . .'*

Impulsively I began to stroke her forehead and her hair. I couldn't remember ever having done it before. For a while her mouth went on moving; then she relapsed into drowsiness, into sleep.

My arm began to ache. I saw, through the window, the roof of a taxi driving up to the door for me. The rain went on pouring throughout my journey back to London. Was this the last journey?

Yet it was not the death of my mother that we heard of next.

One evening there was a telephone call from Robert. Elspeth and Viola and I were eating our supper at the Breakfast-Bar. I took the receiver from the wall.

'I wanted to let you know, old boy . . . Annette died.'

'When?' Half-baked question. I saw Elspeth and Viola listening to follow the conversation.

'The funeral was this morning. I didn't bother you with it – you've got enough troubles of your own.'

'There's nothing for me to say.'

His tone of voice changed. 'It's a little awkward for me, that I've got to go abroad immediately.'

'Where to?' The USA again! I thought.

'Didn't you know? . . I thought I'd told you. I'm going to the Soviet Union. I shall be away some weeks – I'm going down to the Don, among other places. I shall be making speeches, meeting writers – the usual . . . I'm desperately tired. I could well do without it.' There was a pause. 'I'd like you and Elspeth to cheer up Veronica now and then. If you will . . .'

I said that of course we would.

There was a longer pause. Then he brought himself to speak about illness.

'How *are* your troubles, old boy?'

'I came to the end of my antibiotics,' I said.

'When?'

'Ten days ago.'

'Then – then it looks *all right*?'

'I daren't even think so, yet.'

'Bless you!'

I put the receiver back, and I was thoughtful about something else: when he returned from the Soviet Union would he marry Veronica? We should see.

CHAPTER V
SAILING AWAY

One breakfast-time soon after that, we got the telephone call about my mother. The formula: Your mother passed away peacefully in the early hours of this morning. Peacefully? I supposed it might be called that.

'Now,' said Elspeth, 'do you know what you've got to do?'

'Yes. The Staff Nurse told me. I've got to go down to the hospital and collect a doctor's certificate and take it to the local Registrar.' I thought I'd made a pretty good start.

Elspeth smiled. 'Do you know what else? *Did* you read the booklet?'

I couldn't lie. It was a booklet called *What To Do When Someone Dies*. It had been purchased by Virginia years ago, a sensible move when Elspeth and I went on holiday, travelling from place to place in Canada and the USA by air. I said:

'I'll read it now.' I meant my tone of voice to say, That's time enough, isn't it?

She went into another room and found the booklet. She put it on the Breakfast-Bar and I opened it. Actually I had previously glanced through it. I read through it now. It told you simply, sensibly, usefully, what to do.

Elspeth was sitting beside me. 'I'll telephone your sister just after mid-day,' I heard her saying. 'That'll be just after seven in the morning there.'

'Thank you,' I said, going on reading.

I'd come to the section about undertakers.

Many years ago I'd received my instructions about all this from the person in question, inimitable instructions –

'You don't need to spend any money on me when I'm gone. You can have me cremated. But don't go to Glossop's.'

252

Inimitable instructions springing from pride and diffidence –
pride and diffidence to the end, I thought, and beyond it . . . (She
had had my father's body cremated, and she had gone to
Glossop's.)

'You have to watch out with undertakers,' Elspeth was saying.

'You don't need to tell me that.' I'd read Jessica Mitford's *The
American Way of Death,* unforgettable book.

I could see that the booklet, in its quiet useful way, was not
conveying a substantially different message from Jessica
Mitford's.

'They take advantage of people being incapacitated by grief,'
Elspeth was saying, 'to run them in for all sorts of incidental
expenses.'

I'd suffered most of my grief, I thought, along the way during
the last few years. My feelings now were mainly relief for all
concerned, my mother being first among them – called at last.
Elspeth went on.

'Poor people who don't like to say No, who can't afford it. It's
sometimes quite shocking.'

I said, 'I think you can take it that I'm not lacking the power to
say No.' I smiled at her with amusement.

She smiled back at me. 'That's all very well. But just you
watch out! They'll ask if you'd like this or that, and clock up
everything you say Yes to.'

'Then I'll say No to everything.'

She laughed. 'Darling, you can't do *that.*'

'Watch *me!*' She'd put me on my mettle, she and Jessica
Mitford and the writer of the booklet.

'Watch *me!*' I repeated.

I was going off to make arrangements for my mother's funeral
in the indomitable spirit of one going off to do battle with sharks.
I felt a passing spurt of exhilaration.

Elspeth said: 'Remember, you can't say No to having a funeral
at all!' She was laughing at me.

I laughed back at her. 'We'll see about that!'

As I was leaving the flat she called after me, 'Don't let them
take you anywhere by car – they'll charge you up to twice as
much!'

'All right.'

I needed cars throughout the whole day as it was pouring with rain again. What a New Year! As well as with the possibility of a monetarist Conservative Government coming to power that year, 1979 began with awful weather. Storms and floods – 'unprecedented' the daily newspapers called them, with journalistic disregard for historical records and the meaning of words. (We seemed to read of *unprecedented* storms and floods every few years.) Squalls of water sloshed against the windscreen of my taxi on the way to the cottage hospital.

I collected the doctor's certificate and my poor old mother's belongings – or rather, I took the broad gold wedding-ring for my sister and told the Staff Nurse to dispose of the clothing among the other patients. And I experienced a tremor of dismay. Slackly, or perhaps because I'd jibbed at facing death, I'd instructed the hospital to call an undertaker for me. I asked the Staff Nurse. Glossop's it was. I was dismayed. I'd let the poor old dear down.

The taxi was waiting and drove me down to the Registrar's Office, where everything went according to what the booklet had told me. I was briefed about how many copies of the Death Certificate I should need. Sometime I had to go back again to the hospital: I told the taxi-driver to take me instead to Glossop's.

It was time to join battle with the sharks.

Glossop's had a little over-manicured front garden, always the subject of my mother's distaste. I dashed through the rain up to the front door and was let into a panelled hall and then a panelled waiting-room – all very chapelly, I thought. There were flowers and a respectful atmosphere. Mr Somebody-or-other would see me in just a few moments.

In just a few moments I was shown into the room of Mr Somebody-or-other. I noticed that he was fairly tall, fairly young, sober and sedate and respectful; but there seemed little else to notice – it was as if all noticeable features had been wiped off him, perhaps for the purposes of his profession. He sat down at a big desk. There were flowers somewhere nearby.

He wrote down some of the details necessary for the occasion, ascertained that it was to be a cremation, told me where the crematorium was – I knew, of course, having been to my father's funeral there – and then got down to business.

'You'll be wanting a Service?' he said. 'Most people do.'

'Do you mean a religious service?'

'Yes . . . '

I said, 'Then, No. There'll only be my wife and myself and our two daughters present, and none of us have any religious beliefs.'

'Ah, yes.' He paused. 'But sometimes the deceased would have wished – '

I interrupted him. 'My mother didn't have any religious beliefs to speak of, either. So I'm afraid it's still No.'

'I understand,' he said. 'In that case,' he went on, 'perhaps you'd like a short reading?'

'No, indeed,' I said. 'Glossop's arranged my father's funeral and had a reading. My mother objected to it. Very strongly.'

Very strongly seemed to me only the truth. ('They had somebody *reading*. I don't know what they'd got to do that for. *I* didn't tell them.') This was one of the reasons I'd been told *not* to go to Glossop's.

'I think you'll feel you need *something*,' he said. 'You'll have some music?'

'Yes,' I said with éclat. And then I added, 'I suppose it will be piped music?'

'Yes.' He had an apologetic expression – not knowing what I was briefed to reply if he'd suggested somebody playing an organ for which one had to pay a fee.

'I should like you to play some Bach,' I said. 'But not organ music or choral music.'

He made a note of it.

I was feeling pretty pleased with the number of things I'd said No to. Elspeth and Jessica Mitford and the writer of the booklet might have been proud of me. I felt exhilarated yet slightly tense. The heights of the battle had yet to be scaled.

The heights of the battle were immediately before us – he raised the subject of the coffin.

'Our quote for the coffin is inclusive of the whole funeral,' he said, 'with the exception of the crematorium fee and the doctor's certification fee.'

'Yes,' I said, remembering Elspeth's observation that I couldn't say No to having a funeral at all.

'Now,' he said, turning over the pages of what appeared to be a catalogue of coffins, 'our Charlwood is very popular. I think you might be very satisfied with it.'

'And how much does it cost?'

'Including VAT, £437.'

'No,' I said. 'I should like something that costs less than that.' (I hadn't much idea whether £437 was a lot or a little, but I didn't doubt that I was right to say No to it.)

He looked thoughtful. 'I think perhaps we can do you one for something less than that.' (Perhaps, indeed!) He paused and turned over some pages. 'Yes. Here's one. Our Ruvigny. That costs rather less.'

'Oh yes?'

'We can do you our Ruvigny for £285.'

As I gave no sign, he began to describe the Ruvigny, what wood it was made of, what metal the handles were made of –

'Brass handles!' I interrupted. 'What on earth do we want brass handles for?' I went on. 'Come to that, do we need handles at all?' The booklet had prepared me for brass handles: no handles was entirely my own inspiration. I felt really exhilarated.

He looked at me.

'If you'll excuse me a moment, I'll make an enquiry,' he said, and went out of the room.

I supposed that he must have gone out to consult some higher authority. I should have loved to think he was beginning with 'I've just got a customer in my room who's a shark . . .'

When he returned he said:

'I think we *can* manage something less for you. It's our Rock-Bottom – £242.'

At first I thought Rock-Bottom must be the name of another coffin. I said:

'Thank you. I'll accept' – I suppressed the impulse to say, Your Rock-Bottom, and said – 'your offer'.

He did some more writing. Then he proposed the date and time of the funeral. The rendezvous was here. 'Will you be coming by car?'

'No. We shall be coming by train from Victoria.'

'Would you like us to have one of our cars to meet you at the station?'

'No, thank you. We can easily get a taxi at the station when we're ready.'

'Of course.' He paused. 'And flowers? Would you like us to order some flowers for you?'

'No, thank you. I know the flower-shop just along the road, here. I'll go in and see them about it after I leave here.'

'And then you have to go up to the hospital again?'

'Unfortunately yes.' It was still pouring with rain.

'I believe one of my colleagues is going up to the Crematorium shortly. If you'd care for it, he could pick you up at the florist's and drop you at the hospital – it's on his way.'

I nearly said Yes, just to give him a break. However I said truthfully, 'I hadn't planned to go up to the hospital immediately.' There was a pub near the florist's – I needed it.

'I understand.'

Poor sod! He did some final writing, which seemed to take him a long time.

I gave my attention to an enormous vase of flowers about a yard away from me on my right. It was what's called a flower *arrangement* – very rightly called so. Another squall of rain dashed itself against the windows. I heard him say:

'And now, would you care to see the deceased?'

Just before I'd left home Elspeth had said to me, knowing that I had never seen anyone who was dead, 'You realise that they'll ask you if you want to see her?' I hadn't known what to say.

Now it was easy. I heard myself saying –

'Yes, of course.'

He said, 'I'll just make sure everything is ready,' and he went out of the room again.

I waited. The rain dashed itself against the windows again What had I *said?* . . He came back.

'Yes. Will you come this way, please?' And he opened another door.

I followed him through it. He stood aside. I saw her.

'*There* she is!' I exclaimed, my feelings suddenly lit with affection and warmth – I might have been looking for her in a room where there was a party going on, and have suddenly spotted her talking among friends. There she was!

She was lying in the middle of the room. Her feet were towards the windows at the end of the room, the back of her head towards me. Her hair was sweetly done up into the knot on top of her head – one sometimes saw it done up just like that nowadays on ladies walking along Knightsbridge.

I went forward to look at her. She was lying quite high in what seemed like a little wooden box on top of something; pale as when I'd last seen her, composed, still – called at last.

I heard the undertaker go out. I moved round. The little wooden box made me think of a boat. She was lying in it as if it were just about to float off. She was covered in what looked like a white satin nightdress with an embroidered bodice, embroidered in multicoloured silks and lurex gold thread – there'd have been a row, I thought, if she'd known they were going to do that! The long white dress, the silks and the flowers round about, and above all the way she was lying as if she were floating, suddenly made me think of Sir John Millais' painting of Ophelia – which I hadn't seen for donkey's years and couldn't even remember well.

So *there* you are! I thought. Floating, ready to sail . . .

It was the moment when a superstition of my childhood, over half a century ago, sprang up in me. I'd heard people saying – I recalled it exactly – that you must touch a corpse if you didn't want to dream about it.

'Goodbye, my dear,' I said aloud, and touched her forehead.

Her forehead was cold, much colder, whether from death or refrigeration, than I'd expected. Poor old forehead . . . I remembered stroking it that last time while she was still alive, just alive – *'That's good . . . '*

No more, now. I'd said goodbye, I'd touched her, it was time to go.

As I turned away I looked at her for the last time. There she lay, floating in the little boat, ready to sail away. Ready to sail away to nowhere. Nowhere . . .